MW00913294

Crybaby Lane

The New Royal Mysteries, Book Two

By
Laura Ellen Scott

pandamoon
publishing

© 2017 by Laura Ellen Scott

This book is a work of creative fiction that uses actual publicly known events, situations, and locations as background for the storyline with fictional embellishments as creative license allows. Although the publisher has made every effort to ensure the grammatical integrity of this book was correct at press time, the publisher does not assume and hereby disclaims any liability to any party for any loss, damage, or disruption caused by errors or omissions, whether such errors or omissions result from negligence, accident, or any other cause. At Pandamoon, we take great pride in producing quality works that accurately reflect the voice of the author. All the words are the author's alone.

All rights reserved. Published in the United States by Pandamoon Publishing. No part of this publication may be reproduced, stored in a retrieval system, or transmitted in any form or by any means—for example, electronic, photocopy, recording—without the prior written permission of the publisher. The only exception is brief quotations in printed reviews.

www.pandamoonpublishing.com

Jacket design and illustrations © Pandamoon Publishing
Art Direction by Don Kramer: Pandamoon Publishing
Editing by Zara Kramer, Rachel Schoenbauer, and Forrest Driskel: Pandamoon Publishing

Pandamoon Publishing and the portrayal of a panda and a moon are registered trademarks of Pandamoon Publishing.

Library of Congress Cataloging-in-Publication Data is on file at the Library of Congress, Washington, DC

Edition: 1, version 1.00

ISBN-10: 1-945502-73-8
ISBN-13: 978-1-945502-73-6

Dedication

This book is dedicated to Mom, Dean, and Rexine. It is also dedicated to the spirit of my very distant cousin (?), Oley Odin Jensen, who wrote a journal about emigrating from Denmark to America in the 1800s. His words made my words possible.

Crybaby Lane

Chapter 1

December 26, 1796
Somewhere between the Scioto and Little Miami Rivers

The only good thing about being the last surviving member of the Monongalia Boys is that the blankets are all Joseph's now, as he huddles in his tiny, inadequate shack, waiting for the snow to stop. But here in the doorway is Peter Horup, his new friend. The one he sometimes forgets is real.

The snow swirls in behind Peter, who wears leather and fur from his homeland.

Peter has never served, neither as slave nor soldier.

"Close," is all Joseph can manage. It's the only word he's said in days, ever since Apple Boy fell and died. Apple Boy was their pet name for James, and it was charming when there were apples still. Joseph cannot recall James' last name, and that will be a problem when they make his marker.

Peter pulls the door behind him, but the wind still forces snow though the gaps in the wood. The structure isn't even fit for beasts, and instead of protection, it merely provides more darkness.

Peter is younger, having split off from a failed homesteading effort. His people, he said, were from Norway, and most of them preferred to stay near the Pennsylvania timber camps rather than push west. The ones that came with him, his brothers and their wives, were killed by Indians.

Peter's own wife will join him later, when he has a house built and he sends for her.

Joseph cannot imagine that Peter will be successful, where Joseph, Gordon, Gregory, and Apple Boy failed. But they were old when they claimed this land just last Spring. Bachelors, all.

One by one, gone. Gregory's gut swelled up after he caught and ate a pike from the river. Then his gut went down and he died. Gordon wandered off and didn't come back. Joseph supposes he is dead, too. It hardly matters. In this rough territory, they had all deteriorated quickly. They were mature, but not seasoned. Not as farmers, anyway.

Peter sits next to Joseph now and wraps him in a leather and fur clad embrace. "Happy Christmas," he says.

"Is it Christmas?"

"There about."

The old man nods, his head swaddled in heavy rags. He reaches behind and finds his flint. "Shall we spare a log for Jesus?"

Peter pulls a handful of twigs from his coat, grinning. He places them in a pile on the black dirt at the center of the shack. "I thought the same, old father. I'll pull a plank from Gregory's."

Joseph loves it when Peter is affectionate. While he waits for Peter to return, he arranges the kindling just so. His hands shake, and he recalls a time when they were steady—enough for work, enough for fight.

Gordon, Gregory, and Apple Boy James. The Boys, they were called. The Boys, they called themselves. All dreamers, baptized in strife, now free and ready for the good life.

Who would have thought that nature would defeat them, after man had done his worst?

Peter returns, plank in hand.

"It's too big, my boy."

"Seems just right, father."

And down, down it comes.

* * *

When Joseph regains consciousness, he sees the gray sky sailing at speed, and he knows he's being taken out to die in the storm. The only warmth now is around his ankles where Peter drags him. They are headed down into the woods. There is mercy in the snow that fills in the gaps between the rocks and ruts. It makes the journey a little easier.

When Joseph attempts to lift his head, he cannot. Not even when Peter stops to curse and catch his breath.

It seems the route has become impassable. They are paused at a small, rocky drop that was once a home for fox kits before Apple Boy hunted them. Peter is above Joseph now, trying to work out another way to get him further down into the forest. The younger man swings into view, his fine, thick boots planted on either side of Joseph. Peter lifts him under the arms like a child and carries him to the edge of the outcropping. It's not so far down, but it's enough. Joseph imagines that somewhere down there, perhaps under the snow, Apple Boy is at rest.

Joseph tries to hold onto Peter, but he hasn't the strength. And in the struggle, he discovers a detail, perhaps that last detail he will ever understand.

Peter is wearing all the blankets now.

Chapter 2

He waits in the frigid, airless pantry for Helen, the home health care worker, to go home for the day. Viola is worn-down and giving one syllable responses to Helen's relentlessly upbeat, holiday chatter. When Helen finally leaves, he takes his first, tentative steps out of hiding.

Viola speaks out, strong and clear: "Alone at last."

A smudge vibrates at the feeder attached to the windowsill. The day's seeds are gone, but the little gray bird perches on the edge and stares into the house, expecting. Witnessing.

* * *

"Alone at last," Viola says to the house and herself, as if they are frustrated lovers. This is the joke she's been saving for the day after Christmas, because even though she is the last of the Horups—with no children, no husband, and no living siblings—peace is hard to come by. She's been inundated with holiday company, in addition to frequent visits by her nurse, Helen, and the new handyman, Seth, who Helen says is a bum.

She waves away the complaints of a tufted titmouse singing *peter-peter-peter* at an empty feeder.

Viola plucks a fresh, flat shipping box from the top of a stack and begins to unfold it. It's slow but pleasurable work, especially the part where she runs the fat tape along the seams with a gun-type dispenser that she holds two-handed, like a man painting lines on a highway. Highway painting would be a wonderful job if she ever needs employment.

Crybaby Lane

She hasn't minded the weeks of unannounced drop-ins by her lawyer, the Quilting Society president, or the women who are constantly trying to get her to join that red hat fiasco, but a person only needs one set of carolers a year, if that. This year Viola has been serenaded by a half-dozen of these roving gangs, and frankly, she never wants to hear *White Christmas* ever again. Or *The Twelve Days of Christmas*, for that matter. Life is too short for that nonsense.

When the box is ready, she layers in all the wrapping paper saved from her gifts, smoothed out, and refolded. Then goes in a few of the presents, too. Soaps and powders and scarves—that's what people usually give her. Two engraved copper bells. A DVD of *Gone With the Wind*. A picture book of dogs dressed as angels. She normally stops here because any more items will make the box too heavy for her to maneuver, but when Seth comes, he can help.

Seth is a looker, with his sandy hair and dirty red skin. He came to her door in the middle of the Thanksgiving blizzard, offering to keep her driveway and paths shoveled so she wouldn't be stranded like her neighbors, and right away she thought he looked like a surfer, straight from a sunny beach.

With Seth around, she can put as many things in the box as she likes. She unplugs a table lamp and lays it on top of the presents. In the nearest powder room, she collects the spare rolls of toilet tissue, as well as a half-used bar of soap, and those go in the box as well.

Seth visits at least twice a week, and when there aren't odd jobs for him to do, he sits with her and they chat over decaf or watch the television together. She tells him her stories, the ones about growing up as a member of the most powerful family in New Royal. The Horups were there at its founding more than two hundred years ago.

Seth is great company, and only occasionally cautions her that some of her stories include commentary she should not repeat in public, and that is amusing. She rarely goes out anymore. When she does, the occasions are stuffy and ceremonial, with dimwits like the Mayor or the University President sucking all the air out of the room. Fools like that don't deserve her stories.

She kicks off her beige deck shoes, and puts one in the box. The other will go into a new, fresh box, as this one is sufficiently full. She folds down the flaps and reaches for the tape gun, but it's not where she left it.

A sudden shadow towers over her. She has been tiny all her life, peaking at four-foot-ten, so she's accustomed to this feeling but not at all accustomed to intrusion. She looks up at the man who casts her in darkness, and she gulps a wee cry.

He's come back.

* * *

Seth Shute's hands are red from having held them under the cold faucet, but at least the bleeding's stopped. His palms and fingers are covered with fine red scratches that will be gone in a day, but still he hates the idea of touching her with them.

He crouches over Viola to lay a finger on her neck. She's gone. At five p.m., the house is dark except for the long windows that let in cold light from a dying sun. Viola is so slight that her body looks like someone's dropped a raincoat on the floor.

At least there isn't much blood. He rises and pinches his eyes to hold back tears. The tears come anyway, stinging his snow burnt cheeks.

"We had some good times, V."

He takes a sentimental record of what has been. No gig is forever. Still, Viola was a lucky get, and a decent storyteller, too. He's even developed a taste for lukewarm, milky tea.

The telephone, a land line of course, sits on a tiny marble table, and right next to it is Viola's purse. Yawning open, too, as if to say: "Take what you want, you've earned it, hot stuff."

Seth rifles through, looking for just a little cash. He only needs enough to get a head start.

He considers calling his mother, telling her how he screwed up again, but he realizes that's a bad idea. He doesn't know why; he just knows it is. So, sniveling, he dials 911. The operator answers and he says, "Miss Horup is dead. You better get out to the farm." Then he hangs up.

Time is of the essence, as they say on TV.

But Seth dawdles. He can take anything he wants.

Over her body again, toeing her gently. No response. Then he picks up the tape gun and seals Viola's last box for her.

A shock of white hair stuck to the teeth of the blade.

* * *

Seth's mother, Marla, finds out soon enough.

Over the next several days, her son becomes famous, both in New Royal and on some corners of the internet, where his escape has become a reality show. Seth Garan Shute, a "Person of Interest" in the bludgeoning death and robbery of a 97-year-old woman, has made his way east and now travels the I-95 corridor, hitchhiking and taking busses at a leisurely pace.

7

He shows up on the nightly news each time he patronizes an establishment with a security camera.

The first night he has dinner at a Hardees in Breezewood, Pennsylvania.

The next night he makes it to South of the Border.

The night after that, he buys several candy bars at a BP in Savannah.

Each night brings new footage of his continued, baffling freedom.

Marla wishes they would stop saying Seth is a homeless drifter. He's not homeless, though he does drift.

* * *

Back in New Royal, Detective Rasmussen holds press conferences every day, and he's beginning to look as foolish as he feels. His brand has always been "college town cop," with his long hair in a ponytail and a Bulldogs scarf around his neck, but lately he wonders if he shouldn't try to skew more toward his own age. Ms. Horup's murder is easily the most important case he's ever caught, and the community is obsessed with every detail. They don't have confidence in Rasmussen or his scruffy style.

When he says to the crowd of reporters, "We have reason to believe he's in Florida," they laugh at him. Everyone knows Shute is in Florida. The last image of him came from Chik-fil-A in Jacksonville.

"Tell us something we don't know," says one of the reporters. "Like why hasn't Shute been apprehended?"

Rasmussen gets hit with some version of that question every day, and his usual response is to ignore it and stick to the script scrawled on his notecard. But tonight, he's tired, so he says what he believes, which is a mistake destined to go viral. "It's hard to catch someone who doesn't know he's being chased."

The entire room bursts into laughter.

January 1, 2017
South Florida

West Palm Beach has a zoo, and it's open on New Year's Day. Seth uses the Discover card to pay the entrance fee. Viola had four credit cards, and Seth figures that if he keeps rotating them, never using the same one twice in a row, he'll never get caught.

Storm clouds hang over the palm-choked complex, and Seth discards the park map. He doesn't need it. This is a cozy little operation, shaped like a wheel.

A teenager works the ticket kiosk behind a plastic window. She's distracted by flickers from a hand-held device that seems too big to be a phone. Did they still make Game Boys?

The girl gives him his stub without looking him in the eye.

"Any recommendation where I should start?"

She looks up at him as if she's never been asked this question before. "We got a white alligator," she says. "He don't do nothing, but he's a white alligator."

"Albino?"

The girl shakes her head. "Albinos got red eyes. This one's got blue eyes. It'll freak you out."

"Okay, then."

As his hips hit the turnstile, she calls out, "Hey, wait."

"Yeah?"

"I forgot. Alligator's off exhibit. He's got worms." The girl is wearing a tag that says *Rexine*, and she leans over her ticket machine to put her face up close to the Plexiglas. "You should really go see the elephants. They're like, everybody's favorite. Don't miss the elephants."

Elephants are great. "And they'll be where?"

She raises her palm and flicks it like she's batting a tether ball. "Oh, they're *way-way-way* in the back. They need a lot of room."

"Gotcha. Thanks!" Florida people are nice, and the day is warm. New Royal is always so bitter this time of year. And then he remembers.

"Happy New Year!" he calls out to Rexine, but she's already back to her device, engrossed in its mysteries.

* * *

Rexine's snap of Seth Shute collects 43 likes by the time the first police cruiser arrives. She's telling all the commenters that she called 911 before posting the pic, but that's not true. When the first officer reaches her kiosk, he asks, "Is there a way to lock this facility down?"

"You mean like for a Code Adam?"

"Exactly." The officer is pink and anxious.

"That's for when a kid goes missing. Ain't no missing kids today." Cops all seem the same to Rexine—wound up tight and overdressed for the weather.

He presses. "We need to contain a potentially dangerous individual."

"I know. I called it in. You're welcome, by the way."

"So shut. It. Down."

"Not my call. If there was a kid missing, that'd be different." She raises her phone. "Mind if I take your—"

"Put that away and implement the lockdown."

"You'll need the supervisor's okay for that. I can call him, but I need to use my phone…"

"Call him."

As she dials her Uncle Steve, she says, "Officer, maybe you don't want to trap your potentially dangerous individual in there with all these little kids and their families running around?"

But you can't tell a cop anything.

"Oh hey, Steve. There's police up here want to talk to you. Yeah, okay." She signs off, but not before she peeks at the picture, again. 107 likes. *Wow.* "He's on his way."

The officer's partner has finally come down to the kiosk. He's black, but just as uptight. Poor dude. Oh God, a piece of gum would be great right now. Cops hate it when you popped your gum. Makes them itch for their weapons.

From one distance comes the whine of Steve's EV—no one's allowed to call it a golf cart—and from the other distance a feathery song of emergency. The cops hear it, too.

"Shut this facility *down*," says the Pink One.

This is going to be the best New Year's Day, ever. Rexine says, "I can tell you where he is, you know."

Now Steve is humping the little green cart over a parking lot speed bump, forced to stop for a line of toddlers holding onto a tether.

The siren forms. The officers are worried about that. Their perp is going to hear it, too.

Officer Black: "Where is he?"

"He wanted to see the elephants. *Way-way-way* in the back."

"Let us through."

"Sure thing, sir." She presses the turnstile controls, and the cops ram through. "*Way-way-way* in the back," she repeats.

When the officers start running, every adult in the park freezes. The kids just point like dummies.

Steve finally makes it to the ticket kiosk, and he's breathless, as if he's been running too, instead of poking along in his little toy car. "What the hell, Rexine?"

"I sent them to the elephant exhibit."

Steve groans. "You crazy kid. This time you're fired."

"I know it." Her phone is burning up though, so it's all worth it.

* * *

There are no elephants at the Palm Beach Zoo. Officers Belasco and Daigle find that out the hard way. By the time backup arrives, Belasco and Daigle are panting, bent double at the edge of a swampy lake. Several signs describe what animals a patient observer *might* see, and elephants aren't among them.

No Seth Garan Shute, either. Instead, the officers are surrounded by dads with trays of nachos, moms with iced teas, and kids with pickles and blue snowballs, running around like terrorists on the enormous wooden deck that overlooks the water. There'd been a pause in the feasting when the policemen came pounding onto the boards, but these are zoo patrons who are motivated by rest, shade, and sustenance more than anything else.

Seats are at a premium, and a filthy man sleeps across a bench in the full, brutal sun, exhausted from seeking non-existent elephants. A mother, followed by her ten-year-old, blue-tongued twins looms over him.

"Excuse me," but she cares nothing about being excused. "We need to sit down."

The man wakes, and when he sits up, the woman and her boys recoil. He reeks, even by Florida standards. This interaction sets off a wave in the social ocean, one that laps back to the policemen.

Belasco tilts his head at Daigle. Daigle takes a cleansing breath. Both officers remove their batons from their belts.

They part the crowds as they approach Seth Garan Shute, who is trapped in the apex of the deck. He says to the woman who demanded his seat, "You might want to find a shadier spot."

She agrees, corralling her children and moving them back nearer to the concessions.

Seth considers an over the rail, watery escape, but he's more afraid of alligators than cops. His hands go up, and the crowd quiets, and all faces turn to the unexpected dramatic finale to their day, now accompanied by the swelling soundtrack of sirens.

Seth covers his head as Belasco and Daigle approach. At first the beating is awkward, and Daigle and Belasco sometimes hit each other's clubs, but soon they achieve a vicious rhythm. One that takes Seth Garan Shute to the very edge of the world.

Snacks are abandoned as cell phones are raised high. The finale to his internet fame is recorded from every angle.

Chapter 3

The box arrived on Friday, and I had to go collect it at pick-up because the delivery guys wouldn't come up to the third floor of my building anymore. So, that was a thirty-pound package that I carried on foot back to my apartment, where I humped it up onto a rickety folding table already overloaded with my books, laptop, and all the coffee cups I couldn't be bothered to put in the sink that was all of five steps away.

I'd hike for miles across icy streets to avoid getting my driver's license, but I wouldn't rinse a cup until I ran out. Even then, I'd just get Starbucks if I could afford it.

My home office. Where the magic happened. I shoved the box to the center, and an old tube of lip balm fell to the floor, and when I went to retrieve it, I found two others, a pink highlighter, and a pair of earbuds I'd thought were lost forever.

I slit the box tape with a butter knife. This was the moment every writer dreams about. It was my first book, stacks of advanced reading copies marked "Uncorrected Proof. Not For Sale," shining up at me.

Mean Bone: The True Story of The Beast of New Royal
by Crocus Rowe

The cover was black with a human ribcage on it, but bleeding through the bones was an infamous photograph of Brianna Shaler and her two daughters, Nuala and Mina. The one where they were all together eating sandwiches on a bench in a park. The reason the photograph was so famous was that it had been taken by the girls' nanny, Jeaneane Lewis, a student in the Crime Writing program at NRU, who *just happened* to find their bodies in a pond one cold spring afternoon nearly seven years ago. Uh huh.

I'd told my agent that I thought the cover made it seem like Brianna and her daughters were trapped in a birdcage, and she thought I was trying to be funny. That was something I never anticipated, that when I signed the contract I had signed away my right to complain.

In the corner of the cover, lurid text promised of shock, horror, and small town tragedy. Per the packing slip there were forty-two copies for me to distribute. I was supposed to try to create some "local buzz."

If my email inbox was any indication, any copies I might give away would end up as kindling.

One good thing—the official release date wasn't until May. The publisher had wanted to pull the trigger in March on the anniversary of the murders, but I managed to talk them out of it by threatening to walk. I was surprised they bought it, as my threats weren't usually convincing.

I flipped through a copy, letting the words blur by. I was supposed to take a selfie with the box and post it on social media, with some sort of declaration of joy like, "My dreams are finally coming true. #SQUEE!"

Instead, I went to my bathroom and got sick.

* * *

To combat depression, I'd taken up running in a sort of half-assed way. Come Monday morning the sun was out, full force. A sunny winter day in Ohio was something you didn't take for granted.

I ran on a tar and chip path that looped out into a grove of oaks and dying ash, and tilted my face to the bright sky like a goon. No investment in real running gear yet, so I was still doing my route in old jeans and Chucks, but my hair was fresh-done and straight-up stiff, making a gumby-tent under my gray hoodie. The colorist called it "Avalon Flame." My hair was sherbet orange on the razored sides and a crimson coxcomb up top. I must have been quite a sight out on the trail.

I never met a punk who ran for the sake of running, but then again I'd never been to a colorist before, either.

The fool's gold morning bit cold, and my breath puffed out the time as I veered onto the access road that divided the Honor Farm from the free world.

Two old-timers waved from their bench. They wore barn coats buttoned up and puffed out like pregnancy smocks over their bright orange overalls. For years, the Honor Farm prisoners were indistinguishable from civilian grandpas in baggy blue jeans and farmers' hats, but the state now required all inmates to wear their NRCCI jumpsuits. Before the jumpsuits, it wasn't unusual for an Honor Farm resident to give in to temptation, stretch out a thumb, and take a ride with a passing trucker.

Which was usually no big deal. They never got much farther than Sully's, the first bar on the edge of New Royal proper.

That color, though. My pride hiccupped, which was the only way I knew I was proud in the first place. The orange they tried to cover up was an exact match to the major hue in my new 'do.

Then, like clockwork, The Joke: "Hey, honey, slow down! He stopped chasin' ya."

I slowed down, ran backwards a little, and stuck out my thumb hitchhiker-style, reminding them of their lost privilege.

The smiles were gone.

The old, fuck-the-world me would have just flipped them off. Once upon a time, perhaps they had been murderers, rapists, gang members, or child molesters… Now they were just old men. I returned to my pace, and it was easy to forget them.

Next up, the northern edge of Horup's farm, where the mansion rose from the contours of hillocks that stayed green even in winter. The patrician brick building had been dark and lifeless since the crime tape came down, but now there was action again. Several vehicles, mostly vans, were parked out front.

Progress. The estate had been settled quickly after an even quicker investigation, and it was time to clean out Viola Horup's things.

97 years of things.

I cut across a thin strip of woods that was the last undeveloped acreage owned by NRU. Beyond the woods was an old part of campus where the original four buildings stood, dwarfed by a ring of newer buildings, most of which were residence halls. A spongy green quad joined the original four: Parmenter, Smith, Nguyen, and Jarvis.

At the front entrance of Jarvis I jogged in place, just in case I needed to keep on running, but no one called me out for trespassing. No one was even around.

Shouldering through the heavy doors and breathing hard, I managed to turn the echoing hallway into a horror movie. With classes starting in just a week, there should have been *some* action on campus—instructors copying syllabuses or students registering last minute, but so far, nothing. Then again this was a weird week, bookended by Martin Luther King Day and the inauguration. Anxiety kept everyone home.

Crybaby Lane

I liked the big feeling of being alone in a building designed to hold hundreds. I hiked up two flights of dim stairwell, then down the main hallway to a tendril corridor were office numbers that ended in *A, B, C,* and the dreaded *D.*

Perfect place to find a body. That's where my head was at. I'd spent the holiday season devouring murder novels and not talking to anyone if I could help it.

Finally. Alma Bell's new office, which used to be Murgatroyd's office, and by extension, mine. It had a window, which made it a prize get when Murgatroyd "vacated her position." She was about to head off to the Chillicothe Reformatory for Women, and I still couldn't deal. By taking me on as her assistant, Elizabeth Murgatroyd had pulled me out of the shadows, and now she was the one slipping back into them.

Her sentence was twelve months, which she should have fought. Which she *was* fighting, but then she just gave up, right after the new year. In a sense that was the same as me doing twelve months, too. I was looking at a long stretch of being alone with my self-doubt.

I was worried the lock had been changed, but no. The key worked, and when the door cracked, there was an explosion of sound and movement within.

Alma was in there. "Oh, Jesus!"

"Shit! I'm sorry—"

Alma Bell sat rigid behind the desk, her hands pressed onto the surface that only had a laptop and a phone set on top. No papers, no photos, no books. Not yet, anyway.

I'd screwed up. "Seriously, I didn't think anyone was in the building."

"This is *my* office now." She slapped the desk lightly. She was freckled, morning-tight, and no make-up, with her curly hair wadded into a knot bound with a rubber band. "Or do you come with it? I'd rather have a printer."

It was a bitchy joke, the sort Murgatroyd would have made, and I laughed even though I wasn't supposed to. I kind of wanted to be like Bell, some day. She was a runner too, but an expert at it. At 55, she had great bones and was the envy of peers who would never wear out another pair of Saucony cross-trainers.

I also wanted to be like Murgatroyd, except not in prison. "I am so sorry. Won't happen again. I was just dropping this off." I laid my key down on the desk.

Bell scraped it into the top drawer where it made a lonely clink. "Thank you." Her jaw was set, and the lines around her mouth did not relax.

"You okay?"

Bell ignored the question. "Are you going to see Liz before she goes?"

"I'm on my way to the hotel after I run an errand. You have a message for her?"

"You can tell her she was right." Bell rubbed her forehead with her index finger. "The Dean put the brakes on filling her line. Pending a program review, he said. In the meantime, we must make do with a one semester, non-renewable hire."

"I don't really know what any of that means."

Bell was half-jealous of my ignorance. "Liz predicted this. That the Dean would come gunning for the program, first opportunity he had. This is Phase One: Operation Crap Job. Bad pay, no future. No dental on the insurance. Our top two candidates turned us down, almost laughing." She nodded at the phone. "I came in here this morning only to find a message from the one who finally said yes. She's backing out, less than a week before classes are set to start. Left *a message on my office phone*. Not email. Not my cell. Shenanigans like that? Makes me want to ruin her career."

"I'll take the job."

"Funny."

Not funny.

Bell said, "Stick around. I might have another little gem for you to take to Liz." She dragged the phone set towards her as if it were a loaded gun. She punched in a number, the shape of which was weirdly familiar to me. Murgatroyd had dialed it a dozen times. East-southwest-northeast-west-north-south-north-west.

The crone-fingered genuflection that raised Doris Wethers.

Though chair of the department, Wethers was almost never at home or in her office. She was always on a jet, a boat, or in some special box at a prestige sporting event. No one knew how she'd made her money; it certainly wasn't in academic administration. The Doc once said Wethers had been voted most likely to die of an aneurysm, mid-cackle at an absinthe party with corrupt political officials in Prague.

Bell wasted no time on niceties with Wethers. Instead of hello, she said: "Did we have a fourth choice?"

Wethers' voice was strong, as if some tiny but mighty version of the department chair was hidden inside one of the desk drawers. I overheard a lot more than I should have. Like this: *You aren't looking for a colleague, you're looking for a pall bearer.*

When Bell finally hung up, her posture went slack.

I asked her, "What happens now?"

A *c'est la vie* gesture with her fingertips. "Tell Liz we're replacing her with an equity office nightmare, because he's the only one who will take the job on two days' notice. A student seducer, in addition to being a former Master's student here. She'll find that amusing. By the way, love the hair."

"The Doc sent me to her lady."

17

Nodding. "Liz is going to be okay, you know."

Caught off guard, my throat tightened the way it did every time I thought about the Doc's immediate future. "You don't know what she's facing."

"I know Liz. We've been colleagues for almost twenty-five years."

"I know."

"No, you do not know. We were among the first women tenured in the department. We were never friends, but we are bonded by cause. Cause can be more powerful than friendship." She could see I didn't believe her. "This was her choice, Crocus. She has her reasons, and we all need to respect that."

"Really. So, tell me how it makes sense that an affluent, privileged white woman with no prior record has to do time for a fucking third-degree felony?"

The F bomb froze the conversation for a moment. Bell said, "That's the kind of thing Liz would say, isn't it?"

"I'm sorry."

Bell dismissed it. "Don't be. All I'm saying is she builds walls with her words, but that doesn't have to be your style, too. You're okay. Liz will be okay. The rest of us? I'm not so sure."

* * *

By the time I left the office, the weather had gone from bitter to cruel, like mom with her third gin at Thanksgiving. The gusts were wicked, and when I ducked between Parameter and Nguyen for protection, the corridor of brick walls only made the blasts worse.

I fumbled for my phone. Maureen had sent a pic: Shute's "before" picture, something a kid posted just before the police caught and nearly beat Seth Garan Shute to death.

Suddenly, a tall, skinny man in a NRU warm-up jacket shouted, "January sucks!" as he skipped by me on his way to who knows where. He was only the second person I'd seen on campus that entire morning, but his passing misery provided a much-needed boost.

"February's worse," I yelled after him. I leaned against the wall like the weather meant nothing. Besides, *Maureen*.

M: Did you see that clown? How did he make it all the way to Florida without being caught?

I texted back with Rasmussen's bonehead reply to the same question: **It's always hard to catch someone who doesn't know they're being chased.**

M: WTF did he even mean by that?
C: R's not a great public speaker
M: Always looks like he just stumbled out of a bar
C: I can't criticize the dude's style
M: I can. Viola deserved more respect
C: Some murders are more formal than others
M: ???
C: Sorry. Trying to sound smart. Gotta practice
M: Weirdo

Then she sent a series of gifs that danced and jumped all over my phone. People falling on their bums while trying to look cool. Sprinkled in were several emojis of black cats.

Subtle. I texted back: **No.**

Maureen, in addition to managing the New Royal Pet Market, worked with a cat rescue called 9Tales, and she was holding onto a black kitten named Zero that she was always saying would be a perfect for me.

But there was no way I could take on a pet. Not now, not here. Life wasn't stable enough. I wasn't sure it ever would be.

There was no quick comeback from Maureen.

Passive aggressive has always been my favorite kind of aggressive, so I took the bait: **Maybe after the book comes out. After the tour.**

It was gross writing something like that when I still lived in a cheap apartment that reeked of food—not my food of course. I only ate stuff that came factory sealed in a cellophane wrapper.

The phone stayed dark, and the frigid wind hit me again. Nature's dope slap.

Maureen was done for now. She was in control. Not in a mean way, but she had a lot more self-esteem than I did, and she used it.

* * *

I gave up waiting and headed across town, leaning like a mule into the weather. The wind arm-wrestled with my hair, but the match was a draw by the time I reached Veritas, a wine boutique that opened at ten a.m. I went up to the counter and said, "My friend has decent taste in wine, and she's going to prison tomorrow. Today she wants to be drunk. What do you have that's good?"

The shop manager was small and well-muscled. With ferrety grace, he pulled two bottles of Châteauneuf-du-Pape Cuvee Reserve from a nearby rack, carrying each by the neck between his ring and pinky fingers, as if he needed his other fingers for more important work. He placed them on the counter.

I looked at the price. Then I looked at the manager. "You're kidding me."

He said, "I run a wine store in a prison town. You asked for my expertise, you got it. Or," and here he revealed himself, "You could always go to the 7-11." It sounded as if he had never spoken those words together before: *Seven. Eleven.*

So, the fucker recognized me, big deal.

Then I remembered once seeing a pack of Newports in the Doc's handbag. I never saw her smoke or even smelled it on her, but she never gave away her secrets easily. "You got any cigarettes here?"

"We have cigars." He was going to be difficult about this. Something about me always brought out the bitch in people.

"K. You got any, uh, elegant cigars that are sort of like cigarettes?"

"To go with the wine?"

This was beginning to feel like a trap. "Sure."

The manager zipped sideways, and when he came back he held a tiny, golden tin with a hell of a price tag up to my face, closer than it was safe for him to do so. If he knew who I was, then he should have known what I was capable of. Lucky for him I had somewhere to be.

I pulled my wallet from the pocket of my hoodie. Back when I had nothing to lose I used to carry a big old biker's wallet, complete with a chain, even though it was empty most of the time. Now I counted out crisp bills from a modest brown folder, slow so the guy could watch. The total came to $193.77.

As I handed over the cash all traces of the wine dude's attitude disappeared.

* * *

Transaction complete, I hustled two blocks over to the Hampton Inn where the Doc was spending her final hours of freedom. My knuckles were red from exposure where I gripped the twine handle of the pretty little sack of wine and smokes. The manager had thrown in a fancy candy bar for free, which impressed me until I saw it was "organic" white chocolate. It probably sat on the shelves for years.

The Hampton was a nice one, so that meant I was stared at in the lobby by other guests, up until I showed them my social passport—the bag with its bottles and embossed logo.

I knocked on the door of the suite.

When the Doc opened up, it was clear she already had a load on. Her normally tidy hair was mussed, and her smile was kind. No one would accuse a sober Elizabeth Murgatroyd of being kind.

"Morning."

"Oh, how lovely," she said, laser-eyed on the wine sack in my grip. She whisked it away and took it into the kitchenette, leaving the door swinging.

Drawer slam, drawer slam.

The errant corkscrew was on the dresser. "You looking for this?"

"Ah. Thank you."

The two double beds in the room were still made, but the one nearest the window was a little rumpled. If the Doc had slept at all, it was on top of the spread. I crossed to the big windows where the drapes were half open to a fourth-floor view of downtown New Royal and its busiest intersection. Down there, cars were boxed in by school buses and supply vans, and holographic hangtags glinted from windshields. On every corner, someone hunched against the sunny, blustery cold, smoking. Ears poking out red.

No one in New Royal seemed to own a hat.

"Everything okay, Doc?"

Murgatroyd appeared with a glass of wine as big as Donald Trump's ego. "I'm going to miss the inauguration."

I looked around for a place to sit. The chairs and the sofa were piled high with clothes and books that should have been packed and stored already. Murgatroyd was stalling.

I crawled onto the unspoiled bed and piled up pillows into a makeshift chaise. With my arm behind my head, I exposed my pride and joy—the words "So much depends" tattooed on the inside bicep. The whole text of "The Red Wheelbarrow" snaked along in a single line ending with "white chickens" at my wrist.

I'd gotten the tattoo in prison, where I took a class in American Lit. I loved it. Murgatroyd said it was my "English major tramp stamp."

She was a mean person, but her meanness meant the world was working as it should.

"Crocus, dear. What should I pack?"

"You don't pack anything, Doc. You can have certain things sent to you, or you can buy what you need at the commissary, but anything you walk in with, they'll take away."

"What about soap and a toothbrush?"

"They'll set you up with the basics."

"Like a hospitality pack?"

"Uh huh. 'Cause it's Nice Lady Prison. There'll be a chocolate on your pillow. No pillowcase, though."

"Well, I don't know anything about it. You're the expert." That was Murgatroyd's idea of a joke, referring to the years I spent inside for chopping a guy's fingers off with a hatchet in a 7-11. The Doc had a terrible sense of humor.

"Tell me again," I said. "Remind me why this has to happen."

Murgatroyd's speech seemed poorly improvised. "It'll be good for me. I'll get some writing done." Drinking her wine like soda pop, she walked over to the window to gaze out at a frozen New Royal.

So, this was how she spent her hours, her minutes, waiting for the prison transport van.

I hated it. "You think you're Martha Stewart or something? I don't think you get it, Doc. You're only doing a year, but it's going to feel like ten. Prison is *boring*."

"I'll be out in weeks, dear. Perhaps months. The Chillicothe facility is experimental."

"Sorry. Not Nice Lady Prison, then. *White* Lady Prison."

"I can't complain. Anyway, boring is a luxury for those without imagination. The Liberal Arts trains us for survival in dull conditions." She paused, as if she needed to parse her own bullshit. "How did you get on with Eva? It looks marvelous, by the way."

"Why do I have to get on with a hairdresser? She acts like a drug dealer."

The Doc turned and gave me a head to toe appraisal that made me squirm inside. There was the old power, the almost psychic command. The hair thing had been a compromise; she'd wanted to me to buy new clothes, too. A *blazer*, but I drew the line.

I counted the days I'd been wearing these "running jeans" without washing them. Maybe the Doc had a point. No one should risk the honeymoon itch unless they've been boning. And I didn't bone, per se.

She said, "It's going to be a new world for you."

"You can take the girl out of Ohio…"

That expensively manicured hand was up. "Regional bias is our biggest challenge."

The word *our* made my cheeks hot. In a few months, I'd be on the road, traveling to support a book that had my name on it, but the truth was, Murgatroyd had written most of it before giving me the draft. *Our* challenge, and *our* little secret, too. *Mean Bone* wouldn't have been possible without a lot of unethical and frankly illegal action on Murgatroyd's part—withholding evidence and obstructing justice, for example.

Double dealing was why she was going to prison. It was why her house was burned down, too. You walk the razor line, you get punished by the good guys *and* the bad guys.

I said, "I don't want to be someone I'm not."

The Doc may have been three sheets to the wind, but she wasn't going to give up the point. "You have made a career out being anyone but who you really are. Don't be hurt by that. I'm envious, in fact. I can't seem to get away from myself, no matter how hard I try."

Yeah well, drinking isn't trying. "Three emails today," I said. "Before breakfast. All from people begging me to stop the release of *Mean Bone*. Someone from the Mayor's staff called yesterday. If I could pull the plug, you know I'd think about it."

"Unsolicited attention for a book is always negative. No one, and I mean no one, tells you you've done a great job unless you beg for their approval first. They should call it a book crawl instead of a book tour. You'll soon discover that it's more dignified to sit out on the street with a harmonica and a tin can."

"You're not making me feel better."

"It's just local push back. Meaningless, but understandable. The dreamy little citizens of New Royal would love to go back to the way things were."

I almost said, *me too*, but she had her eye on me, like I'd better watch it with the self-pity.

She placed her glass on the side table. I knew nothing about stemware, but the glass looked fancy to me, out of place in a hotel. Did she bring it with her? Ten bucks said she only had the one, too.

Then I saw it, a hotel pen lying angrily across a couple of scratch pads. It looked like she had been making a few notes.

"What's that?" I said, nodding to the desk.

"Work."

"You've been working?"

"That surprises you? I'm always working. Nature of the beast."

She walked slowly into the sitting room area of the suite, and lifted the opened bottle high to check the level. Pacing herself and measuring time. Prison was only a few glasses away. When she came back she was holding the bottle by its neck, down by her side, as if she were going to water the plants with its expensive contents. It hadn't taken long for her to shift from celebration to utility. The wine was a tool, now.

She poured another. "You should be working, too. It's the only way." Refilled. The wine glass seemed to take the light with it, like magic.

I had to look away. "What do you mean?"

"Do you know what they are going to ask you, as you go around the country trying to sell *Mean Bone* to bored housewives who are on the brink of becoming pen pals with serial killers?"

"No."

"Two things. One: where do you get your ideas?"

I smirked—writers always complained about that question.

Murgatroyd said, "That's not funny. It's a real question. Think about how tragic it is. People honestly don't know where ideas come from."

"Sorry."

A flutter of her fingers. "Just come up with an answer that takes the question seriously, an answer that respects the asker. Any writer who blows that question…well, let's just say they might be sociopaths."

"Wow. Okay, and the second thing?"

"Oh, yes." She faced me and made me look at her while she looked at me. Terrifying. "The second question is always: what are you working on now?"

With that the Doc had sliced down to my most pressing fear. "Shit," was all I could manage.

"Shit, indeed. Stop your whining and start thinking about the future beyond *Mean Bone*. I've given you a career, Crocus. Don't blow it."

The next book. She was talking about the *next book*.

The one I was going to have to write for real.

* * *

I stayed with her through the day and into the late afternoon. By then she'd stopped talking intelligibly and was weaving. She needed to give in to sleep. Plus, the wine had run out.

She begged me to get more. I told her I was going to do just that, but I went home instead.

At 7:00 am the next morning, I woke, as always, to the noise of students in the hallways of my apartment building.

The Doc was half way to Chillicothe, by now.

She'd sent three texts at about three in the morning.

1. **Viola. No way SGS did it.**

Seth Garan Shute.

2. **Dog Rasmussen**.

I could imagine the Doc, sitting up in the darkness of her room, her clothes askew and that awful taste in her mouth. But she'd be in her head, her kingdom.

3. **I knew that old bat. She was tough. Follow the gossip.**

And there it was. My assignment.

* * *

Later that afternoon, someone shoved a large brown envelope under my door. Inside was a head shot of the Doc that had been taken by a photographer in the University's public relations office years ago. In addition to the photo was a printout of her faculty bio. Both the photo and bio had been purged from the faculty website as soon as the Doc was charged.

She had them delivered to me. It was one of the ideas that came to her the day before, just as she was sinking into incoherence. "You're in charge," she said, not so much slurring as making her words sound rich and decadent. "In case anything happens to me."

She wanted me to make sure I controlled the story, should she die in prison. I told her she was being ridiculous, but that she was thinking in this vein rattled me.

In the professional head shot she's freezing the photographer with her gaze, something she attempted to do in her booking photo, but with less success. That picture was of an aging woman, caught up in her lies, who was not as remorseful or ashamed as the world needed her to be.

But the photo I held in my hands was that of a warrior, whose power and authority was unassailable.

Chapter 4

"Viola, it's 90 degrees. You can turn on the AC."

The foyer of the mansion is stifling. Liz has a key Viola gave her two years earlier, when the old woman was on a Y2K apocalyptic kick. Back then, Viola warned Liz that, "the lights are going out at midnight, so you might want to consider taking refuge from the looting, raping hordes in a building that was built before the lights came on in the first place."

"Won't you be here to let me in?"

"Oh hell, Elizabeth. You know I'll be in bed already."

Now Viola takes her time welcoming her visitor, while simultaneously complaining about the intrusion.

Liz hangs her pocketbook on a coat hook. "Just thought I'd meet you half way."

That suspicious eye. "I don't like to be rushed."

"And I know better than to knock twice, but do you know you have a wasp's nest out there?" Liz braces for the hug as those doll-thin, white arms reach out from the dim hallway, pulling the rest of Viola with them. In stature, the women are evenly matched. Both are tiny but strong.

Viola is wearing a lacy white sweater over a baby blue boatneck top, as if it's early spring on Cape Cod. "I'll get the boy on it. Come on into the sitting room, and we'll get smashed."

The boy is a grandfather named Matz who marched in the 60s for civil rights.

"Don't call him boy. Poor man's stuck in some *Driving Miss Daisy* purgatory."

"Yes, that's a very good use of your energy, telling me what to do. Besides, I've known him since when he *was* a boy." Viola, suddenly quick on her feet, beelines to a well-stocked drinks cart made of the same dark wood as the wainscot paneling, and the cart's array of crystal carafes look as if they hover in thin air. There is a full, formal bar at the end of the room, but in a place this expansive, drinks on wheels only makes sense.

Viola says, "Bourbon?"

"I'm not much of a daytime drinker." Liz wonders which of the sitting room's dozen or so chairs will make her look the least like a child. The room is furnished with oxblood leather wingbacks trimmed in captain's button-studs and square club chairs in bronze velvet.

"Nonsense, Liz. You're a single woman in your late thirties, tied to a life of academic pursuit. You should spend most of your days half in the bag if you can."

"Jesus. That's a little rough."

"Oh, that was no slight, my love." Viola busies herself over the cart like a scientist, and when she turns she has in her hand a faceted tumbler, three quarters full. She walks it over to the nearest conversation area, and sets the glass on a low, burled-oak table. "I only mean to say that you've very nearly made it. You're almost to safe ground, and you should celebrate that."

Liz understands. Viola has never married, either. "Maybe a little white wine?"

"There you go. You have to start somewhere."

Viola returns to the drinks cart and pours Liz a bourbon just like her own.

Liz accepts it without comment and settles into a wingback, letting its anachronistic quality overtake her. The entire room is arranged in what she imagines a Victorian gentleman's club must have been like. The long, brilliant windows on one side illuminate many paintings, most of them portraits, on the other. She's been here a few times before, but this room has always been the most impressive. The original Horup may have been a robber-baron wannabe, but he was clearly constrained by an Ohio aesthetic, as were his descendants.

Apparently, they abhorred the clutter that usually attends dynasty-building.

Viola eases into her own wingback, decidedly more comfortable about it, smiling at her drink and practically daring the world to deny her privilege. She winks at Liz and says, "Sleeveless. Nice guns."

Liz smooths her simple white tailored blouse. "Let me guess. Underneath that boatneck sweater you've got biceps like ivory powder horns." She takes a pull on her drink as Viola laughs. The burn of liquor is so much more powerful in the daytime.

Viola says, "Oh! I need my papers," and she gets up again, casting about. She had them ready, but now she doesn't know where she put them.

She finds them. A sheaf of typescript about half-an-inch thick, held together by a black spring clip. She brings it back, sits down, then remembers she needs her reading specs.

Liz works at her drink, watching the old woman do piece-by-piece the sort of thing that should be whole, collected, prepared. They'd set this meeting weeks ago.

And yet Viola *is* prepared. It's just that she has come to an age where everything is volatile, unstable, always shifting. The centrifugal force that is the art of growing old.

Liz has terrific patience. The bourbon is good, especially in the smothering heat of the house.

By the time she drains her tumbler she is angry with every adult child who was ever impatient with their scatterbrained mother.

* * *

Viola, finally settled, reads to Liz from the typescript. And as she reads, the octogenarian transforms, becomes the words. The words of a young man, naive and vain, then the words of an old man, full of regret for horrors he set in motion. It takes an hour to complete, and Viola's voice remains clear and steady. Her outer body is failing, but her inner body is strong.

Liz listens, especially to the final pages. Fixes another glass for Viola, and helps herself as well. As a soon-to-be tenured teacher of writing at New Royal University, she knows all about what the written word can do. And yet she weeps as Viola reaches the final page, revealing a guilt that is centuries old.

"Bullshit," Liz sniffs. "But that's complete bullshit."

Viola grins, hardly affected by the alcohol. In fact, it seems to have energized her. "Liz, believe me. I have the original." She lays the manuscript on the table, pushes it towards her guest.

"You have the journal? Where?"

"So it's not bullshit, then? Don't worry, it's safe."

"Let me see it."

Viola is thrilled by the request, showing a large grin of artificial teeth. "No. But you can have this," she says, pushing the typescript towards her guest.

Liz picks up the manuscript. "Why did you want me to have this?"

Viola's eyes glow bright as a pirate's. "In case," she drawls, so far the only hint that she might be drunk. "In case something happens to me."

Liz Murgatroyd laughs out loud. She's never heard anyone say something like that before, not in real life.

"Don't piss yourself, sweetheart." Viola taps the pages with her fingertip. "I'm serious as the grave. Knowing who you are is vital. Same thing for a town. Wasn't easy finding out that everything I thought I knew about Peter Horup was—" She is about to say *a lie* but thinks better of it.

Then Viola stands. "Get up, I want you to see something." She goes over to one of the long, elegant windows and looks out, her hands clasped behind her back. Liz follows.

The view is a tumble of green, a long rolling hillside that doesn't stop until it hits evidence of civilization. "What you're looking at is mine for 200 acres or so. And that low, gray complex there?"

Liz knows it. From this distance, it looks like a tiny farm. "The prison."

"Damn right. Look at that blue sky, look at all that green grass. And right there, simple as can be, a place where men are suffering every day. And we got two more of the same in New Royal, all because Peter Horup was afraid of a priest."

"Is that really going to matter now?"

Viola sighs. "Time means nothing, Liz. What happened two hundred years ago is the same as if it happened yesterday. You think, despite having lived here a few years and going up for tenure and all, you still think you're just passing through. Well I have news for you, hon'. New Royal is your home."

Chapter 5

When John steps inside the foyer of the Horup mansion, the odor isn't nearly as bad as he expects. Not great, but not devastating either. The hallway is lined with cardboard boxes stacked three deep on either side, turning the otherwise spacious and grand entry into a single file tunnel.

A woman emerges to greet him, and even through a paper mask, she exudes an easy authority.

"Amanda Carlos. I'm the estate agent." She pulls down her mask. "You're the archivist?"

"John Hock. For the next five days, yes." He gestures to the stacks that top out at his shoulders. The ceiling is much higher, possibly twenty feet, and a stately, gleaming chandelier hangs over the boxes like a depressed god. "Looks like your team moves quickly."

"We didn't do these. Ms. Horup did. We're onsite to *un*pack them. Here, this is for you." Carlos offers John his own paper mask and a box of disposable rubber gloves. "Non-latex. I've got caps, too."

"Do I need one?"

"Viola kept things clean, so no. Not unless you believe in paper mites."

"I don't."

"Good man. Follow me." She leads him through the passage to the great room, with its vaulted ceilings and long multi-paneled windows that are half-blocked with even more boxes. Again, only shoulder high.

As she walks, she talks. "Hoarding is one of the few problems where being rich isn't necessarily a benefit. And you can probably tell, Ms. Horup was on the short side. Good thing she had a lot of square footage at her disposal."

There are two masked workers in the great room, armed with notebooks and plastic bags. They wear the paper caps, and John doesn't blame them. The smell of rot is strong in here. One worker cuts the seal on a box with a stained corner and draws out a china statuette of dancing child. After examining it for identifying marks, he labels it with an orange sticker and marks it in his log. Once the entry is complete, another worker whisks the statuette away. The next item pulled from the box looks like a small black veil or a dead octopus. Regardless, it's garbage. The worker flings it into a plastic bag before changing into fresh gloves.

John's brain chants, *I need this job, I need this job, I need this job.*

"Don't let the tidy stacks fool you. There's no order here," Carlos says. "And that smell is just what you think it is. Any one of these boxes is likely to have books or jewelry or an old cabbage in it. Bless her heart, Viola Horup liked to put things away. It's the weirdest thing I've ever seen."

John says, "Did she keep cats?"

"No."

"Well, that's a plus, then."

They move on through to the next room where a grand stairwell teems with more boxes straining against a carved balustrade. "Your assignment won't be as messy, though. You're from the library?"

"No," John says, testing the steps. Even though the estate is enormous, Viola Horup's collection makes for a cramped environment. John, at just 5'8" and a little thick in the middle, feels too big for the place. "I teach at New Royal CC. I'm on contract for the library."

Carlos is confused.

John says, "No, not the Correctional Center. That's NRCCI. NRCC is the community college."

"Oh. What do you teach?" She continues the climb. Her calves, even under business trousers, are very well developed. In her line of work, she must climb a lot of stairs.

"History."

"Really." As if she pities him. At the top, she leans on the newel and waits for him to catch up. "Do your students like you?"

"They say they do." He's breathing heavily after only one flight, which probably doesn't improve Carlos' impression of him.

"My youngest will have to go there in another couple of years."

"Yes?"

"The tuition is cheaper. Then it's off to the real college." She turns a corner to lead him up one more box-laden flight to the third floor, where the ceilings are lower and angle with the roof.

"Here's the study." Carlos opens the door but it stops halfway, jammed by more neatly packaged clutter. "Good luck."

John takes a moment. It's a crazy room with a stucco ceiling and exposed wood rafters, stuffed with dozens of boxes through which a narrow path has been cleared, putting him in mind of a wound struggling to heal. This is the work of a lifetime, not just a week. He enters sideways, sucking in his gut.

Behind him Carlos asks, "What's your area? In History, I mean."

Nice that she's aware that there are sub-disciplines within History. Certainly, his Chair didn't seem to think so. This term he's saddled with two sections of Early American, two sections Western Civ, and one section Digital. He's self-trained in the last area, one of the smartest career moves he's ever made. Maybe the only smart move. "My dissertation was in Ohioana."

"Fantastic." Her voice is flat. "Then you'll love all this…stuff. Horup told everyone she was writing a history of New Royal, but as far as we can tell, she never wrote a word. Anyway, the contents of this room were specifically bequeathed to the New Royal University Library. You ever been there?"

"Of course I have."

"Sorry. I just wanted to make sure you knew what we're dealing with."

"I understand," says John. The boxes obscure the room's furnishings, but he spies the outline of a large Shaker desk, and there is an oval, leaded window that lets in the kind of hard sunlight that makes things harder to see, not easier. "I'm to identify items of unique historical value."

"And send the crap to the shredder. I think you're going to find a lot of coupons and cable television bills for the most part, so don't get your hopes up."

John turns slowly, taking it all in. It feels as if the slanted ceiling might just give up and lay its burden directly on his low, round shoulders. The rafter beams are just begging for a dangling noose, but the most unsettling aspect of the study is the absence of a computer. It's like a kitchen without a cooktop.

He is about to declare that the job at hand is impossible, but Carlos beats him to it. "Look John, just do what you have to. We finish by Friday, and that's that. To be honest, the library board isn't very excited about Ms. Horup's gift. They were hoping for something a little more…" She rubs her fingers together in the universal gesture for "fungible."

John nods. "It's too bad. She had a good idea."

"What?"

"The history of New Royal. There isn't a decent one, you know."

"Well, maybe you'll find inspiration here. Then you can write that history on your Spring Break. Good luck." As she leaves him, her close-lipped smile says it all: *in your dreams.*

"Spring Break," he whispers. Carlos' joke was about how he was spending his Winter Break, but it isn't very funny. In public, beta dudes like himself would call a woman like Amanda Carlos "all business," but in private, online? Oh, man…

He treads carefully through the boxes until he reaches the odd little window.

It's a beautiful sight with rolling hills and majestic trees, except for one thing spoiling the view: the prison rising up in the horizon.

And there, a sudden addition to the compromised pastoral. A woman with orange hair moving fast from west to east. Looks like she's in blue jeans. A jogger or a runner—he wasn't sure what the difference was. This one seems to be in between. As she gets closer he can make out her face, and he feels like he knows her.

It's possible. He tends to lump certain people all together until they make themselves more important in his life. ·

* * *

It comes to him on Wednesday, when he's only half way through the job. The running woman is Crocus Rowe, from all that mess with those dead girls. She got a book out of it. Some people are just lucky like that. Funny to see her out this way, especially since John had only just interviewed at NRU to replace her mentor, Elizabeth Murgatroyd.

Running by the farm is part of Rowe's routine, apparently.

"Goddamn it." John yanks his hand from a newly opened box, and a drop of blood oozes from the pierced glove. He daydreams too much. Carlos was right about the contents of Viola Horup's study—there isn't much of value, and the work is dull. There are family letters and photographs, but nothing of real historical value. Viola came from a time where one saved the newspaper from a date of national tragedy or triumph. There are also items of sentiment—corsages, wedding favors, and even cigars—mostly detached from provenance.

He changes his glove.

Does he have a shot the NRU job? It's only a one semester position. Still, it's a step up—okay, a half-step up—from where he is now. And the committee seemed to like him. They especially liked his technical acumen. *You could take care of our web page,* said Dr. Wethers, as if that would be some kind of treat.

No, I could not, he wanted to assure her. *I'd rather pull out my own eyes.* But that's not true. If it means the difference between having the job and not having it, he'll clean the Department's refrigerator with his toothbrush.

* * *

As he works, John builds two piles known as SAVE and RECYCLE, the latter being large enough to be taken out at the end of every day. The SAVE pile is small enough to sit on the desk top next to a Chock Full O'Nuts coffee can of nails and pins. The nails and pins came from Viola's boxes—a perverse attempt at a security measure.

On Thursday, John despairs of the work. The study looks more cluttered than when he began, and he doubts the value of those few unique items he's set aside. That's the way with a job like this, though. It's always most chaotic before the breakthrough. If there is a breakthrough.

Carlos checks in. "How is it going?" She looks around the room, clearly unencouraged. "Find any gems?"

John bends over his task, not because he's engrossed in it, but because his spine needs a good cracking stretch. He peers into a dusty, crammed, plastic bucket. A bucket of worthless sentiment.

"You like to cook?" he asks.

"No."

"Too bad. These are the Horups' top-secret family recipes." He raises the bucket by its wire handle, letting it swing. "Found six for coca-cola salad."

"You're kidding me."

Of course he is. He isn't going to sort through all the little brown stained notecards and flaking pieces of paper. "Nope."

He dumps the bucket on the RECYCLE pile, the cards floating out like worthless scrip.

"Well, I'm obliged to tell you we're running out of time. No need for you to hurry, just know we're shutting down this operation at 5pm tomorrow. Oh, and you got a call from the school office. Someone looking for you."

"My office?" John removes his gloves and fishes out his cell to check for himself. No bars and mostly dead, of course. "They say what they needed?"

"Someone said they'd catch up with you. Sorry, I didn't take the call. Dave did."

"Just as well." He snaps on a fresh pair of gloves out of the box. "Anyone calling from the Community College before classes start only has bad news."

Carlos lingers in the doorway, as if she's forgotten something. "I could swear Dave said the call was from the NRU. Or, what he said was, it came from 'the school,' and you know what that means to these hicks."

John's heart does the Cuban slide, but he acts like this information is no big deal. The last thing he wants is for a woman like Amanda Carlos, or any woman for that matter, to think that there are things in this world he wants, and that he must beg for them.

"Maybe I can take a break and check in with Dave, then? Where's he stationed?"

"Operations. Trailer out front."

"Fantastic."

As soon as Carlos leaves, presumably to explain to some other contract chump that Friday comes after Thursday, John's up and shedding his gloves again. His hands are a wreck. Did he get the job? Of course he did, of course he did. Who else could fill old Murgatroyd's shoes so quickly and cheaply, without a promise of tomorrow?

* * *

Outside, as the wind picks up, the flaps of Viola's once carefully taped boxes heave in their current state, crushed flat and stacked next to a pyramid of black bags all full to bursting. The trash truck will arrive on the last day, but the "treasure trucks" have been coming and going all week. That's Carlos' name for the moving vans that cart away the so-called good stuff. The load crew is working a lot faster now that they've been joined by a few non-English speaking day laborers who aren't paid to care about the cargo.

John leans against the operations trailer, and he's not crazy about making this call during so much hustle. Dave isn't super hospitable. He just shoves the scrap of paper across the desk and doesn't look up from his Toughbook. At least Dave lets John use the sat phone. Outside.

The trailer gives John the creeps anyway. It smells of panic sweat. He thumbs in the unfamiliar number, wincing. His hands burn from every prick and slice, and his fingers stink of antibiotic ointment. Why he hasn't made a bigger deal out of his injuries he doesn't know, except that he wants Carlos to think he has everything under control.

He's surprised to hear a familiar voice answer. "Dr. Buonopane?"

"Johnno! I was just about to leave the office. I'm glad you got back to me."

Of course. The hiring committee has been in touch with Buonopane. "You have news for me?"

A dry laugh from the old professor. "They're contacting your references, son. I'm not supposed to tell you that, but I was too excited when I received the call."

"Ah. That's good news, I suppose." Just not as good as he wants. It's sad that he still lists Buonapane as a reference. It's a little bit like keeping a picture of an old, long-dead cat in his wallet. Buonapane directed John's Master's thesis eleven years ago.

"I told them you were marvelous, Johnny. Supremely talented."

"Thank you, sir. Did they talk to you long?"

"About twenty-thirty minutes. They had a list of questions."

"Any tricky ones?"

"No, no. Just the usual. They were mainly interested in your classroom experience, which is the way with these Term appointments. I talked up your research, though. Just in case."

One of the vans, full now, is being directed out of Horup's driveway. John puts his finger in his ear to drown out the noise. "Well, thank you for calling, sir. I do appreciate the news."

"Not at all, not at all! Where are you, sounds like a construction zone?"

"No, sir. I'm at the Horup site."

"Oh my, is the clean out this week? How exciting."

"Yes, sir. And thank you for putting my name forward. But I do have to get back to the job. We only have until Friday on the contract."

"I completely understand. And John, if you get this position, we'll need to have coffee on campus."

"Every day, Dr. Buonopane. Every day."

"Yes, yes!" the old man shouts.

"Talk to you later, Dr. Buonopane."

"Oh, but John?"

"Yes, sir?"

"They asked about Akron."

John Hock removes his finger from his ear and stops breathing for a moment. They know about Akron? And why would they ask Buonapane? He wasn't even there.

"John?"

"Yes, sir."

"I did have to tell them."

John Hock watches as a new, empty van pulls up to be loaded. "I know you did."

* * *

John returns to Viola's study, fantasizing about how he would like to kill Gerald Buonopane. The fool. The gossip. What does he even think he knows? Akron is where John Hock earned his PhD—*earned* it, despite everything that had transpired. Buonopane had nothing to do with it.

It is in this funk that John reaches into one of Viola's booby trap boxes and pulls out a freshly bloodied hand for his trouble.

"Fuck this." He's ready to walk off the job until he remembers that it is now more important than ever that he finish up and collect his check. His pride can only get in the way. He dumps the contents of the box, without examination, into a black bag and then moves that out into the hall for pick-up. The occasional nail or pin pokes through, but he doesn't care. He repeats this action with four more boxes before he whistles for one of the day laborers to collect the trash.

It is, after all, what Amanda Carlos wants him to do. Clear the room, without sentiment. She never valued his expertise in the first place. She merely needs his credential, such as it is. She wants a sanitation worker masquerading as an archivist.

He can do that.

* * *

By late Friday morning, John Hock has cleared more trash out of Viola Horup's study than in the previous four days put together. With the last of the cardboard boxes, he's even stopped dumping their contents into bags. He notices that workers in other areas of the mansion are doing the same, just ripping off the tape and moving on.

Enough with the "treasure."

By the time he pushes the last box out into the hallway, he's breathless and dizzy. The study is nearly empty, and particles flit through the air to remind him of its fluid nature.

The last thing to go is Viola's Shaker desk. It takes three men to haul it out, and John helps by holding the door.

Fucking Akron. It's like that dream every academic has, where a single skipped gym class in high school leads to the rescinding of all his degrees.

Is the room starting to tilt, ever so subtly? Viola's study is the only room he's ever been in that seems *smaller* after being cleared out. He reaches up and touches the exposed beams, trailing his sore fingers along the ancient grain. They are closer, aren't they? Just a little lower than they were the day before.

He skipped breakfast that morning. Too depressed to eat.

John walks over to the odd little leaded window and leans his forehead on the glass. Sure enough, there she is. Crocus Rowe running her path, like clockwork.

NRU isn't going to call, he knows that.

"You okay, there?" Amanda Carlos speaks from the threshold but won't cross it, like some real estate vampire. "Looks like you're just about done. What about that eave cupboard?"

First thing that morning, he'd moved enough boxes to reveal a square wooden door in the wall where the ceiling was too sloped to stand under. "It's locked."

"Get a crowbar from Dave."

A crowbar would be perfect, if only Carlos hadn't suggested it.

"I have keys." He shows her the coffee can, emptied of its sharps but now full of keys. He found keys everywhere, too.

"Why on earth did you keep those?"

"I like keys."

"It will take hours."

And she's counting those hours until she can hand him his envelope and say goodbye once and for all. John grabs the can and drops to his knees, crawling into the acute angle where the ceiling meets the floor. He has nothing better to do, does he?

Akron, for God's sake.

"So, Amanda," he says, putting his hand on the little door that has probably not been opened for a generation. "You want to get a drink later? Rumor has it, this is a paying gig."

Carlos smirks, or maybe that is her actual smile. "I'll check back in an hour."

"Wait, don't you want to see what's behind Door Number One?" John pours out his key collection, and starts swiftly moving them into piles based on style and age.

She shakes her head no, with a bit of sadness. If locked door mysteries had ever intrigued her, that time was long ago. "I'll ask Dave to bring the crowbar up for you," she says. Which is the kindest thing she'd said all week.

* * *

By the fifth key, the lock works crumble, and the little door pops open by default. A small cloud of rust and dry rot race out into John's face, but that's only a minor nuisance. There is enough light to see inside the storage space, which, to his delight is not crammed full of trash as he had expected. In fact, the area is relatively clean, though dusty with the odd tuft of insulation poking out.

In the center crawl space is a single piece of furniture.

A cradle. A very big, white cradle.

It's easily five feet in length with flat sides made of planks of wood, no bars. Like a lidless coffin, mounted on rockers.

He wipes the dust and sweat from his brow. He knows what this is, doesn't he?

It's a senility cradle. In some 18th century communities the elderly in decline were swaddled like babies and kept in cradles to keep them safe and comfortable until they politely expired. Then the cradle could be used as a coffin when the time came.

Why the hell is this one in storage behind the wall?

Oh, God. What if there is someone in it? Some ancestral Horup, mummified in the dry air of the eaves? He crawls forward, careful on the old boards, not designed for foot (or hands and knees) traffic.

Once inside, he can just about stand if he tilts his head.

Cracks of light come from the tightest corners. Desiccated acorn husks are underfoot, evidence of squirrels.

As John's eyes adjust, he makes out a pale bundle in the cradle. Oh, God. Oh, shit. He reaches in to touch the fabric. Just a normal, ordinary cotton sheet, though rougher than anything one could buy at Walmart. Beneath it, something hard.

"Don't be a baby," he whispers, tugging the sheet upward.

To his great relief, out tumbles a book. Books he can handle. Even old ones like this. It is leather bound and large, like a ledger.

Finally, he's found something! He can feel it. He escapes the storage space on all threes, using the sheet to carry the book since he shed his gloves. Out in the main room, he places the book on the floor, balancing it on the wad of fabric that is striated and discolored from where it lay creased all these years.

The letters *AH* are carved into the reddish-brown cover. There is little adornment, otherwise. John grabs a fresh pair of gloves and puts them on before attempting to open the book. The conditions for examining it are hardly ideal, but after the week he's endured, he deserves a little satisfaction.

He lifts the cover as gently as he can, crying out as a nearly invisible string that bound the book snaps like a hair. It is very frail and the same color as the leather.

John uses both hands to open the cover onto the cloth.

The deckled pages are tragically foxed, but there, on page one, in brown ink:

The Personal Journal of Abraham Horup
Clerk of the Orphans Court
New Royal Ohio Territory

March 1, 1805

I am Abraham Horup, the first appointed Clerk of the Orphans Court in New Royal, a settlement of the new State of Ohio. New Royal has only this year become chartered by referendum vote of all eligible house holders now living within the boundaries of what was once known as Horup farm. We are a new municipality though not new to the territory.

I maintain a ledger of the nameless. I record, track, and place motherless babes, the number of which keeps pace with the growth of our new town. I also witness, certify, and store wills and testaments.

There is no written down history of our settlement, so I have already begun one in this journal, an unexpected gift from my father, Peter Daniel Horup, on the occasion of my employment. He gave it to me out of love, with a card that read "Mr. Cradle to Grave, Esq."

I have thought long and hard about what I can make here, and I decided that this will be an informal document, combining my understanding of how our town came to be with reflections on my civil duties. I am sure that was not my father's wish in giving me this gift, but as the Court Ledger belongs to the citizenry, so do these pages belong to me. I will practice here.

How We Came to the Ohio Territory.

The Horups were the original family when we arrived in this territory in 1798. I was 16. This may be a source of confusion, but the Horups who founded the settlement were distant cousins of my father's family, and we had never known of them before my father received an offer of employment should he choose emigrate from Aoleboruup, which he did. We left Denmark for Sweden and then sailed to America. The journey took seven weeks and we had to bring our own food. For most of the journey we ate hardtack and drank coffee boiled up by the ship cook. Hardtack is not so bad as people like to say, and it is preferable to anything else that spoils. My mother despaired when the fish she had so carefully packed in oil turned bad mid-way through our ocean journey.

Myself, I liked the hardtack. I could keep it in my pocket, and that gave me great satisfaction. Our ship quarters seemed very cramped, but then we landed in Boston and traveled by rail and then a much smaller steamer to New York City, where we lived for three weeks in a flat with two other families. They spoke German.

New York was full of thieves, or so my parents assured me. I do agree that certain draymen were insistent, daily offering to move us from our flat to more fulsome accommodations for a mere fifty cents apiece. My father told me to ignore them, but that was difficult to do as they were teaching me useful English phrases I might not have learned otherwise.

Crybaby Lane

Father chanced into a building job, helping to frame a store. After that, he took two more similar jobs, and with that money we moved west, into the country, on our own. The travel was risky, but at least we had somewhere to go and family waiting for us. In Pennsylvania, we met many travelers who were not so fortunate.

Our cousin Horup's Christian name was also Peter. His family was abundant in number and robust of health, even the daughters, of which there were four. When we arrived at the farm, we were one of five tenant families plus a gentleman named Carsen. We lived in timber-built shanties that my father said were former slave dwellings. Our cousin often alluded to his release of slaves held by the former owner of the land.

The five families were these: the Jensens, the Calhoons, the Johnsons, and the Siversens. The families contracted to earn their own parcels after some time farming the main. I am told that is a happy thing, to own your own land and raise a family on it, but I am a bachelor, and I have developed a bachelor's preferences.

There were no youths my age when we arrived, but the Horups' young daughters doted on me, sometimes competitively.

At the urging of Mr. Horup, the shanties were, one by one, razed and replaced with better houses. The materials were acquired and paid for by Horup, but the homes were built by my father and the other men of our tiny enclave.

My father was less grateful than I expected. He explained that we were merely improving Horup's holdings.

Horup, if it is not yet clear, is the first and continuing Mayor of New Royal.

Today's work.

Of the three babes brought to me today, only one was a boy. I put his name down as "Peter," as a small tribute to my father that only I will know about. We bundled the three and sent them to Crybaby Lane. This is the informal name for the path that has been worn through the church's formerly held land. The name memorializes a tragedy that I will address in later entries.

* * *

Like every grand home of the era, the Horup Mansion is equipped with two sets of stairs.

John heads for the servants' access. The unremarkable wooden door is at the end of the floor where anyone would mistake it for a closet, but it opens to an uneven staircase that twists down three floors and empties into what they once called the summer kitchen, long transformed into a walk-in pantry. Before he descends, he zips his parka up securely. The passage is narrow and the turns are so tight that the polyester shell of the coat sometimes scrapes the rough plaster walls.

No windows. He'll have to feel his way down. During the week's cataloguing and clear out, Carlos declared these back stairs "off limits," because they are too dangerous for heavy traffic. John pauses at the second floor to recover his breath and steady himself. He can't afford to draw attention, not at this point.

Near the bottom, he's relieved when he turns the last corner to see two slivers of light bracketing the bottom and top of the pantry door. When he lands, he stands quietly.

No sound. Nothing. Nothing for a good, long time. He puts his still-gloved hand on the knob—old glass—and attempts to turn it as slowly as he can.

The knob is frozen.

Damn thing is locked. Carlos? Of course.

A single, firm twist is all that is required. The lock is tougher than the frail works of the crawl space, but it gives way, and the door to the pantry floats open. He enters a room of empty cupboards and shelves, barely illuminated by tiny window panes in a side door that leads out to the garden. The plumbing and the gas to this room has long been shut off, but the valves are still there, and every floor tile has some sort of crack or chip in it.

John considers the garden exit, but it's in full view of the loading vans. On the intersecting wall is another narrow door, leading to the cellar. He recalls a boxy, external storm entrance directly in the back of the house. He isn't sure what he will do once he gets out, though—he'll have to return for his car and his paycheck—but right now all he wants is to get off the grounds, unobserved.

The runner. Crocus Rowe. If he follows her route, will he end up at the NRU campus? There he can grab a bus that would almost take him home.

The door to the cellar is locked too, but this time the old key has been left in it. He turns it, and opens a thin maw of cold, stony darkness, smelling of mouse shit and damp.

He waits too long at the precipice.

Bam! Amanda Carlos is standing outside on the kitchen porch, her face filling one of its little windows. She smacks the frame once. An urgent muffle: "What are you doing in there?"

John steps back, and Carlos enters the pantry, bringing in fresh air and her clipboard.

"I thought I heard a cat," he says. "This crazy yowling from the stairwell. I followed it down here."

"A cat." She's skeptical, but in her world the possibility is too powerful to ignore. She sees the open cellar door. "Damn. Was that open?"

"Yes." He's improvising like mad. "I don't hear it now, though."

Carlos pushes past, and he recoils. She picks up on that. "You look ready to go home, don't you?"

"I'm done up there. There's one more piece you'll need to move. A big, heavy cradle. It was in the crawl space."

"That was it?"

"Yes, ma'am." And as soon as he says it, he realizes he's overdone the humility. With a woman like Carlos, "ma'am" is a tricky word. She probably expects it from her illegals, but it makes her wary coming from John.

She looks straight at John's parka-bundled chest. "You're stealing from me."

"What? No!"

"Please. I know what a thief looks like. Every job comes with a guy like you." She crosses her arms in a *you've been caught* pose, which is only fair. "Hand it over."

The journal is tucked inside the coat, held in place against his chest. It is, as far as he can tell from peeking at only two pages, a career maker: a document of New Royal that promises to challenge the assumptions of its so-called noble history.

But now John's caught. Not just caught, doomed. A dismissal from NRCC was guaranteed. That, plus missing out on the NRU position *and* blowing a prestigious future as New Royal's preeminent historian... This what they call a career-fail hat trick.

Carlos' eyes narrow as he touches the zipper on the parka with his gloved hands.

"Yeah," John says, a new idea coming to him. He withdraws the journal, and lays it on one of the barren counters. "I could really do something with this. It's an early account of the history of New Royal. This was what Viola was talking about, I think. When she claimed she was writing her book."

Carlos steps over to examine the journal, handling it without reverence. She opens and thumbs through it with her bare hands, unconcerned by the flakes that flew away from the pages.

"Riveting," she deadpans. "It always fascinates me the things people are willing to throw their lives away for. I mean, seriously. You really think there's big money in local history?"

"No." A tremendous heaviness, laced with cold, courses through his veins. His eyesight blurs, and the whole top of his head begins to ache as if he'd been poisoned.

"John?"

He can't answer her. His throat has closed. He turns and faces the darkness of the cellar, gripping both sides of the doorframe. Nothingness wants him down there. He was sure he heard a cat down there, crying, but then he remembers he'd made that part up.

"John!" Carlos grabs the back of the parka and tries to pull him away from the cellar door.

Once turned back to the light, he takes her arms and says, "I am so sorry, Amanda, but this is going to be violent."

* * *

Hours pass before Viola Horup's estate is quiet enough to convince John that he's alone in the house. It is dusk before he climbs out of the cellar to see that all the moving vans are gone from the front drive. The operations trailer remains, but there are no lights on inside it. John's car, a thirteen-year-old, rattle-trap Ford Focus is the only vehicle left—along with Amanda's. Will anyone remember that? Probably not. Dave has never looked him in the eye, and the day laborers treat him like the invisible man.

Aching from his injuries, John limps out onto the kitchen porch in his stockinged feet and steps into the barren garden where the underlying sticks and gravel stab him into an awareness of…well, his ridiculous depravity. Under one arm he carries the journal and in the other hand his parka, gathered together in a makeshift satchel. Inside that are his blood-soaked shoes.

And the gloves. Viola's pins and nails and those frustrating, beautiful gloves. Meaning there are no fingerprints where they shouldn't be. Total accident of fortune, that.

"Thank you, Viola," John says to the hard, slate sky. He's never been lucky in his life, but perhaps the cosmos was saving it up for this day, only.

When he reaches his car, his cell phone begins to ring, miraculously. The screen was shattered in the fall.

"Yes?"

"John Hock?"

"That's me."

"Well, John, I'm Alma Bell, from the Crime Writing Program at New Royal University. I think I have good news for you."

* * *

45

Darkness is a concept she no longer understands.

She cannot move, see, or feel anything other than the coldness underneath her that smells spoiled. She has a vague sense of where she is, but no sense of time. Though she is in Viola Horup's cellar, broken on the floor, it feels as if she's suspended in mud or trapped under a snowdrift. Her senses are only picking up the most rudimentary information.

Amanda Carlos is dying, but it isn't at all like they said it would be. Her soul is not rising, her thoughts are not illuminated. Rather, she is de-humanizing, becoming a thing. Like an old flashlight from the bottom of a junk drawer. Turn it on, a flicker, and then fading, fading, fading.

She should have stayed unconscious, protecting a slim reserve of life until someone finds her, but just the mere action of waking—this is what is going to kill her.

Stay still, stay still.

Her hand moves in opposition to her will. While it warms and works, the rest of her body shuts down. Her hand, creeping with great effort towards the breast pocket of her blazer, is killing her.

Chapter 6

I walked into New Royal Pet Market, my boots creaking, and the twitchy clerk who smelled like mouthwash all the time pointed me to the back of the store without my having to ask. There was Maureen, hopping around in a collapsible play ring with a fuzzy, fat yellow pup that was going to hit a hundred pounds inside of a year. She was training it, or trying to anyway. To me it looked like she was feeding it chunks of goopy treat every time it moved.

The puppy's owners were a man and his gap-toothed daughter, who was maybe eight. Maureen was working just as hard at training them as the pup.

"Huh! Ooo! Eh-*eh*!" Maureen raised her arms like an evangelist over the jumping dog, a gesture that made it sit and tremble. And piddle, just a little bit.

"See," she said to her clients. "Be big and you don't need the N word."

The N word being *no*. I'd seen this demonstration before. It was the bargain package, $150 over five lessons, so it was the most common course. And least effective, according to Maureen. She snuck a peak at me through the fringe of her long red hair. These two, the dad and the daughter, weren't going to learn much. They adored the puppy too much and not enough.

I loved watching Maureen work.

After the lesson was over, the puppy and her human slaves left the store, breaking several rules before they got out the door. Maureen cleaned up the food crumbs and the pee, and then put away the gate.

"What a life, eh?" She doused her hands in Purel.

I pointed at the pricey bags of dog food on the endcap. "Is that stuff really made of buffalo?"

"No, dummy. That's just the brand name."

"Why does that make me a dummy?"

She shook her head. I was beyond educating, just like the yellow puppy and its owners. She said, "That was my last client today. We can go do something, but it needs to be cheap."

"Because that was your last client." Bookings were dismal in winter.

"Yeah, sorry."

Didn't matter to me. "I have money if we need it, but we don't."

"What are you grinning about? I thought you were all depressed and shit." Maureen was being rough because she didn't like the Doc. She thought Murgatroyd was manipulative.

"Yeah, but my head's on straight now. Might have a project cooking." I followed her back into the employee area. The transition from all that color they used to sell pet products to the dirty white walls of time sheets and stock intake was like going from hot water to cold water.

"A writing project?" Maureen unfastened her training apron and hung it on a hook before writing something down on an overloaded cork board. Then she grabbed a blue North Face jacket that no one could doubt was hers. Among the cat hairs, two or three long red hairs were stuck to the fleece. If she noticed, she didn't care.

"What do you think about going over to the Horup place, snap a few pictures?"

She was half zipped. "You're kidding me."

"There's nobody there. They hauled out all the old lady's stuff last week. Vans pulled out on Friday."

The rest of the zip came up slow and thoughtful. "You're going to write about Viola Horup?"

"I might."

"This a Murgatroyd thing?"

"It was her idea," I admitted. "And yours, too. You're the one who thinks the investigation was sloppy."

"I think the investigator was sloppy. That's a little different." She held her hair out with one hand as she wrapped a narrow blue knit scarf around her neck more times than most people do. "So what's the play? A little trespassing to get the creative juices flowing?"

"Just a drive-by, nothing illegal. I just want to get a feel for the scene. You in?"

Finally, a real smile. "Sure," said Maureen. "A good old-fashioned creep-around. Almost as good as going to a horror movie." That was almost like saying we were going on a date.

"I'll drive," she said.

It was a joke. I didn't have a car.

* * *

Thing was, at 4:00 p.m. on a winter Sunday, the sky was already wavering, losing its promise. The roads of New Royal were mostly empty, stained with salt and bordered with an inch or two of scraped up snow and gravel.

Maureen steered the van like a boat. Pet people drive vans.

We went past the University, which seemed abandoned, but we both knew the dorms were packed with returning students. All the Welcome Back parties had happened the day before, and now everyone was hunkering down.

Maureen said, "My Uncle Dana was in the shop today. Said he dropped off his daughter Jenna yesterday. It'll be her second semester. She hates school."

"It's better than jail."

"Yeah, well. She blew it. Shitty grades, and now her scholarships and insurance are in peril. So, Uncle Dana drops her off and says, by way of so long, 'Lay off the pot, sweetheart. Do your homework. Go to class.'"

"Words to live by." We both laughed like old ladies.

"No shit, though," said Maureen. "Kid's depressed. Growing up's a drag."

"Not to argue, but going to college isn't really 'growing up.'" And as I said that, I could hear how boring I was, relating everything to going to prison. That wasn't fair. There were other experiences to be had in the world. Poor Jenna. "You think she'll make it through?"

"No idea." Maureen shook her head, never taking her eyes off the dimming road. "Uncle Dana said that as he was driving away, he looked in his rearview at her, and his heart broke. She looked like she was a little kid again, asking to hold his hunting rifle."

Now as we cruised through a post-rapture version of New Royal, I felt sorry for Jenna. If she was depressed, she shouldn't be going to school in a place this gray. In winter, the city of New Royal was in a perpetual state of Sunday morning. And of course, there was all the weird feeling from the inaug-alypse piled on top. White people didn't know what to make of each other anymore. Unless you dressed like me, or you smelled of kibble and cedar chips like Maureen, it was hard to get a read on folks.

We passed a guy in a parka and a red MAGA hat, trying to get his car going by revving it till it screamed, and Maureen said, "There's one in its natural habitat."

The car was coughing black smoke. "Well," I said, "At least with him, you know what you're getting."

Maureen nodded. Then we were quiet. We were supposed to have gone to the women's march the day before, but we both found reasons not to. Watching history being made on TV just wasn't the same.

When the Horup mansion finally came into view, I said, "Maybe this needs to wait until tomorrow. Any pictures I take in this light are going to be useless."

Maureen grinned. "It does look kind of creepy." She slowed, and I thought she would keep on rolling by, but then she stopped at the beginning of the long gravel drive. There were deep tracks from the vehicles used by the clean-out crew.

"Hey, wait," I said.

"Gate's open."

We were going in. Maureen stopped the van halfway, and leaned forward over the steering wheel to look up at the house. The dark shuttered windows looked like sleeping eyes.

"This place," she said.

"What?"

"Well, you lived out in the county, so maybe the Horup house didn't feature in your dreams and nightmares."

"Excuse me?"

"Confession time. Viola was a big deal in my childhood. If I could get Dad to haul us all the way out here on trick-or-treat, it was worth it. She always gave out full size Hershey bars while she complained about the ghosts in her house. She said they kept her up at night."

I looked at the house, imagining the thrill of being a kid stepping up on that porch.

"Look, Cro, I'll tell you something. I went to Viola Horup's funeral, and I cried."

"Oh, Maureen, I'm sorry. We can go back."

"No, I want to be here." Her breath was condensing on the inside of the window, so she wiped it with her jacket sleeve. "To be honest, I think it was good she got to go out quick and unaware, but still herself. Not sick and fading. I remember she would have jack-o-lanterns on the stoop, and a bouquet of lit candles beside the door. She kept the hallway dark, so she could creep on up and make an entrance. We'd put our faces up to the side windows to peek in, and every year some stupid kid would say 'maybe she's dead.'"

"She sounds like she was cool."

"She was."

While Maureen was half in the present and half in the past, I was trying to drink in as much of the shadow-swallowed landscape as I could. We should have waited until morning. There was a compact car parked under the bare but drooping branches of a tree that gave me an odd, cold prickle that I told myself was normal.

Paranoia was the official, national preexisting condition, a frantic backdrop for the next terrible thing.

I said, "Whose car is that?"

"Looks like it's been there a while. Aren't any lights on at the house."

Maureen edged the van along until it was up behind the car. It was an Audi, silver and unassuming, but not cheap, either. She turned off the van, shuffled around below her feet until she pulled out a ratty knit cap and pulled it on down over her ears.

"Nice coat, crap hat," I said.

"Call me 'Miss Ohio.'"

"Yeah, but what do you think you're doing?"

"Let's go knock on the door."

The drive-by had turned into a surprise visit. Anyone with any sense would have insisted we leave right then.

"Hold on." I fished my phone from my jeans and stepped out of the van, my boots making a racket on snow that was already compressed into a pebble and dirt flecked crust.

"Don't slip on the snirt," Maureen said. She'd fallen in love with skiing her junior year in high school. Something turned her off it, but she still used the lingo from time to time.

I did a slow pan of the darkening landscape, taking a video with my phone and ending it at Maureen, who had walked over to the Audi. Her hands were jammed deep into the pockets of her zip-up, and she gave the car a good, hard stare.

Ice glazed its windshield. She said, "I scraped this stuff off the van this morning."

I stopped filming and put the phone in my jacket. "So the car's been here a while."

"Belongs to an auction house," she said, pointing at a magnetic sign affixed to the driver's side door. *Barrow Estates & Liquidators*.

We walked up to the front of the house, letting that Styrofoam crunch of snow do all the talking. The porch was long, made of brick, with just a few short steps up to a large white door. On either side, a series of windows, long and skinny, set low. On one was an empty bird feeder, attached with suction cups.

I could just imagine eight-year-old Maureen peering into one of these windows, waiting for the spectral, witchlike presence of Viola Horup to welcome her with candy.

But then I noticed a problem. The key lock box was open and empty.

Maureen went ahead and knocked.

We had this moment, this stupid, horror movie moment.

"Try it," I said, as if it was more her duty (or right) than mine.

The white door swung open to a chilly, cavernous entry. You can feel it, when there's no one there, but I still said, "Hello?"

Maureen turned on her cell phone for light. "It's not as big as I remember."

"Really? Seems vast to me."

Now it was Maureen's turn to hesitate.

I teased her. "You think Viola's going to come skating out of the shadows?" The smell of cleansers and wood polish was intense. Then the soft *foom* of the heat pump kicking on almost made me jump.

Again, I yelled, "Hello!"

"No one's here."

"Then we should call someone. The property isn't secure."

"We really should."

And then somehow we were both across the threshold. "Have you ever been inside, before?"

"Once. On a tour with my mother. Some Christmas thing with tea."

"We need to call."

"Call who?"

"Like, maybe NRPD."

"Because they're your pals, right?" Maureen turned and gave me that sort of withering grimace you only see on fifteen-year-olds.

I followed her down the hallway, the light from her phone showing us gleaming floors and pristine walls. She was wearing soft-soled shoes, so her steps were silent. Mine sounded like half a horse was coming through. "So you know your way around?"

"I was ten, Cro."

"Wait, hold up." I pulled out my phone and replayed the video I had just taken. There at the end, I'd caught the sign on the Audi. I zoomed in on it and at the bottom of it was *Estate Services: Amanda Carlos. 216-880-8828.*

I punched in the number as Maureen watched. She seemed to agree that calling the agency was reasonable, and certainly less of a hassle than calling the cops.

It went to voice mail. I said, "Um, hey this is one of Viola Horup's neighbors, and I was just driving by the property, and it looks like—" I walked to the door and pulled it open, letting the cold in. "Like the place is wide open? The door an all? You might want to send someone around to check it out."

I hung up. "Asses covered."

"*With lies.*"

"Shut up."

We leaned away from the enormous shadow that was the great room, but poked our heads into the smaller ones we passed as we moved in a straight line down the hallway. Nothing there, no creatures running about, no unsettling sounds or pentagrams scratched into the molding, and best of all, no Audi driver laying prostrate in some closet or bathroom.

"The rooms are just rooms," I proclaimed.

"Except this one." Maureen had reached the end of the hall. "I think this is a work room or something."

I followed her inside. She was right. The room was cold with long counters. And a nasty sink, crusted with scale. "A kitchen, maybe?"

"Why would the kitchen be so gross when the rest of the place is so awesome?" She shined her cell on a gray metal fuse box set inside the plaster wall. It was open with its switches labeled and re-labeled in fading cursive ink.

"There are probably a half a dozen hell holes in a place this old." I found some hand-written pages on the countertop and used my own phone to check them out. "Looks like we're expecting the electrician to come by."

"What the—"

"I mean an *actual* electrician." The Electrician was the nickname of the murderer in *Mean Bone*, and once upon a time he just happened to work for Maureen. I tapped the pages. "These are instructions for someone to do a complete inspection. Signed *AC*."

Maureen walked over to the counter, added her light to mine. "As in Amanda Carlos? So, she drives to the house, leaves her notes, and then what—decides to walk home because it's such a lovely, icy day?"

"Oh please, Nancy Drew." I tried to laugh her off, but we had, in just a few dark minutes, given each other near-fatal doses of the creeps.

Maureen read out loud from one of the notes. "'Cellar door off summer kitchen. Nonfunctioning box.' Underlined." She turned around and shone the cell phone across the walls, stopping when she found a narrow void that resolved into a door.

"That's just a closet. A pantry."

"Uh huh." But Maureen had already grabbed the knob before I could warn her off.

The cellar air embraced us, enriched by a metallic smell.

Cold blood. Then our cell phone lights found a tangle of humanity in a black pool.

Maureen made a small, desperate sound, so I pulled her back from the top of the steps. No healthy person expects their imagination to create reality.

Down at the bottom, the woman's head was turned away but one arm and one leg were clearly visible. Her shoe was gone, and one red-painted toenail poked through a snag in her stocking. Her hand was clutched around an object that reflected back at me. A cell phone.

Whatever had happened here, she'd tried to call for help before the end.

I cast about and spotted an old, dome shaped switch on the inside of the door frame. I knocked it with my elbow, and a ceiling light hummed to life.

"Oh, Jesus," said Maureen.

The black pool remained black, but now we could see the woman's face under the sprawl of her hair. Lids sunken, lips the same color of her pale skin. She looked like a blank version of a woman awaiting detailing by her maker.

I was halfway down the stairs before I stopped myself. I suppose I should have taken comfort in the fact that the old instincts—the ones I'd developed on the EMT squad—were more powerful than the self-protecting instincts I'd developed since.

Maureen asked, "What is it? Why'd you stop?"

Her voice rang off the cold, hard walls. I don't think I'd ever seen an empty cellar before. I stared hard at the broken woman below. Then I started walking back up to Maureen, backwards.

"Damn it, Crocus, you have to see if she's alive."

"She's not."

"You can't know that—"

"Just go out on the porch and call 911. If she's alive—and she's not—techs will get here soon enough." When I reached the kitchen, Maureen hadn't moved. I said, "She's been down there for days. 10 more minutes isn't going to make a difference, unless you want me to go scrambling through a crime scene."

"She's a *person*, for God's sake."

I took another look down at those stockinged legs, the artificial color of flesh now made more necessary than ever. "She's not a person, she's a body. So please go back out on the porch and call this in. Try to retrace your steps exactly."

A slight click in Maureen's demeanor. "You come with me."

"I'll be right behind you."

"What are you—"

"You know what I'm going to do, so don't ask."

* * *

When I joined Maureen out on the brick porch, she was staring out at the night sky, flecked with hard stars and a shy moon. The snow glowed, and didn't look so dirty anymore. Maureen's arms were crossed, and she didn't want to look at me. That was okay.

Down the drive, it looked as if her van and the iced over Audi were disappointed in each other.

She said, "They're coming."

"I'm sorry about this."

"It was my idea."

"No, I mean what happens now. They're gonna want to process the van."

"You talk like a TV show."

"I know. They might want our clothes, too. At least our coats, anyway."

Her lips twisted. "I pity the guy who has to check my coat. There's all kinds of hair on it, and only some of it is mine."

When we saw the first lights coming up, they were unearthly and hypnotic in the winter night.

Maureen took a cold, quick breath. "Did you get what you need?"

"Yeah."

She shuddered so I wouldn't miss it.

I said, "What would you have done?"

"The same," she said. "It's still…awful."

It was, and that was important to remember. I wasn't Murgatroyd, I couldn't just do the job and ignore its violating aspects. I imagined all that data whipping through the black spaces between the stars, and I felt a certain sickness. The kind that passes but leaves a mark.

I sent the pictures to myself. I knew that when I got home I'd have to look at them, examine every pixel. Figure out how this was part of Viola's story.

"You deleted—"

"Maureen, please." Of course I had.

The first cruiser arrived at the end of the long, bent drive, its headlights bouncing as it encountered hardened ruts of ice and snow.

Maureen pulled out her phone and recorded its approach.

* * *

We were all on the porch together, Maureen, Rasmussen, and I, standing like rocks in a stream of officers pouring around us. The detective's eyes were small, fatigued almonds that closed slowly, with significance, and inside my head I heard violin music like we were all in an Errol Morris documentary.

But the detective's calm was an act. When Maureen's attention was drawn to the shimmering reflective lettering on the Medical Examiner's jacket, Rasmussen gave me a dark look. *We meet again...*

I tried to make a joke about it, but Maureen thought I was being rude. She'd never seen Rasmussen in person before, so I think she was weirdly star struck.

I remember, through the strains of music flooding my mind, there were a lot of *You did what* questions that didn't sound like questions at all. And Maureen was bending over backwards to give him answers that stopped just a hair's breadth from the complete truth.

I should have told her that fast-talking and eagerness to please were both tells, but as it turned out, Rasmussen wasn't tuning in to Radio Duplicity. He took notes in that sleepy way of his, and when he was done, he thanked Maureen.

He only nodded to me.

I got it. He couldn't spare more civility than that.

* * *

Later, Maureen and I watched the action from the back of a squad car wearing big old cop parkas that had been loaned to us by guys who were inside the mansion now, measuring every possibility. I was right that Rasmussen wanted our outerwear, so we gave it to him without hassle. A lawyer would have had an aneurysm over that.

We were somber, letting the weight sink us down into our private thoughts.

The colored lights were swinging off the snow, crisscrossed by the passing forms of officers, bundled against bullets and weather, contrasted against the techs in their sterile gear. All of our drags were so genderless.

Maureen was damned quiet. I was alert for any signal that I should hold her or pat her hair, but she wasn't needing that kind of comfort. Lots of people like to say *shit just got real*, but they don't know what they're talking about.

One thing I knew. Neither of us was going to cry, not here anyway. Not in front of these people.

And that was okay for me. I'd been through the dead people thing, before. Losing it doesn't help anyone.

Maureen tilted her head against the window, and waves of red light swept across the bones of her face. Her eyes were black. "Why didn't he ask us more questions?"

"Rasmussen? His curiosity is satisfied."

"Seems pretty limited, his curiosity."

I pulled the sleeves of the parka down over my hands for extra warmth. "He believed us because he has no reason not to. We're just dumbasses, messing around."

"I guess they get that a lot. Your coat kind of reeks."

"Somebody had an Italian sub for lunch is my guess."

Maureen sniffed her own shoulders. "My guy just does coffee. Why'd Rasmussen give you the eye like that? I thought for sure he was going to call bullshit on us."

"You saw that," I said. "It doesn't have anything to do with this. That's just an old grudge he's nursing."

"Because Murgatroyd."

"Because yeah." And that was why it was *only* a dirty look. Rasmussen was counting on the fact that I was no Murgatroyd. At best, I was just her guileless muscle.

So far.

"Don't be disappointed, Maureen. Rasmussen's instincts aren't all that good, or if they are, he works hard at keeping them under control. Not like you. You have good instincts. You knew something was wrong. That's why we went in there."

"Your instincts are solid, too," she said. "That's why you *didn't* want to go in."

"So does that make us a good team or a bad team?"

She swallowed. "Just makes us a team, is all."

I tried to burn the whole scene and what we had seen into my memory. I'm not a notetaker. "They think she fell."

"Well, of course she fell."

"I mean on her own. By accident."

Maureen pulled herself out her own dark dream, so she could help me with mine. Ticking off the possibilities. Thumb up. "She fell." Index finger next. "She was pushed." Middle finger. "Horup's mansion is cursed."

"Are you accusing me of being overly-impressed by the venue?"

"Who wouldn't be?" Maureen's three fingers tilted forward into a gun. *Boom.* It was supposed to be funny. "Thing is, saying it's *just* a fall is sort of like trying to prove a negative, isn't it?"

"That's exactly what he's going to say."

"Who?"

"Seth Garan Shute's lawyer."

Chapter 7

Seven women wait at the start, but as the promised half-hour delay turns into three hours and counting, two leave in tears. There's work to go to, other children to care for. Marla Shute has taken off her coat and is half out of her shoes. The waiting room at the NRCCI is hot, despite the brittle temperatures outside.

Finally, a guard comes to lead the remaining women to visitation. He's bored by them. Marla recognizes the name on his golden tag: *D. Cutler.*

He waves them into a narrow elevator, and as they are piling in, a tiny African-American woman says something like, "Nearly two thirty," as she wedges herself into the corner.

The guard says, "Tell your boy to keep his nose clean, then."

The casual cruelty, the cold implication. It's the sort of thing that a mother practices her whole life to fight against, but these women shrink against the elevator walls, terrified at the power of the man who now jabs a button on a panel that closes them all in together.

Most of the women are probably in their forties and fifties, but like Marla, look older. She wants so badly to exercise the one shred of privilege she still has. Besides the guard, she's the only other white person in that confined space. She wants to say to him, "I know your mother."

But she doesn't. The elevator groans and shakes, and Marla stares at a pimple on the guard's hard shaved jaw. A person like him, the kind who would do a job like this, chances are he doesn't care what his mother thinks.

Instead, Marla says to the pimple, "I heard that Hanky Bell's son was a guard here."

The pimple's host gives a soft grunt. "Before my time."

The other women in the elevator turn their terrorized expressions to Marla. She is to shut up.

Fair enough. No point in trying to make friends.

When they reach their floor, the guard leads the women to a room of carrels and bolted stools arranged in a U-shape. In each carrel is a monitor with a telephone receiver.

Video visitation. The notion is chilling, but it's so much easier to schedule one of these sessions than an actual, in-the-flesh visit. Somewhere on the floors above or below, her son is being led to his own terminal. They are in the same building, and she can feel it, but does he?

She picks up the phone and obeys the instructions on the wall:

Touch Visitation Icon

Enter PIN

Touch Green OK

And just like that, her son is on the screen right in front of her. He's a wreck, but she's practiced her face and now smiles sweetly at his. Taped nose, shattered cheekbone, and the eye that isn't gauzed looks like it belongs to a mad animal—glowing, pinpoint, red. This is the good eye.

Marla almost wishes the cops down in West Palm had beaten Seth a little bit harder—not so much as to kill him, but enough to keep him in the hospital longer. But those bastards were expert in their savagery, crushing only those parts of his body that would most readily return to their natural state, at least in appearance.

They said he could walk, but that's hard to believe. He cants to one side, like it's all he could do to stay balanced on his stool.

"Ma." It's an echoey sound, like from inside a can. Not his voice at all.

"Seth, honey."

"You could do this on 'puter."

"You think I have a computer?"

His head rocks back in what she assumes is a laugh. His laugh used to be so easy, infuriating even. Now it's heartbreaking.

She wants to see it again, though. "Did you know Petey Prickles used to be a guard here? From the funny papers."

No response from Seth.

"Well, not really Petey Prickles, he was made up. But the guy who drew him, Hanky Bell? His family lived up on the lake, and they say he based Petey on his own son."

The good eye blinks slowly. "That where the kid gets into trouble all the time? I 'member it."

"Right. That comic strip was around since I was a kid. They don't run it anymore."

"And Petey went on to be a boss up here?"

"I guess so."

"That fucked up."

Marla agrees, silently. She is worried about crying in front of him. She is worried that if she looks away from Seth, he will disappear. "I've got some of the records that Mr. Huebinger asked for. All the files from Dr. Jacobs, at least." Huebinger is Seth's court-appointed lawyer. "But I don't have any from…Kansas."

"You can say Leavenworth, Ma."

Seth can be so sharp when he wants to cut her down, but so dull at everything else. He's been in a variety of institutions all his adult life, including the army, each time swaggering in as if he owns the world. Each time, staggering out, beaten, broken.

"Huebinger says we need a complete medical picture. That your history could be a factor." Marla speaks carefully, avoiding saying things like *in your sentencing*, especially since Seth hasn't even gone to trial yet. Her son already suffered two concussions that she knew of, but who knows what might have happened to him in federal custody.

Seth shakes his head. "I didn't kill her, Ma. I jus'…"

"I know, honey, I know. I still need the information. You're going to have to help me with the release forms."

Frustration in the way he breathes. He says, "Liked her. Liked Viola."

Marla finds that hard to imagine. "She always scared me, I'll tell you the truth. Even when I was a little girl, I'd see her riding in the back of a convertible in the Pioneer Parade, and I was terrified of ever getting that old."

A sucking noise from under the bandaged nose. Seth bobs his head again, and now Marla is worried he might be unable to move his neck.

He says, "She old as balls."

That would have been shocking or funny if it wasn't so true. *Old as balls*. Marla must remember that one. "But you were inside the house. You talked to her."

"Ton of times. She thought I was hot."

Marla lets herself laugh. "She should have seen you ten years ago. Would have given her a heart attack." That year he quit high school, he looked like a young, dope-addled Robert Redford, always half-naked, always ruddy, no matter the weather.

"I'm not a murderer, Ma."

"Oh, hon'." A creeping sensation in her veins. "You're so many other things, no one's listening."

Thief, thug, drug dealer, swindler, solicitor. Kidnapper. What sent him to Leavenworth after only a year in the Army was a drunken scheme to rob a Muslim cab driver. Somehow the cabbie ended up in the trunk of his own vehicle with a head wound, while Seth and his two army buddies took a five-hour joyride. When they were caught by the MPs, Seth was the only one who told the truth about what happened, and he served four years of a fourteen-year sentence. His buddies served eighteen months apiece.

Seth was the one who grabbed the bat—snatched it away before they could kill the guy, and tossed it into the dark Baumholder night. That's what he told Marla, anyway, and she believed it. He would have been better off had he lied. Had he let the killing happen.

It was the only time she'd ever been out of the country, to testify at his tribunal. Hell of a thing, traveling the world. She never wanted to do it again.

"Seth," she says. "We need to be realistic."

"I didn' kill her."

"But they have everything they need to say you did. And all we can do, short of hoping some other old lady gets murdered in New Royal, is plan for the likely outcome."

He wobbles slightly. Getting tired. "You think I got brain damage?"

She certainly hopes so. Marla lowers her voice. "Did they hurt you on the ride?"

The prison transport from Florida to Ohio was known as the "shuttle from hell," and she'd read horror stories about how those vans, driven by contractors, were packed with offenders with no regard for the severity of their crimes. Violent felons, first-timers, men and women separated only by a sheet of Plexiglas.

"They kept me shackled," Seth says. "But I didn't want to move anyway. Didn't have no AC at first. No heat later. And the windows were blacked out."

"Were you scared?"

The question confuses him. "There was only one other dude with me, spent the whole ride crying or asleep. So, it wasn't too bad."

Wasn't too bad? Sounds like being buried alive to her.

"Hey, Ma?"

"Yeah, 'hon?"

"How come I can tell the difference between a six-by-nine cell in Florida and one in Ohio?"

"I'd say it's the cold. Changes the air, even inside."

"Huh."

"Seth, what was it like inside the mansion?"

The one eye closes. He's thinking, remembering. Then it opens, information gathered, complete. "We drank tea. She told stories about before she was born. She put everything in boxes and taped 'em up."

That is about what Marla expects. The rich are diseased.

"An' she was pretty racist."

Marla doesn't think Seth cares about that one way or another. "The Horups had slaves, my mother said."

"Nah, that's wrong. Viola said they bought the land from slaveholders. But her grand-dad was a freedom guy."

"An abolitionist?"

"Right. Half her stories were about how he stuck up for slaves. So, fuckin' weird."

"Is it?"

"Well, if we watched TV or something, she'd turn into this old cracker, saying 'nigger-this, nigger-that.' Especially with the news on."

Marla notices *D. Cutler* has returned, just a little less puffed up than he was on the elevator escort. He moves through the video visitation center to inform each woman that her time is nearly up. He speaks quietly and gently, probably because there's a man in a suit observing him from the doorway.

Marla says, "Yes, well. For some people, decency is merely a matter of timing."

D. Cutler had makes his way to Marla and taps her shoulder.

Seth sees it. Jerks his head up.

Marla says, "I have to go. Remember you need to help me with those medical releases. Huebinger is going to bring the forms." She pulls her coat up and around, even though she's over-warm. Without a handbag to fuss with, she has no other going away ritual.

"Ma, wait."

She stops, one hand clutching the wool together at her breast, trying not to notice the murmurs of grief and goodbye spreading throughout the room. It's tough not to break down when everyone else is breaking down. Just like it's tough not to sing in church. Something leans hard in her throat—the challenge against her strength.

She says, "Yeah, baby?"

And that sets him off. Her calling him baby. His eye is full wet, and he makes a terrible sound. Along his shoulders, a rolling tremble of despair.

"Why'd that girl lie to me about the elephants?"

* * *

For a small town, New Royal has a good selection of decent grocery stores, but no one really wants a selection, do they? They go to the ones they've always gone to, even if the mom and pop store they shopped at with their own moms and pops has been swallowed up by a Walmart Supercenter. Same with Marla, who doesn't mind the Walmart at all, even though she works at the Kroger across town. She stepped inside the Whole Foods exactly once, but turned around and left before she cleared the produce area.

It's after nine at night. A safe time to shop. She needs two lasagnas, packaged peas, bread, dish soap, Charmin. Wine is not on her list, but she grabs a box of Franzia Zinfandel to get her through to Wednesday. That's when she'll meet with Huebinger, the lawyer, and hopefully she'll have Seth's medical records, too. People always came through her line at the Kroger with "beer" or "wine" written in ink on their lists, like they were going to forget to drink or something.

Now, she's stacking the frozen goods in her mini cart, leaning on the handle like her mother always did, browsing all the brightly lit packages she didn't have the cash for this week. She'd given up two shifts already because of Seth.

But then she turns to go down the ice cream aisle, and there's Helen Nemuth, unavoidable as a cold.

Marla and Helen used to work together at a senior daycare that was shut down for reasons she never understood. Then Helen went off to work for an agency that specialized in in-home care. When she was contracted out to work for Viola Horup, everyone thought Helen had lucked into a gold mine. Viola was old, rich, and given to eccentric generosity.

But most folks didn't understand how things worked. Helen had her own little mini-cart, stocked with what Marla recognized as "essentials," for a woman living on her own. Helen's husband left her as soon as she turned forty, ran off with a woman even uglier and older than Helen. Then he dropped dead of a heart attack within the year, so things do even out sometimes.

Helen's son lived in Portland, which was code for something, right?

But it's Helen's cold stare that shakes Marla awake and reminds her that she is the mother of a killer, and no longer the clucking queen of Walmart.

Marla says, nodding at the cart. "No job yet?" She half-expects (hopes?) that Helen will come at her, fists whirling windmill-style. A throw-down is welcome, sometimes.

But Helen has too much grace for that. For instance, you'd never catch her leaning on her cart like she couldn't walk without it.

Helen's face folds, she's about to cry. She shakes her head, *no*. Gently.

Marla nods in response.

They have become old birds.

When they embrace, they hold each other hard because no one has the inclination or guts to be physical with women like these anymore. You take touch where you can get it—lessons learned in Senior Care.

And Helen says in Marla's ear, "I should have never said, I should have never said."

Helen is claiming responsibility. She thinks she is the reason Seth killed Viola Horup. And that's just ridiculous, but Marla will take it for now.

* * *

Helen comes home with Marla to sit with her and drink that wine. Might as well. The house is dim except for the light coming from the television and the kitchen. The furnishings are old, and not in an antique way. This stuff comes from Goodwill. She had to sell the good pieces the last time Seth got in trouble. She's kept the lights low ever since.

Marla and Helen lean forward at once. It's on the news. Another woman found dead in Viola Horup's basement.

A uniformed police spokesperson talks about it on TV to a reporter as they stand in front of Horup mansion. In the background, Marla recognizes Rasmussen by his posture. He's looking at his phone, shaking his head when another officer approaches him. Then he looks up, sees he's on camera and walks out of frame.

Helen says, "Hey," but Marla's way ahead of her, phone in hand. She's dialed all but the last three digits of Huebinger's number when the spokesperson says, "There's no indication of foul play at this time."

Neither woman is surprised to watch the bottom drop out of hope again.

Amanda Carlos' LinkedIn portrait floats across the screen, while the disembodied voice one of her male colleagues expresses the shock and grief of Carlos' corporate family, Barrow Liquidators.

"She was young," says Helen. "No family of her own, though?"

"I guess not. Or maybe they can't talk right now." Whether Carlos' family loved or hated the woman, there would be unspeakable pain, and what she lives in every day because of Seth, can't even compare.

And then one last thought makes her physically sick. Seth is responsible for this one, too. If he hadn't done in old Viola, this woman would still be alive.

She looks sideways at Helen, wondering if her old friend will absorb that hit, too.

Chapter 8

My file was called *Viola*, but so far all I could think about was Amanda Carlos.

It seemed as if everyone lost interest in her after only a few days had passed. After all, it was only accident, with extra macabre sauce.

But I couldn't let it go. Partly because I hadn't been sleeping well since we found the body, and what happens to me when I don't get enough rest, is I start grinding on all my problems and mistakes, past and present.

I checked with Maureen. She didn't seem to want to talk about it anymore, either. In fact, she was a little abrupt, telling me she was needed at the store, but there was something else going on. She wasn't in the mood for me. Or she was worried about being with me.

I kind of felt the same about her.

It was as if we'd made out, and now we needed some space between us. But we hadn't made out—that was a future I was still gunning for, made a little tougher now that we were liars before lovers. That makes for bad foundation.

It's not that we weren't talking to each other, but we weren't talking like we did before Amanda Carlos. Without Maureen to confide in, I was left on my own with the pictures I'd taken and sent to myself.

When I first opened them up on my laptop, I let myself cry. Correction—I *made* myself cry. There are exercises you can do to keep human. Like crying, like remembering how good garlic bread is, like speaking with a stranger about the car they had in high school.

I was going to write down everything I saw in those pictures, and put every question I could think of on a yellow legal pad, scribbling around a coffee ring. I wished I had a whiteboard and colored markers like we used at Murgatroyd's cottage, but all that stuff was long gone. Burned up in the fire, along with all the Doc's archives and furniture. She had this pristine yellow sofa, made me feel like I was leaving a smudge every time I sat down.

My apartment, in comparison, was a broke-ass, second- and third-hand nightmare. It was getting harder and harder to pretend I was comfortable here.

First thing on the page? *No cobwebs.*

There I was, staring at the bent around body of a woman who had died in an unheated stone and brick room during the cruelest part of an Ohio winter. And my mind was on the unsettling cleanliness of the cellar?

There had been a moment when I was on that sixth or seventh stair, headed down to her, that I almost reached for the rail, but saw its jagged splinters suspended in space and realized I was about to contaminate the scene.

Broken rail. Not easy to spot in my pictures unless you were looking for it, because the angle was all wrong. Whatever had sent Amanda down, she'd smashed into that rail and shattered it. I looked at the rail again. Carlos was a trim woman; she must have hit it with a lot of force.

And she still ended up at the bottom somehow, with her torso and arms turned towards the lowest step, but the hips twisted away, as if she was trying to roll back up when she died. There was a science to reading these things. A science to interpreting the direction of her hair and the thickness of the blood pooled under her head, relative to the distance of one cast-away shoe.

I was no scientist.

Blood. A tremendous amount of it, set and gone dark. In the photo, it looked like a crumpled blanket beneath her, spreading out from her head and shoulders. But I'd seen the blood, whiffed it up close. That color and texture, the spread thickened by its coagulate nature and further arrested by the cold—I don't think there's a name for it.

Again, on that stair, I had seen things that I couldn't see here. But now, when I really looked, there was so much I'd missed.

"Amanda," I said out loud. Her black hair flowed over pristine, vacant flesh, as if she were in mid-fall on a theme park ride where they take your picture before the big drop. There was a deep, dark pocket where the strands seemed to eddy just above her cheek.

A little shock. I sat back quick, as if she could reach out and get me.

No wonder I'd rushed down those steps like an idiot. This was…familiar to me.

I hadn't thought about it for years. The day I came home from school and found the cellar door open at my house, and my dad down at the bottom. His blood on the floor, a mere puddle compared to Amanda's pool. His body, a giant's that would have hidden hers completely.

I was in second grade. I ran down there, conquering my fear of the open-backed stairs, and I shook him awake. Then I helped him stagger up the stairs where he cleaned himself up before my mother got home from work. She was a cashier at the only drugstore in town, a prestige gig compared to most.

Days after, I found two of his teeth, whole with roots, clear across the basement under a big rusty sink we never used because it was full of junk. I kept the teeth. They were yellow. I thought I could do spells with them, someday.

I loved my Dad, but maybe I shouldn't have. He survived the fall in our basement because he was drunk as fuck, home during the day because he was unemployable.

Amanda Carlos died because she was sober and on the job.

Thing is, that's how this crap goes, every single time. If you want to walk away from a disaster on your own two feet, be a despot or a drunk.

Dad's teeth were so far away, as if someone had thrown them. No one would have ever found them because the basement was never cleaned, and I was the only one small enough to reach that almost invisible corner. Question was, why was I looking?

I returned to the pictures of Amanda Carlos. I wanted to find the thing—her shoe or her eye—that would tell me the whole story, somehow.

Same with Daddy's teeth.

I came up with nothing.

* * *

So, I'm an idiot, right? Working hard at something, studying it… That wasn't me, that's not my thing. I closed my computer and went off for a run, but a careful one, seeing as I was jittery from lack of sleep. I also didn't want to do my usual route towards campus, because it was the first week of the Spring semester, and my emotions just couldn't be trusted. I was primed for stupid choices.

I ran through downtown, jogging really, trying not to trip on uneven pavement. I trotted past the courthouse and into what we always called "lawyer alley," a series of old colonial looking buildings that served as office space for attorneys, financial consultants, and realtors. If you wanted to see jay walkers and lonesome smokers, this was the place.

And there it was: Barrow Liquidators. I'd passed their shingle almost every day and never paid it a second thought, but who would? No one cares about the third little pig in his brick house until you need him.

My gut said *go on in* while my brain said *don't be a dummy*.

The interior of Barrow Liquidators was very office-y, an eggshell box of pristine furnishings and uncommitted art, with a heads-down receptionist just beyond the foyer, guarding a glassed-in bullpen full of desperately personalized desks. All unoccupied.

Amanda's stood out. It was piled with flower arrangements.

The receptionist was a blond dude who looked dressed for court. "Can I help—" He looked up at me and stopped. His name plate said *David Michals*. "Oh, God you're the one who found her."

I realized I should have cooked up a cover story for being here, but maybe this was better. "Yeah. Sorry, I was just walking by and... Is that her desk?"

David nodded. "The flowers are from clients. They've been coming all week."

"Pretty. May I take a closer look?"

"Oh sure." He was dying for a distraction and led me back into the agents' bullpen. "I'm driving this batch over to her house tonight. Her children are devastated, of course."

"So where is everyone?"

"I know. Waste of space, right? The other agents are at sites. January's busy in this game."

The game being appraising and selling dead peoples' things. I don't know what I thought I was looking for, but the burst of color from Amanda Carlos' desk top memorial was irresistible in this otherwise drab and sterile environment.

David rattled off the names of the individuals and agents who sent various arrangements, as if that was important. Then he paused on the biggest, a huge peacock-sized array of white and yellow blooms, fanning out. "And this one," David said, "is from the Horup team. There were a lot of contractors on that one."

"And everyone chipped in?" I said.

"Well, most of them did, and then Mr. Barrow put up the rest."

"You worked the site?"

"I'm not just a pretty face. I coordinate operations on the large jobs."

There was a gleaming white card tucked into the arrangement. I took it out to read it. "Wow, you got everyone to sign it."

David made a funny, sad face. Then his voice lowered as if someone might hear. "And boy is my hand tired."

"Aw, that's sweet. Seriously."

I glanced at his work, admiring the fact that he'd tried his best to change it up as often as possible. "There must be two dozen names here."

"I'm a little OCD that way."

"To your credit." I was about to put the card down, when I saw a named I recognized: John Hock. He was Murgatroyd's replacement. "Hey, I know this guy, Hock. He worked at the Horup house?"

"He was the archivist we brought in from the University Library. I don't think he found much. I'll tell you one thing you won't hear on the news. Ms. Horup was a bit of a hoarder. Most of what we took out of there was garbage. We sent a truck to the dump every day."

"That's too bad," I said, replacing the card. I thought of how vast and empty the mansion was that night. Hard to imagine it full of trash. "So that means Amanda Carlos was very good at her job."

"Oh, she was terrific," David said, his voice losing some of its practiced chipper quality. It was as if it suddenly dawned on him that the Amanda Carlos he saw in his head was completely different from the one I saw in mine.

Every office has someone who knows exactly what's going on and what should be done under any circumstance, and it's rarely the big boss or even a manager. I'd just assumed that the go-to person at Barrows Liquidators was David, but now I suspected he'd only just recently stepped into the role—one that was previously occupied by Amanda Carlos.

"Well, thanks for letting me barge in here. It has been a rough week for all of us, I guess," I said, pulling out my little brown wallet. I gave David a twenty-dollar bill. "My contribution to the flowers."

He didn't have heart or wherewithal to refuse. David looked at the bill in his fingers and said, "Do you want to—" and he paused, mid-thought, realizing how weird it would be for me to sign the card.

"No thanks," I said, and he was visibly relieved. I said goodbye to David and walked out of Barrows Liquidators slowly and quietly. It was, after all, a makeshift funeral home, deserving all the decorum my punk-ass could muster, but when I hit the sidewalk, I broke into a full out run.

John Hock, eh? Murgatroyd's replacement. I recalled Alma Bell's bizarre endorsement—that he was an "equity nightmare," who was a little too close to his students, apparently.

Yeah, skill and discipline were overrated. All that got you was twenty-five years between books, sad to say. But then maybe that was what Murgatroyd was saying when she told me to "follow the gossip." I didn't know what the Hock connection meant, if anything, but fate had hit a fly ball, and I was gonna go for it.

* * *

Gov Doc met on Thursdays that term. I hadn't even missed the first class. I didn't intend on getting more than a peek at Hock in action, but then Roth Thierry, a six-and-a-half foot, sweaty rage-nerd with an endless wardrobe of black Slayer t-shirts, just assumed I was there as a sub for Murgatroyd, and things sort of snowballed from there.

Crybaby Lane

When I walked into the classroom, I recognized most of the eight faces in front of me. Grad students who should have taken Government Document Analysis first year, but kept putting it off, because…Murgatroyd. In particular, Thierry had known attention issues, ones that he could control when the stars aligned just right, but he would never have survived her. The course was notorious, top to bottom. Not only was it research-intensive, but Doc M insisted that it be scheduled in Jarvis 424, a cramped, windowless, oppressive room that felt like the hold of a fishing boat.

I started with some garbage about the syllabus not coming back from print services. Thierry's eyes fixed on my new orange 'do, and he smiled like he was in heaven.

Thierry said, "You found that corpse over at Horup's." In addition to his body being big, so was his overall vibe. Usually when he piped up, everyone else would roll their eyes, but this time his classmates were on the same page.

"Yeah, why the hell were you even there?" This from some girl I knew had three names, but that was all I remembered about her, except she was a back-of-the-room loner who only spoke up when she wanted to rip Thierry to shreds. Nice cohort, here.

Mel Something-Something. Her first name was Mel, I remembered that much.

I said, "I was following a lead." I hopped up on the top of the table—the Professor's end—cross-legged in my hoodie, ripped jeans, and bar-laced Chucks.

That's when Alma came in with Hock. He was who I was there to see, anyway. He was shiny, happy, bursting with something like pride in a corduroy jacket just a hair too small for him.

And then Alma said, "Hello everyone, welcome back. This is Professor John Hock, and he'll be in charge of Gov Doc this semester."

Thierry thumped the table. "I knew it was bullshit. No way would they let a TA teach a grad class."

"RA," I corrected him. "Research Assistant. Not even on the teaching track." As if my lack of credential was itself a credential.

Alma gave me her best gorgon stare. She wasn't thrilled to see me, but Hock reached out to shake my hand.

"Good luck with the book," he said.

I slid off the table. Hock was a little guy. He and Thierry were going to have issues.

Alma said, "We'll leave you to it then, Professor Hock. Crocus?"

Thierry thumped the table again. "Wait up, where you going to be?"

I said, "Not sure. I'm kinda getting thrown off campus right now."

"No one's throwing anyone off campus," Alma said. "Come along. And Mr. Thierry?"

"Yeah?"

"A grace period, yes? Until we're all acclimated."

We left Hock on his own then, and he looked untethered, as if he might float away. Poor bastard.

* * *

As we left the classroom, Alma angled me towards the stairwell. Maybe she wasn't throwing me off campus, but she sure as hell wanted me off the fourth floor and away from the department.

"Not that it matters," she said, "but what was that all that about?"

"Just checking out the new guy is all."

All around, students and professors filed into their assigned places. Because the semester had just begun, the hallways smelled of fresh floor wax and paint where the wall trim was touched up over break. For me, the sentimental pull was strong. The bulletin board was plucked bare, awaiting a new season of flyers, and the drawing that someone scratched into one of the metal double doors had been buffed away, leaving a cloud where there was once the open, nude torso of a female figure—a carving of a goddess on a cave wall.

"Hock? What are you trying to stir up?"

"I'm just following my instincts. Trying to figure things out. Don't you think it's interesting that the dude you hired to replace Murgatroyd was one of the last people to see Amanda Carlos alive?"

Alma's face tightened. "I don't know how you found that out, but try this one on instead: I think it's more interesting that you were one of the first people to see her dead."

"I was just going by the property—"

"Why?"

"I just was."

"And you found a dead real estate agent. In the cellar of a house you had no business entering. Pardon me if this song sounds eerily familiar."

"Excuse me?"

Alma waited for me to get it on my own. She was talking about Jeaneane Lewis, the subject of *Mean Bone*. That was her line, too, that it was a coincidence she happened to be the one who found Brianna Shaler and her daughters dead in a backyard pond.

The crime that put New Royal on the map, for better or worse.

"This is different." Immediately I could hear how stupid I sounded. Liars and guilty people always said that. Even in that crowded, noisy hallway, it was as if the ghost of Jeaneane had just sidled up in her hospital gown to join the conversation.

"Look, Crocus, I don't know why you're creeping around crime scenes—although I bet I can guess—but you need to be more circumspect. It doesn't take a big leap to see a pattern."

She was right. "Murgatroyd said I should look into the Horup case."

"No kidding." Imbedded in those two words was a criticism of her former colleague as well as an accusation: I didn't have what it took to make my own trouble from scratch.

Added to the general shuffle of bodies was a crew of special needs students in matching blue t-shirts, rolling an enormous recycling cart down the hall. There was nothing to recycle yet, so this was just a training run, but when they came down the hall, students found their classrooms a lot more quickly, as if the cart was one giant, slow bowling ball, knocking pins out of its way.

I said, "Hey, can we just talk a second?"

That was the last thing she wanted to do, but she was too polite to deny me. We headed towards her office, and once there I noticed she'd finally brought a few things in to cheer it up. A plant, her books, an old poster from an opera. It was in Italian.

"Nice," I said.

She sat in the big chair behind the desk, I sat in the little one, scooting up close. As it should be.

"So," I said, "What *is* the deal with Hock?"

"Christ, Crocus. There's no 'deal.' It's a small town, and we gave him a terrible job."

"But that was a real grade school move, walking him to his first class."

She knew that. "Seemed like the least I could do. He's had no real orientation, and technically, he isn't even an employee yet. The paperwork's in virtual limbo with HR."

"You like him?"

"Oh my goodness. Liz isn't going to care about that."

"This isn't just for her. I mean, she got me started, but I'm asking the questions now."

"Well, good then. I suppose that is your strength. The human element."

We both knew what Murgatroyd would think of my so-called strength. "So, what do you think of him?"

She was fidgeting a little, moving pens around for no reason. Still getting used to her new environment. "I think there's no point in getting attached. He's basically a temp. I feel sorry for him. He dumped NRCC in a heartbeat, leaving them with five classes to re-staff. They must be tearing their hair out."

"Well, he seems awfully happy to be here."

"He does, doesn't he? Though I don't know why a Gen-Xer is playing around in a millennial economy." She meant that to sound glib and clever, but there was an icy core to her statement, like when my Grandmother talked about mortgages and credit cards. She never had either, because debt was her biggest fear. The lack of a career was Alma Bell's biggest fear, and she couldn't imagine what it might be like to swim from contract to contract.

My own point of view was a bit different, since I was all set to reap the rewards of a job well done—mostly by someone else.

Alma was eying me.

"What?"

"Liz sent you out to Horup's."

"Uh huh. She said she knew her."

"Everyone knew Viola. Her murder is about as high profile as you can get. Liz doesn't think that Shute kid did it, does she?"

I shook my head.

Alma relaxed. "Well, the implications are potentially folkloric, aren't they? Especially with a second death. This town's going to demand that another beast be dragged out into the light."

"If you're trying to tell me I'm in over my head, thanks." I got up to leave, but she had another bullet in the chamber:

"You know, I read an ARC of *Mean Bone*. Well, I skimmed it from a pdf on my tablet. It's a hazard of the job really, losing the ability to become immersed in someone else's narrative. I catch myself saying 'I look forward to going through this,' when students give me their essays, but I never say I look forward to *reading* the work, anymore. That's a whole other practice."

Typical memoirist, telling me the story of how she read as opposed to what she'd read. I said, "So, what did you think?"

"It was better than it should have been."

My hand on the door knob. "Awesome," I said.

"I'm not impressed by your emotions, Crocus. You shouldn't be, either."

I left, on fire.

Writing 101.

Chapter 9

As soon as Bell and Crocus leave, John Hock gets a good eyeful of his class, including the thump-inclined, round shouldered, and oddly fragrant, Mr. Thierry. John's been warned about this group. Sure, they're graduate writing students, but they also think about murder more than is healthy, and from what he's seen so far, they're socially inadequate, to boot.

The faces. It's important to *see* these kids. If he has an ace up his sleeve it's the fact that he's a newbie instructor taking over for the least liked Professor in the Department. Job one—don't be Elizabeth Murgatroyd—is already in the can.

But he isn't Crocus Rowe, either. She leaves behind a charismatic residue that John wants to scrub away.

His amiable schlub demeanor melts as he strolls behind the lectern to fire up the projection system. He enters the password that's taped on the console, as is the practice in every classroom in every public institution of higher education everywhere. The system clicks on quietly, and the screens, both on the computer and on the wall behind him, slowly come to life.

How many first days has he experienced? It's not the same for professors as it is for students. Students are always powered by the assumption that the arc of the semesters and their accumulation is a long train ride into adulthood. But for professors the trip is circular; they are already where they were headed in the first place.

He thumbs the wall-mounted switches, experiments with the lighting and settles for near total darkness except at the rear of the room. Then he pulls up the course website.

"There's the syllabus," he says, coming out from behind the lectern. For a moment, the projected type bends around him until he takes his seat at the head of the table.

The projection skims only the top of his head, but his face is in darkness. "Just putting that up so it looks like we're getting down to work."

An odd giggle. A familiar thump beyond. He has their attention. "I assume you all heard about what happened at the Horup place last weekend."

"Oh man," comes Thierry's over-enthusiastic reply. "That's all we been talking about."

Hock nods, and the projected light massages his skull. He's heard the whispers all over campus, like it was a welcome back present. This new, mysterious death.

Young people crave random sacrifice. It gives them something to practice against. It brings them together and makes sex make sense.

John begins to create his NRU self.

He says, "Well, her name was Amanda Carlos, and she was a real estate agent. I know because I saw her just hours before she died. I did appraisals for the estate."

The silence is electric, broken too quickly when someone other than Thierry utters, "Holy shit."

John rubs his hands on his knees. He will tell them so much without telling them anything at all, and by the time he finishes, he'll be their new Teacher Crush. That should be useful down the line, if things don't go all Akron on him.

That's the best-case scenario, a sort of foggy outline of a new future if he doesn't screw this up. No one else sees that outline, but John Hock is beginning to believe in luck.

In the meantime, he'll be happy just to make them forget Crocus was ever there.

"Yeah," he says, letting his voice drop. "We were... Amanda and I. We were just getting to know one another."

* * *

March 16, 1805
From the Journal of Abraham Horup

Some History of The Rectory

Mr. Horup was an experimental man. Though Lutheran, he sold a parcel of his land to the Catholics. This was a daring move as the papists were generally distrusted in the territory, but our cousin was of the opinion that the benefits, especially in terms of increasing the population of our little community, far outweighed the risks.

However, rather than establishing a public church, the church used the land to build a seminary for the recruitment and training of priests in a pastoral, contemplative setting. A large, three floor dormitory style building was constructed on a spent sorghum plat, alongside modest stables that were already in existence but disused for many years. The rectory was not considered an attractive structure. Also, its remoteness was a limiting factor in its success and appeal. The story goes that the first batch of young priests were prone to frustration with their new environment, and over time were replaced by foreign-borns.

In 1801, the rectory was set alight by a German, barely more than a boy.

By then, there were fifty or so from the original families, and more came in to serve the priests with small shops and the like, making up 112 who lived and camped or had built houses in the vicinity. This was recorded in a letter from Peter Horup to the diocese.

My father woke me up from my bed and said, "Come on, Abe. There is a fire."

I thought we would help to put it out, but when we arrived at the rectory, all the tenant families stood back together, most in their night wear. We watched from the tree line. It was too late.

About half the priests survived, but some were crippled as they jumped from the third-floor windows. All that lived went away. Back to where they came from, we assumed.

The ruins of the rectory stood untouched for nearly a year. Eventually, at Horup's urging, the Church tried again, and the influx of tradesmen brought in to rebuild the facility greatly transformed our quiet settlement into something very town-like, and we began to call ourselves residents of New Royal. This was a satisfactory transition to Peter Horup, since it was one of his daughters (Elea Pauline) who thought up the name. She was unaware that the practice of calling a place "New" meant that there was an original homeland of the same name in Europe, but the growing populace was charmed by the aspirational nature of the name, and we took to it.

When the new building was ready, the Church brought in nuns. They were, by all accounts, less dissatisfied than the priests, and they set about to creating an orphanage. New Royal had no orphans back then, so the sisters took in a good many girls from the eastern cities who were deemed unsuitable for work and who were not yet of an age to be married.

Some of these girls were educable and attended their own classes.

Today's work.

I will pause here for a remark. When a community is a success, it generates orphans. I am not qualified to analyze the root of it. I named two baby boys Peter today. They are being sent to separate homes, so there will be no harm done.

* * *

It's late, and the class was exhausting, but Buonopane will not be denied. Coffee will be had.

The older professor is already at the student center, sweeping crumbs from a table by the time John arrives. The lighting is unkind. Buonopane is fatter, older, and most likely, feebler than when they last met, and John takes a moment to savor that fact.

Buonopane has chosen the worst possible table, smack dab in the center of the food court. There aren't quite as many students around as there are in the daytime, but Buonopane has managed to locate the densest population. All around him, over-caffeinated night students are slinging backpacks and trays. John remembers though, that Buonopane is always happiest in a chaotic environment. Back when John was pursuing his Master's at NRU, Buonopane was present and smiling at every celebration and every protest. And his lectures were intellectual free-for-alls, during which he liked to toss out provocative questions and let the crowd pounce on them like jackals on lambs.

John almost remembers those days fondly. Almost. As Buonopane's TA, John graded student exams, and he learned an important lesson about education. Rarely did the passion of the classroom translate as coherent thought on the page.

Buonopane still hasn't noticed John. There is time to escape, time to call with an excuse. The older professor grins into his coffee while students snatch chairs away from his table, like plucking the legs off a spider.

Is Buonopane a spider?

A happy, stupid spider.

"Professor," John says.

"John! My boy—"

John grabs a chair that is empty but claimed, and he smiles hard at the student who is about to object.

"Thanks!" John says. The kid retreats politely.

Politely. That's something John notices these days. Bad kids are still bad, but good kids have gotten even better. And smarter, too, which could become a problem.

Buonopane wraps his chubby, tweed-bound arms around his former student, flooding John's senses with layers of scent—soap and wool.

"Well, here we are, together again! Like Lewis and Clark."

This game. Ugh. It's easier to play than not. "Like Smith & Wesson."

"Like Burke and Hare."

"Like Jekyll & Hyde."

There is another classic duo on the tip of Buonopane's tongue, but the flame flickers out in the old man's eyes. Forgetfulness in action. He finally says, "Like…Batman and Robin?"

John shrugs. "But without all the sexual tension."

Buonopane laughs hard and loud, generating a shockwave of notice from the young people who surround him. When he calms down he says, "How are you adjusting, John?"

"So far, so good. Just taught my first class. Grad students are a little bit more respectful than community college sophomores, but only a little. Bell seems to think I might have a rough go ahead of me, though. Murgatroyd had her followers."

"Ha. I'm sure they'll be relieved to be shed of her."

"That's a little catty, Jer'. Weren't you friends?"

"Oh, of course we were. I just think she was a terrible teacher with a nightmarish moral code. If someone were to ask you if I was a suitable candidate for a skateboarding contest, you would say no, wouldn't you? And it would bear no reflection on your love for me." He sips from the paper cup and smiles with his eyes.

The assumption of love is a howler.

"But what I am really curious about is your experience at the Horup estate. That poor woman and all."

John nods. "Amanda Carlos. That's what the students wanted to know about, too."

"They say she fell."

"So I heard. I can only imagine, with those old, narrow stairs. It's a terrible shock, of course. I saw her last Friday."

"The house, though." Buonopane sucks his teeth. "Aside from the tragedy, I expect it was a stimulating week."

"Don't be coy, Jerry."

"I am a curious old goat, no point in pretending I'm not. That is why I referred you to Barrow's in the first place." Buonopane had recommended his old pupil for the Horup clean-out when John reached out for a reference on the Murgatroyd vacancy. They'd been teaching in the same town for years without reconnecting, such are the cultural divides between a two-year college and a "real" school, as Amanda had put it.

"Thank you for that, by the way," John says, thinking about that piece of history wrapped in a sheet, and hidden in a plastic storage tub with his tax records, dissertation, and birth certificate. "No, I mean that. *Thank* you."

"Not at all. I'm just sorry for the woman. Well, both of them. Viola and your friend."

"So, you've seen the estate, right?"

"A few times. But that was back when she held events for the University, so it's been years."

"Well, they say Ms. Horup sort of lost it in the last few years. She started hoarding. Place was crammed full of boxes when I got there on Monday. Sad thing, it was mostly crap."

"Oh, dear."

"They assigned me to her study, and I did what I could, but there wasn't anything significant."

"Really."

"Really," John can feel himself nodding too earnestly. "I think I can put 'world's slowest janitor' on my CV now, since all I did was help the auction house throw a bunch of newspapers and recipe cards away."

Gerald Buonopane's face has always been a sort of playground for twitches and tics, and at the moment he is blinking oddly, while still supporting a permanent smile. "No surprises, no treasures, then?"

"Routine junk," John says. "You're disappointed."

"I am. Yes." And the crispness of the old fellow's reply is so jarring, that for a moment John thinks he's been found out. Buonopane makes a noise, and John can't figure out whether it's a snort, a wheeze, or a fart.

"Jer'?"

"I was led to understand that Ms. Horup was writing a history of New Royal. That's why I thought to send you."

"Oh, right. Amanda told me that, too."

The old man is suddenly sad. "I had high hopes, I suppose. Foolish ones. There were rumors—put out by her, mind you, that she was in possession of unique documents."

"What sort of 'unique documents'?" John pretends to relax, leaning back in the purloined chair and crossing his ankle over his knee.

"It was never very clear." Buonopane allows his smile to return full strength. "I suppose it was just an old woman's babble, enticing the old researcher in me."

* * *

After enduring a full half hour with Buonopane, John returns to the office he shares with another term professor whom he's yet to meet. Gossip has it she's a pill-head about to get canned, so it's likely he has the windowless 8x8 space to himself for the next three months.

Sweet. Sort of. He has no future at NRU, either.

Hock sits at the computer, which is much nicer than anything he can afford, and he thinks about sleeping here some nights. He could buy a love seat from a garage sale, stash some clothes and basics in one of the many empty drawers in his desk. No, wait. He looks up. He could put a stash of emergency supplies up there in the acoustic tile ceiling.

Back when he was in grad school, they used to tell stories about a homeless student who had caches of food and notebooks tucked away in the ceilings. The cleaners would chase him out of the adjunct office where he sometimes slept, mostly hidden under a carrel.

"Hey, John." Bell has materialized on his threshold, and she's dressed for the gym.

He wonders if he should stand but then realizes that's foolish. "Professor Bell. Sorry, I was lost in thought."

"You're here late."

"I met up with an old friend on campus."

"How did class go, then? Did Roth let you get a word in edgewise?"

"Ha, yeah. I think it went well enough. Mr. Thierry is a handful, but I know the type. We draw a lot of those at the community college."

"I'm sure." Bell is standing so that the light in the hallway behind her is much brighter than the dim lamp on Hock's desk. It's the wrong dynamic entirely.

He says, "Do you have a second?"

"Oh, I was just on my way to work out."

"Please?"

"Certainly." She steps in a little awkwardly, and the only chair is some beat, wooden thing that couldn't have been University issue, but was hauled in by a professor from the past. A homey but depressing legacy. She chooses to lean against the door frame instead, arms folded but relaxed. "What can I do for you?"

John just goes for it. "I like it here. I mean, I love it here." And that's true. Even the air at NRU smells more collegial than the funk that hovers over NRCC.

"After just one day?" Bell's smile is maternal.

"Well, I did take a Master's here. Things haven't changed too much over the years. But look, is there anything I can do—"

"Stop," she says, softly. "This is only week one, John. In University-world, nothing is possible right now. The job is the job, just as the contract says."

"When do things become more possible?"

"Honestly, given the year we've had? The rules seem to change every day. Just try to be a great teacher, John. Become indispensable. You know how this goes."

"What if I publish? Something important—regionally."

Her expression was clear: *no dice*. "It's great that you are working on a project. That will help with the next job."

"But not this one."

"You're here to teach and help us hold things together for three months. I might be able to get you a course or two for summer, but after that?" Alma Bell shakes her head. "We're in a PR death spiral because of Liz. And we're terrified of how Crocus' book will be received. Research, even among the tenure line faculty, has taken a back seat."

He wants so much to give her a hint, to let her know he has access to something special. Instead he says, "I understand."

She's moved by his acquiescence. "If you have the energy for it, start a club or create a contest. Do something extra. Then I can write you a letter to replace Buonopane's."

"Wait, what? Is Dr. Buonopane's letter a problem? Oh, I'm sorry. I know I can't ask you."

"It's not the letter, John. It's Jerry."

Gerald Buonopane. "What do you mean?"

"Drop him from your resume."

"But he's the most credentialed referrer I have."

"That's why I'm volunteering to bump him. If you earn it." Bell is starting to bounce on her heels. She wants to escape this discussion.

"Why do I need to bump him? Is it Akron? Because—"

Alma's hand is out. "Please, I don't want to hear it. No committee wants to hear it, either. There's nothing more boring than a graduate student over-reaching with an undergrad. That's exactly the point."

John sinks, completely baffled. "Buonopane."

"Is career poison," she says. "He's the one who brought your problem up. Forced us to discuss it. We saw the equity notation in your file, and we were going to pursue it in the least informative way—*through equity channels*—when your old mentor decided to make it a front and center issue."

John is quiet. This is worse than he imagined. Then: "He wasn't even there."

Alma nods. "I thought that was probably the case. Your man had this *tiny bit* of secondhand information. Gossip, in any other industry, and he came forward with it. Volunteered it."

"That f—" He stops the curse from forming.

"Indeed. Are you okay?"

"No."

Bell straightens. "You will be. Just dump that old cod."

He isn't able to look at her.

"I know you don't want to hear this, but John?"

"Yes, ma'am?"

"In my work, I've learned that secrets are almost impossible to keep. Not that I'm defending him, but poor old Jerry probably couldn't contain himself. He had information, no matter how distracting, and he had to provide it. That's my read, anyway." Alma withdraws and reclaims her shadow against the light.

"Secrets are caustic," she says before leaving him. "No one can keep them except for psychopaths."

* * *

Everyone else is bundled up under a cold, crystalline night, but John's body is humming with nerves, and he's running so hot he's able to walk out towards the faculty parking lot carrying his coat over his arm. It's that word, *psychopath*. People toss it around too easily. He feels it like a jab in the gut, even after Bell is long gone. He has secrets, and he's made some extreme choices, but he isn't insane.

There are late classes in session, but most students have left campus or are huddled in the residence halls, de-compressing from the energy/distress of the first week of the semester. Thursdays are Fridays at Universities, for everyone except lower classmen who have last pick at registration time.

He tries to relax inside the fact that he's a stranger here, easy to ignore.

"Psychopath," he says.

"Bitch," he says.

Under the security lights he can see his breath, and both words look exactly the same.

Not many cars left in the lot, but his is by far the least impressive. Far across the lot is the shuttle stop and a Plexiglas shelter where a shadow hunkers down, waiting. Alone. Something about the way the shadow leans, hungrily drawing the red end of a cigarette close, is recognizable.

It's the big kid, Roth Thierry. Mr. Thumps-a-lot. Mr. "Why are we even here?" Thierry makes the sort of silhouette that you would never think belongs to a student. He looks like a guy getting off work or going to work—either way, working class and miserable. Resolute and joyless.

That's when John starts to feel the cold.

* * *

Crybaby Lane

He awoke in absolute darkness.
He awoke in blood.
He awoke next to Amanda Carlos.

The fake brass doorknob sings under his touch. John is vibrating. When he walks into his apartment, which is a jumble of books, unwashed clothes, and old student papers he's too lazy to shred or archive, he puts his key on the cheap table where he was sorting through all the keys he'd collected from the Horup estate.

Straight to bed because it's time to do that, but he knows he wouldn't be able to sleep. He lays naked under two blankets with the bedside lamp still on, but he keeps seeing Amanda Carlos on that cellar floor, next to the empty shelves, the disconnected boiler, and a giant safe that could not be moved. Carlos had claimed there was nothing in the safe, but John wonders.

How he knows he's not a bad man is the fact that pushing Amanda down the stairs was hard to do. She'd taken him with her, too.

Thank God for that handrail. It probably saved his life when he slammed against it, slowing his roll, as it were. Amanda had flung free by that point, and he witnessed her impossibility: she cartwheeled in that dark air, touching nothing, but hurtling unimpeded towards the least forgiving moment of her life. Her eyes, both intact in that moment, were wide open with surprise. Not fear, though. She expected gravity to reverse itself after it had its way with her.

Chapter 10

Follow the gossip.

That was a toughie, seeing as gossip requires having conversations of a social sort. With Maureen being so quiet and all, and with Murgatroyd gone, I did not have many options.

I went for a run and was deep in the thought when I passed the old-timers on the Honor Farm bench, and the routine call of "Slow down, he stopped chasin' ya!" was a slap across my concentration.

I slowed down, stopped, and bent over to breathe. When the ache in my lungs eased, I went back to the bench.

There were two of them, and I'd put their ages at about 150 years, totaled. Their barn coats were buttoned up tight, and their caps were pulled low. One had tufts of ragged white hair poking out from the sides over his long lobed, red ears. The other one's ungloved hands were in a constant tremor, though I wasn't sure that had anything to do with winter's chill.

They were plenty surprised to see me come back. Shaky Hands even had a bit of a smile going, which wasn't his best look. He had long yellow teeth, but only about five of them by my count.

I demanded, "Why do you always say that?"

Long Ears said, "S'just a joke, honey," and his companion gave up a rheumy chuckle.

I came closer. "Yeah, well, it's offensive."

Smiles on both of them. Long Ears, again: "Well, we're sorry, sweetheart."

Shaky Hands looked at his friend. "Dun mean nuffin."

"Then why?"

They seemed a little nervous now, but not because they felt threatened. They looked like kids trying to decide whether to go on a rollercoaster.

"S'funny?"

"It's not funny." I folded my arms, no need to be subtle.

Shaky Hands took a breath, ready to clarify his point. "He stopped chasin' ya. He tired, not that you ain't good looking."

Long Ears agreed. "Means you're a good runner."

"It's not a compliment, damn it. It's a *threat*. Look, a man chasing a woman is trying to catch her, do you get it? And a woman running from a man is trying to get away from him." I was talking a lot louder than I needed to. I tried to calm down. "Your joke is about *rape*."

Long Ears and Shaky Hands took in the lesson politely. They knew that.

"Just don't do it anymore," I said. "Just don't. Not everyone has as thick a skin as I do."

Long Ears looked at Shaky Hands and said, "It's all good then, because we only say it to you."

Shaky Hands laughed at that, or least he smiled uncontrollably as a sound like shaking a half empty box of cereal poured out of him.

"You really think we say shit like that to normal folk? Lord, we would lose the privileges."

There were very few people in New Royal who didn't know I'd once come at a 7-11 clerk with a hatchet, but here were two of them. If there had been a branch or a shovel nearby, I don't know what I would have done. Instead, I stood my ground, glaring at them, and surreptitiously practicing a breathing exercise to get my rage under control.

I wasn't normal, I knew that. But whatever I was to these men made it safe to…what? Harass me? That blew my mind. No one ever did that to me. No one ever catcalled me on the street or treated me like I wasn't a second away from ripping them a new one.

I know other women were publicly disrespected all the time, but I'd managed to keep that shit on lockdown. Except for these clowns.

"You okay, darlin'?"

"Shut up."

"You seem to be having a bad day. I'm just axing if you need help."

Did he say "ax" on purpose? I had no way of telling. I walked back to the path, hands on hips, anger singing through my veins. The breathing exercises weren't doing the trick. I looked out at the rising hills that tickled the sky, and tried to focus on the slow movement of clouds. Way up there was a barn, and behind that barn the grand house it belonged to.

I was looking at the back end of the Horup estate.

Shaky Hands' and Long Ears' regular view. They were out here every day, staring at land that had, until Viola's death, belonged to the wealthiest, oldest family in New Royal.

I turned back to the old men, my heartbeat slowing.

"Hey," I said. "I need to 'ax' you a question."

* * *

After my chat with the old timers, I didn't bother going home. Murgatroyd's second-to-last last message to me was: *Dog Rasmussen*.

Time to dog.

There was another front coming in, and the sky was a vibrant gray that felt like it wanted to ride my shoulders until I admitted that the world wasn't right. Not anymore. The university had been back in session for weeks now, and I was trying not to feel it. I was no longer a student. My life didn't come with "snow days." I was just like other people, like Maureen, and the days were just days, each one an opportunity to store up fuel/food/money for the future.

When you are in college, the future is unknown. When you're out of it, it's known, like a drab form of magic. I guess that's what people on Facebook mean when they babble about how they "adulted," just because they paid a bill or took their car in for an oil change. There was pressure on me to do a little adulting myself. My agent—Murgatroyd's ex-agent—wanted me to set up an author page. The idea was nauseating, but I did it. I had 37 followers so far. Maureen had suggested I adopt Zero, the black cat, and use pictures of him as filler.

Good flipping God. Poor Zero. He was getting to be a big boy. He recognized me when I came in the shop and would lean hard against his cage so that his black fur would stick out. I would have felt worse about not adopting him, except I knew Maureen was taking him home most nights. She said he was an expert car cat, as if that was a thing.

A car cat wasn't going to do me any good, but maybe if I took Zero, that would patch the invisible gap that had opened up between Maureen and me.

At the top of North Russell Street, the New Royal Police Department complex was massive and sprawling, but lacked drama, like a fortress built by a poor man whose only threat comes from the sky.

The desk officer was a woman in her forties, with her hair pinned in place like she was punishing it. She was lost in a form that, by her expression, told a tragic story.

"Can I see Steve Rasmussen?" I asked.

It didn't matter who I was, I'd given her some small reprieve. She said, almost hopefully, "He's down at McDonald's. It's all day breakfast now."

A half block away. I'd passed him. "Has he been there long?"

"Don't worry," she said. "You'll catch up to him."

* * *

When I got to the McDonald's, Rasmussen was eating a breakfast sandwich very slowly, like it might be his last meal. He was alone, still wearing his scarf and coat, and he was reading his phone, using his thumb to scroll while all his other fingers were involved in the sandwich.

His face sort of buckled when he realized I was headed right for him. It was about two in the afternoon, and the place was mostly empty except for some senior citizens trying to pick a seat and a mom with a baby and a toddler in the booth directly across from Rasmussen. The toddler was staring at him. The detective's coat was open over his lap, and his holstered weapon was exposed.

"Detective?" I knew better than to wait for an invite, so I sat down across from him.

Rasmussen was unhappy about that. "Ms. Rowe."

"I was wondering if there was news about Viola or the Carlos woman?"

"You know, I have an office."

"That's what I thought, too. I was sent here, though."

He put his phone away and stared at me. He was making a decision, I guess. "Does your friend know?"

"Excuse me?"

"Does your friend, that redhead Maureen, does she know that you didn't write *Mean Bone?*"

The open hostility was a twist. I mean, he knew I'd bite back, right? "I guess it's tough being a mediocre detective in a town that needs a good one."

"The fuck?" Rasmussen was trying to decide how pissed he wanted to be and still be able to finish his meal.

If the mother of the children heard what Rasmussen said, she didn't care. The seniors had finally picked a place where they could look out on a side street, sip their coffee, and criticize shoe choices, considering all the black ice on the sidewalks.

I said, "You know I have impulse issues."

"If that's an apology, you need to do better." He didn't sound nearly as angry as he should be.

"You're not mediocre. I'm sorry."

"Like I'm going to let *you* get under my skin?" And when he said "you," he looked straight up at my hair.

I touched the coxcomb to make sure it was still high. I'd put it through its paces today. "You don't like my hair?"

"No, not really. Hair's a personal thing, though." He pulled his ponytail out of the depths of his Bulldogs scarf to remind me. "You do dumb stuff to your hair, you're making a choice about the kind of conversations you want to have. Why are we even talking, Crocus?"

There was a shred of egg clinging to his haphazard beard. I focused on it, the symbol of Rasmussen's innate humanity. "I'm just trying to find out if everyone's still sold on Seth Shute as Viola's killer."

Dismissive grunt. "Dude has been arraigned, so yeah."

Like I was the dumbest thing in the world. That was good. It meant Rasmussen felt like he was in charge.

I said, "Because of physical evidence and access."

"If I seem impatient here, it's because I am." He put his half-eaten sandwich down and reached for a napkin to wipe his fingers.

"Please, I'm sorry, I'm trying to work through something. And seriously, you're the only one who can tell me what's solid and what isn't."

He mouthed the word: *bullshit.* This was his house.

Whatever. "So, if I were Shute's public defender, I'd make a big deal about the Carlos death because, well, accidental death is just the default conclusion on an unattended, right?"

No response. Permission to proceed.

"The rest, then, is physical evidence at the scene, which is tricky because Shute was there all the time. He stole the credit cards because that's his nature, but killing an old woman?" I focused on little Eggy. *Hold on, bro!* "That leaves access, and the assumption—and this is me being on the outside looking in, I know—the assumption is that there were people coming and going. Generally high visibility, front door, come-into-my-parlor-types."

"Where are you going with this, fake counselor?"

I leaned forward, tried to tear myself away from Eggbert, and look into Rasmussen's small, perpetually sleepy eyes. "Have you ever heard of Crybaby Lane?"

"Right there." He pointed at me. "That sort of thing. Where you play dumb and then you don't. That's insulting."

"I know."

"We're done," he pronounced. "But let me give you a tip. Don't try to be Murgatroyd. It's no good asking questions if you're only ready for one answer.

That's the flaw in the Murgatroyd model. One piece out of place, and the whole thing collapses. Figure out your own way."

I ruined his exit by eyeballing his coffee cup and the sandwich paper, still on the table. He saw me looking and grabbed his tray to put it on top of the trash can. Pretty sure he didn't usually bus his own table. He fastened his coat up, and with the gun put out of sight, the toddler across the way was able to focus on her hash brown.

He paused at the door, all puffed up. Expecting something from me in exchange for that nugget of nothing.

I gave it to him. "Thank you," I said. Men always want you to thank them for their time, no matter what has transpired.

"Anytime."

"Really?"

"No." Then he pushed open the door against a gust of wind, squinting into the winter sun as if it was the worst. He turned and started walking the half block back to the station, looking somber and put out.

"Way to work off that McMuffin," I said, and then I noticed the mother of the two children staring right at me. "Amazing, right? How he can transform from entitled cop to everyday doofus with a simple zip of his parka."

She didn't laugh. People don't like it when you make fun of guys packing heat.

* * *

At Pet Market, they told me Maureen had gone out on a sandwich run, and when she came back she found me in the cat room where prospective adopters could test drive the varmints of their choice. I was sitting on the floor, swatting Zero on the head with a feather-tipped stick. He was big now, and the only way you could tell he was still a kitten was by his enthusiasm for violence. He grabbed at that feather like he was more than ready for the real deal. Every once in a while, he'd stop going for it, just so he could stare me down.

"What's going on?" Maureen asked. Behind her, the twitchy clerk chewed on his paper-wrapped panini while pretending not to watch us through the glass.

"Well, Zero's telling me he could mess me up, if he wanted to. I also thought I'd brief you on what kind of idiot I can be without your guidance."

"Oh yeah?" Still a little tightness in her voice, like she needed one more day off from me. Too bad. I'd been pulling double shifts in Crocus-world, all on my own.

I said, "Been talking around, trying to shake some information loose." I made the feather draw figure eights around Zero's face, and he was getting mad. "So I went around to see Rasmussen, and I basically told him he was stupid."

"Way to network, Cro. It's not like talking to cops won't be important to your career or anything." Maureen swooped down to rescue Zero from my brutal ways, but he slurped away and came to me, butting his broad, black head against the hand I used to hold the stick. I scratched his ears.

"I talked to some other people, and they were a lot more helpful." I stood up, my feet sort of aching inside my Chucks. I'd been wearing them all day, and they were half wet. Zero leaped up on the cat tower and started flipping around like a black, silky fish.

Maureen was already suspicious. "What people?"

I made air quotes. "Some neighbors of Viola's. The ones across the way."

Though we were behind glass, she lowered her voice. "You're supposed to steer clear of…" She hesitated, not at all comfortable with the terms that townies used to refer to members of the state sponsored population. She settled on "that element."

"It was just guys from the Honor Farm. I wanted to get a sense of what life at the Horup estate looked like from their perspective. You know, before Viola was killed."

"So. You're not here just because you need a sounding board."

"No, I need a ride. Out to Crybaby Lane."

She went placid as a mannequin. These damned townies were never straight with us folks from the county. It was like they were in a cult.

"We can talk about this later," she said. "I have to get back to work." She made a move towards the door of the cat room, but I stepped in her way.

"Maureen, please."

Everything was in her face. "I get off at seven," she said, grabbing the cat from the top of his perch. "I'll come by your place and pick you up."

Zero yowled all the way back to his crate, and everyone could hear him from all over the store. Like a baby's cry, it was the kind of sound that hits you in your heart.

Luckily, I don't take advice from cats.

* * *

Another night-time van trip. Whee! Maureen picked me up outside my apartment building.

"You changed your clothes," she said.

I pretended to be caught up fastening the seat belt. "So what's with all the superstition, Mo?"

"Hey, those old men are superstitious. I'm just careful. A person with your lifestyle restrictions shouldn't be talking to inmates or be seen hanging around places that are off-limits."

"That's sweet, you looking out for me."

"Crocus. You're such a dope," and she put the van into gear.

We drove out to the Horup estate and went past it for some ways. I didn't think you could go past Horup's, as it always seemed like New Royal began and ended there, but then Maureen turned down a one lane gravel road. The van bounced in the ruts. We still had snow to reflect the headlights, but the briars were tall on either side, sometimes scraping the van.

Maureen had been here before, plenty of times.

I looked ahead, trying to see beyond the headlights, but for all I knew she could have been driving us into a lake or over a cliff. The sky was starless, moonless, but we were together, doing something that was probably stupid. Maybe this was going to be our thing.

Then we got to a hole in the bramble, and she turned left into it. We rocked in our seats as if riding tandem camels. The headlights did this *Blair Witch* dance over an expanse of frozen, rutted mud. There'd been plenty of vehicles out here back when the ground was softer.

We stopped. "This is as far as we can go in the van."

"Is this Crybaby Lane?"

"You like saying that a lot."

"It's awesome, like a song from the 50s."

"Well, this is just a farm road. Crybaby Lane is a horse path from the 1800s. At least that's the best guess." Maureen turned off the headlights, and we stepped out into darkness.

Since I couldn't see much, I held onto her jacket sleeve, too shy to grab her hand. I don't know how she could tell where the path was, but we walked along a hard, level patch at the edge of a heavily forested area, and when the way became lumpy with embedded rocks, she took me down a slope into the trees.

The old snow helped with visibility, but I was still nervous, afraid that I'd step into a hole and break my ankle or walk smack into a bear. Every time I pulled my phone out to light the way, Maureen made me put it back.

"Don't ruin it," she said, looping her arm in mine.

So, that was nice. Terrifying, but nice.

We continued down, with Maureen picking out the route. There were pines and rocks and wide, snowy places that looked solid, but she steered me away from them. She kept her eyes to the ground, and I held on tight.

Now in a movie, I would be walking into my own sacrifice. Instead, we were just slip-walking down a steep, woody hillside that should have felt a lot colder than it did.

"Can you see that there's a clearing down there?" she asked. She led me to a long, fallen trunk where she sat down and pointed at the gloom below.

"Not really." I noticed that there was no snow on the trunk. Someone had brushed it off, recently. I took a seat as well. "Why, is that where we're going?"

"We can if you want to. Not much to see down there, though."

That wasn't what the old timers at the Honor Farm had said. They were still going on about ghosts when I got tired of their B.S. "Which way is Horup's?"

"This is all part of the farm, technically. But the house is…" She pointed unsteadily out into nothing before recalibrating and shifting to another nothing. "That way."

"Why's this called Crybaby Lane?"

"Pick a story. Indian burial ground. Ghost priests. Make-out central that doubles as a killer's dumping ground. They all end with the line, 'and from that day on, the path was known as Crybaby Lane.'"

"Everything to everyone."

"Pretty much. When I was in high school, this was where we all went in summer to smoke pot and fool around. Sometimes the guys would put a tent down there. And when we left, the place would be trashed, beer cans, cigarettes, and chip bags everywhere. But then when we came back, it'd be all cleaned up. We all just assumed it was Viola's groundsmen, but it was weird she didn't get after us for sneaking onto her property. Later, I found out different. That's when I stopped coming here. Or, to be more exact, that's when I stopped going down there."

She paused for effect, and I noticed the silence wasn't all that silent. The trees creaked and scraped. Maureen said, "You're supposed to go, *dun-dun-dun!*"

"I know, but I was sort of hung up on a detail. When you would hang out in the clearing, um. That was with guys, right?"

"Oh my God, you're terrible at this. I'm about to blow your mind by revealing the deepest, darkest secret of Horup's farm, and you want a queer memoir?"

"Can't I have both?"

She laughed out loud, and the bowl of the forest laughed back. "Not at the same time," she said. "So my English teacher in senior year was into folklore. She was a pinafore-wearing, crazy hair type, and to look at her you couldn't tell if she was a witch or a Pentecostal. One of the options for the final project was to look into how the truth could be used to tell a story that was clearly untrue."

"Heh," I said. This was right up my alley. "A New Royal specialty."

"Exactly. There must be something in the groundwater. This whole town lies, and it always has."

That struck me as painfully true. And it was probably why I'd never fully acclimated to civilian life in town. I was a terrible liar.

As Maureen settled into her story, her face relaxed, her eyes shined, and the pet store smell came off her in waves. I loved it. If we were going to be together, I'd have to tell her about *Mean Bone*. All about it.

"Anyway," she said, "I got it in my head that I wanted to write about Crybaby Lane, and all the crazy stuff people said went down here. Some of it's cookie cutter, right? Indians and the like, but the ghost priest? I mean, what the hell, right? Like he's just floating around down there, blessing the stones and the tree stumps."

I moaned in my best ghost voice, "*In nomine Patris, et Filii, et Spiritus Sancti…*"

"Cut it out, you'll spook yourself."

She was right about that. I already felt a tingle in my gut. "So what did you find out?"

"Well, I never was a good student, so I just went to my gramma. When I asked her what was so important about this place, she asked me a simple question that I'm now going to ask you: Do you know where you come from, and where your family comes from?"

I nodded. "The Rowes are English, but there's German on my mom's side."

"Uh huh. So, my family is Scots-Irish, like everyone else. Same deal, right? So then she asked me another question. 'Well, what if you didn't know?'"

"I'd pony up for a DNA test."

"Yeah, but what if you're in the 1930s and you're trying to find out about your heritage, but there aren't any records before, say, the around the turn of the century?"

"No church or hospital records?"

"No deeds with your family name. Nothing. It's like your clan showed up on the planet just in time to, I don't know, catch the Chicago World's Fair before spending the rest of their short, nasty lives in a factory."

"That's a little dark."

"Well, Gramma's point was that roots are more important than we think. Even more important for immigrants, which is basically what we all are. So, then she drops the bomb. There's a crazy number of folks from New Royal who can't claim to be from anywhere else, because they just don't know. Except they have one thing in common—the only thing we all have in common—the Horups. Peter Horup, specifically. Viola's great-great-great-great whatever."

"The guy who freed the slaves and founded the town."

"The statue guy, yeah." There was a lumpy, porous figure of Horup in a bad part of New Royal that used to be the good part. He got tagged a lot. "This story is getting complicated."

"It's about to get simple, don't sweat it. Those folks, for generations, sort of just assumed they were all related, at least spiritually. And, they liked to get together from time to time." She nodded to the darkness in front of us.

"Down there?" I said. "Sounds a little culty."

"Only if you think picnics are culty. That's where all the weird stories come from. People getting together in a place they feel is theirs to a certain extent, but to the outside it looks odd. For example, when my Gramma was little, the story was that the old slaves were buried down there. She said there were stones placed north, south, east, west. Those are gone now."

"You believe that?"

Maureen nodded. "I believe the people who were cleaning up after us kids were folks who didn't want to be caught trespassing."

I stared down into the forest, vaguely aware that something had changed since we'd started talking. It was the moon, finally rising behind us. I started to see the path for what it was. "So, you went to class and said, 'this is what my Gramma told me,' got your C minus and collected your diploma?"

"Nah. I did my report on Bill Clinton's depositions. Got my C minus the honorable way, by half-assing it."

"How come?"

"Gramma. She told me to zip it. That there might be kids in the class who knew a lot more than me about Crybaby Lane."

"And that's when you stopped going down there to make out."

Maureen nodded, leaned against me in the new moonlight. "Now I do all my making out right up here."

* * *

It's always feast and famine with me. In this case, I got the girl, but I was pretty sure I didn't have a career. None of my poking around was leading anywhere.

We went to Maureen's place, and I could see why she only took Zero home a few nights out of the week. She already had three cats she was fostering, and I was sure that was a lease violation right there. I told her I'd take Zero, and that was it.

97

We fell into bed, which was fantastic until the cats started crawling all over us. I just watched like an idiot, while she chased them all out into the living room. She'd get one out and another would slip right back in. It took a while, but she did it.

Point of romantic etiquette: if the cats were fosters I didn't have to learn their names, or which was which, right?

It was a nice night. A great night. I was glad I showered earlier. After Maureen fell asleep, I let myself drift back to Crybaby Lane. Fascinating stuff, but it seemed like I was getting farther and farther away from my goal of finding out what happened to Viola or Amanda.

Maybe I wasn't the gal for the job. Maybe there wasn't even a job to do. Rasmussen seemed confident about it all. Of course, he knew about Crybaby Lane—it was merely a well-traveled shortcut with a provocative name, but that also meant that more people had access to the Horup estate than was commonly thought.

One of Maureen's cats had been pawing under her bedroom door, and when it stopped doing that it started to pound up against it. Maureen slept right through the racket. Finally, the door popped open, and all three came in and started climbing the bed, crawling the perimeter and the pillows. The fat orange one started licking Mo's shoulder, and when I shoved him off, he started on me. That was fine, I wasn't sleepy.

My life had changed. Again.

* * *

I woke from a nightmare that wasn't one.

We were back at Viola's doing everything the way we did that night. I sent Maureen out to the porch while I took pictures of Amanda Carlos' broken body.

And then retraced my steps so we could tell Rasmussen everything was as we found it, right down to the last detail.

Except it wasn't.

I woke, pinned under the sheet by the cats. They were all sleeping on me.

I pushed them off, gently as I could, and they complained. Two returned to their original spots, and the big orange one plodded off into another room, and soon I heard the unmistakable sound of him digging an escape tunnel in his litter box.

"Maureen," I said. I put my hand on her back. "Maureen, wake up."

She jolted, the way deep sleepers do. For a second she looked surprised to see me, but then she came to. Her hair was wrapped around her naked shoulders like she was a skater in mid-spin. "What is it? Oh, the cats."

"No, they're fine, they're cool. I just, oh shit, I remembered something. About Amanda."

She scooched up.

"I forgot to shut the door, Mo."

"What door?"

"The cellar door. The one *you* opened. Oh, Christ, Mo. I never shut it again."

Maureen pushed the hair out of her face, her lips in a hard line. She was thinking it through, trying to get to where I was. Slowly, she said, "So the cops don't know that the door was closed when we found her."

I nodded. The orange cat was back, trying to get between us. "That's why it was a slam dunk to them. But why would a woman close the door on herself in the dark?"

"Maybe she grabbed at it to stop her fall."

"She hit that rail super-hard, nothing slowed her down."

"Oh Jesus, Crocus. We were trying to be so careful," she whispered.

"I know."

She reached out and grabbed my hand. "So why didn't you close the door?"

It was such a strange detail, so minor and stupid it didn't make sense, but the dream brought it all back to me like a clanging dinner bell.

I put my phone away and used it to shut off the cellar light. I could no longer see Amanda, but I could see Maureen's moonlit silhouette pacing the front porch. I moved to close the cellar door. She was down there, all alone. And even though she was dead, I was still scared for her.

You don't close the door on someone who's that alone.

"I just didn't," I breathed. "It's like I couldn't. But…I didn't remember that."

Maureen reached out and stroked my neck, pulled me over to her. "It's okay," she said, with a grim, settled voice that reminded me of my mother's in our darkest times. "We're going to figure this out together."

And just like that, a tiny hiccup in my memory became a thing. I lay on her breasts, stroking her body, inhaling her scent, and absorbing her warmth, like I was one of her damned cats. The big orange one. The really big orange one.

* * *

Just before dawn, another nightmare, only this time Maureen was shaking me awake.

"Crocus, wake up, wake up."

I'm a pretty light sleeper, and that's been a good thing before. This time, I wasn't sure what the hell was going on.

"You were crying," said Maureen. "Whimpering."

I felt my face, and it was wet. Did I cry in my sleep? Damn.

We made coffee when the sun came up. Fed the cats and made toast for ourselves. Showered together. I felt a little guilty for enjoying that so much.

"You know I have a problem, right?"

"Are you talking about your PTSD?" She was in a t-shirt. No pants. Flitting from cabinet to sink.

"Yeah," I said. "You know it didn't just start with the Shaler murders, right?" I had been an EMT worker, a first responder at that scene, and in *Mean Bone*, it was heavily implied that my criminal downfall began with the trauma of seeing those little girls dead in the pond.

But a tendency towards unprovoked violence takes some teaching.

She brought her mug, milky but still steaming, to the breakfast bar, where it landed with a thud. "You're telling me what? That you have an origin story I don't know about?"

I nodded. "Boring stuff. Sad stuff. From when I was a kid."

"You going to tell me about it?"

"Someday, probably. Not right now, though." It was already a big enough day without taking a trip down memory lane on a motorcycle with no helmet. "Mo, would you be disappointed if I dropped this whole thing? Looking into the Horup case, I mean."

Maureen came around to my side of the breakfast bar and plunked herself bare-assed on the dining chair next to mine. She put her leg on the rung under me and curled her foot around, linking us together. I didn't know how long she liked to stay naked in the mornings, but I'd pulled on my jeans and t-shirt first thing, and I caught a flicker of disappointment in her eyes when I reached for my Chucks, too. It was just my way.

She said, "I guess I would, a little, but that's just me being selfish. I could get over it. So, what's the plan, tell Rasmussen what you recall and walk away?"

"There's so much I can't do, like talk to Seth or even Murgatroyd. Even with the stuff that's right in front of me, I don't seem to have the *eye*, you know? The pictures, Crybaby Lane. That came to nothing."

"But you remembered the door."

"I *dreamed* the memory of the door. I don't think that's a reliable method of investigation."

"If it's making you unhappy, screw it. But, baby, you are running around with the worst case of imposter syndrome I ever saw, and I don't think you've given yourself much of a chance." Maureen put her hand on my arm. "And besides, maybe you were distracted."

She meant by us. True, my head was probably flooded with idiot hormones.

Maureen leaned in to give me a long, lazy kiss. I closed my eyes like a normal, until she closed hers, then I opened mine again. I didn't want to miss it. When she pulled back, I could tell she'd already made a plan.

"Don't go to Rasmussen," she said. "Not yet. Walk around with this door thing. I mean, that's what you do, that's how you think."

"And just wait for a revelation?"

Maureen's eyes narrowed. "You need space. *Head* space."

"Maureen. I really think I should talk to Rasmussen."

"So he can ridicule you, and tell you a dream isn't evidence?"

Which was exactly what he would do. "It's amazing that you have my back, Mo, but the reality is I only seem to find out stuff a lot of other people know already. Crybaby Lane's no secret. Neither is John Hock's connection to the Horup estate. The only secret so far is what you and I were doing at Viola's house."

Maureen sipped at her coffee, thinking of a comeback.

I lightly rubbed her back. "You know, for someone who just said 'screw it,' you seem to be struggling to accept that there's just no story here, other than the one everyone already knows."

"Murgatroyd thinks there is."

"Well now, that's a big gun to pull," I laughed. "Sure you know how to shoot that thing?"

"You know I don't like to say her name. I'm half afraid she'll appear like a demon. But would she really tell you to go looking if there wasn't anything to find?"

"She was drunk when sent those messages."

"To hear you talk about it, her drinking affects her personal judgment, but not her intellect." She got up and walked back into the kitchen to put her empty cup in the sink. "I'm sorry, I don't why I'm arguing with you."

She was so pretty, so everything. I could sit there all day watching her putter around in that shirt. Suddenly the thought that I might disappoint her, even just a little, was unbearable.

But still. "Mo, I can't do this without help."

"I can help you."

"I mean Murgatroyd. I need *her* help. She needs to tell me what to do next."

Maureen folded her arms, just a little fed up with all of this. "Okay," she said.

"Okay what?"

"Okay, I'll go see Murgatroyd."

Chapter 11

February 2017

So, February was already going to be weird, seeing as we went from a normal icy winter to weather that was a lot like Spring.

But then came the words. Naturally, we blamed the poets.

That's what you do in a small college town when random words on scraps of paper start to appear, stapled to the telephone poles at first, and then in more unexpected places. Single words, and sometimes single letters popped up all over New Royal—even in the woods. A few were handwritten on pieces of heavy stock folded in half, but most were printed on plain old 20 lb. paper, cut up.

Like the one on my shoe. Stuck to the bottom of the left sole was a strip of paper. When I peeled it away, I saw written on it was a single word in cursive: *cradle*.

I crumpled it into a pea-sized ball and flicked it in the direction of the trash can. Missed. Zero went after it, but to me it was unimportant.

No one pays attention to a little slip of paper. And I wonder how many of these were lost before we started to see a pattern?

But then: the lady who ran the Joyful Noise! Christian shop found *never*, *near*, and *collect* on three separate Mondays.

The Einstein Bros bagel store found *birch* and *follow* in their sweepings one evening as they were closing up.

The Subway Shop on the east side of the university received three capital *A*s and nine lower case *a*'s in a single week.

Dutchy's Dry Cleaning produced dozens of words and letters from the pockets of their customers' clothes, which they began checking both before and after service.

A fourth grader found the word *spine* inside a bus shelter.

Crybaby Lane

* * *

My first, full introduction to the word game was when I was cutting across campus, walking under the looming sunset shadow of Jarvis. I was almost past the old quad when I got a text from Roth Thierry.

All it said was, **Howdy.**

Maybe I'd made a mistake with Thierry by treating him like a human being. Since that day in Gov Doc, he'd been "encountering" me in the most unlikely places, trying to engage me in long, philosophical chats about the dumbest stuff. Writing, mostly, although I was convinced he talked more than wrote.

It wasn't a crush, like Maureen kept saying. It was just that I was a listener, and he was going to make me listen to every thought he ever had.

While I was figuring out how to respond to his first text, he sent another. **Look up.**

I did, and after a second I saw a blurry shape at a long window on the top floor of Jarvis. Roth was up there, waving like a giant child from the fourth-floor seminar room, a brick and glass box that jutted out over the sidewalk in a way that always looked dangerous to me, as if it could just calve off like a chunk of glacier right down onto the quad.

I waved back, and almost immediately he texted. **Come up.**

Because Bell was always on the lookout, I needed a good excuse to hang out in Jarvis. Now I had an invitation. From Roth Thierry, but I didn't care. Beggars and choosers, etc.

I took the stairs two at a time, sort of loving the crush of it in my chest. I was getting to be a true runner that way. When I reached the top, I headed to the seminar room, only to find it full of the enormity of Roth Thierry and a new feature: his normally whiffy body odor was now overwhelming—a dense mix of shit and meat. He sat at the table, almost trancelike, his hands flat on its surface. If I hadn't seen him with my own eyes, I would never have matched the waving figure from the window with this sad sack of misery.

I'd always assumed Thierry had a clinical excuse for his eccentricities, and now it was obvious he was having a dark episode. Wearing a black Slayer t-shirt and stained jeans—the same clothes he always did—he was still as I entered, as if the first half of a magic word had been spoken, and he was waiting, breathless, on the rest.

The seminar room was the most desired location for graduate classes owing to the bank of windows overlooking the old part of campus, which meant it was icy during the day, no matter the season, and warm at night, after having soaked up the sunset like a battery. The sun was setting fast now, and Thierry looked runny under its glow.

"Yo," I said. I could feel the weird, almost out-of-body grin taking over my face. "You have a class in here?"

Roth drew a low, unsteady breath, and looked up at me, open-mouthed. He hadn't shaved, his straw-colored hair was matted, and his skin was blotchy.

"They left," he said, as he seemed to be wrapping his mind around the fact of my presence.

They left? That could mean a lot of normal things, but now that I was taking in the scene, I saw that the chairs were not pushed in or stacked. In fact, most of them were askew. If it was Thursday evening and I was looking at a half-stunned Roth Thierry, that meant the class in question was Gov Doc. But back in January, the class was meeting in a windowless tomb. John Hock managed to score a room change, the rarest of academic prizes.

"They just walked out on you?" I didn't bother assuming anything else. "That's kind of cold, man. Was it the lawyers' idea?"

"The what?" Roth looked at me as if he wasn't certain I was real.

"The suit guys in your class." I sat down across the table, and the sunset behind him just seemed to make his odor worse, but it transformed his thin hair into a lovely halo. "There were two that first night. They're fricking 'League of Gs.'"

We had a lot of nicknames for the different kinds of folks in the program. Lawyers were always taking classes, and they stuck out like sore thumbs, even when they tried to be casual.

"Oh," said Roth. "They hate my guts." He giggled softly, like a small girl, and that hit me. No doubt he'd spent a lot of his growing up years learning how to do things like giggle to make people feel better about how big he was.

"Where did they say they were headed?"

"Library."

Hock was a chicken shit, but I got it. He didn't have a future here, so there was no point in getting into conflicts. Best to pull up stakes than engage the problem. I wondered if the students all left together or if they just sort of trickled out, like the Von Trapp family. *Auf wiedersehen, adieu.*

Roth was sweating pure death. My eyes started to water. "The showers at the gym are free, man. All you have to do is show your student ID."

This news was confusing to him, and he was getting a heavy-lidded look that, in my experience, spelled danger. Roth reached behind him and pulled out a wad of paper shreds from his back pocket. He asked, "Do you know what these mean?"

"No. What is that?"

"They're words. They're everywhere." He sounded scared, on the verge of crying.

And suddenly I felt as if I'd walked into some kind of performance art thing, but then I remembered: *cradle*.

"Words," I echoed. Then I tried to make a joke. "*Word*."

No giggle this time. He was all out. He said, "All I wanted was some help. Figuring them out."

He pushed the ball of paper towards me, and I had to take it. I started peeling away the pieces carefully. "You have a theory, Roth?"

cousin

fortunate

used

He said, "Someone's trying to send me a message. These are all over town."

I guessed I'd seen them before, but never paid attention.

Poor Roth Thierry. He was having a paranoid episode, and Hock just up and abandoned him. I said, "You're worried you're missing some pieces, right?"

Big, silent nod. Something was building in him, and that was not good.

"Looks like you have plenty to work with here." I smoothed out more pieces.

unfortunate

tenant

boy

"Look, Roth. We need to get a team on this. Do you have a team?"

"That's why I brought it to class." He trailed off and lost focus. Then, he just exploded, pounding his hand on the table. "Fuck!" he roared.

That had to get someone's attention.

"Damned straight," I said, as if screaming was normal. I flattened the words, moved them around. Kept busy.

Now Roth was breathing funny, almost panting. "Were you really in prison?"

"Uh huh."

"'Cause you fucked up some guy?"

"Um," I played with the scraps. I could hear commotion out in the hall, so I kept yakking. It was my superpower. Doc M always said I was good at eating time, filling silence. "Two guys, actually. One guy I dangled over a balcony until he crapped himself, and the other guy…I wrecked his hand with a hatchet."

"Why?"

Roth Thierry's superpower. He was always the guy who said "Why?" no matter what the discussion. In my current situation, I nearly forgot the most important thing about him: he was a natural jerk. We had that in common, I guess.

And there they were, heading towards the seminar room. John Hock and a campus cop. So maybe Hock wasn't totally useless after all.

"'Why' doesn't matter, Roth. It's the 'how.'" I reached out and scooped up all his little scraps of paper, wadding them back into a ball. Then I squeezed it hard, until it was half the size it was when he gave it to me. "I'm just a hands-on gal, I guess."

When Hock and the cop entered the room, Roth could have exploded again, but he didn't. He just whimpered and let his huge, reeking self go limp. All he wanted was some help, after all.

Whimpers and giggles—they're the same damned thing.

I stuffed the word ball in my jeans.

* * *

After Roth Thierry was escorted away I rushed to the ladies' room to scrub my hands with that that nasty soap from the pump, but it still felt as if his ghost funk was stuck to me. When I came out, Alma Bell and Doris Wethers were having a quiet, serious discussion near the main office.

A Wethers sighting was somewhat rare, but here she was in all her towering, redheaded glory. When she spotted me, her eyes went straight to my orange coxcomb. We had that in common, the hair thing, except I don't think her 'do was even remotely as ironic as mine. The conversation she and Bell were having was obviously private.

Naturally, I horned in on it. "They take Roth to a hospital?"

Bell was still in a sweater set and rayon slacks that screamed *administration*. "I assume so," she said. "His first trip of the semester."

"He usually makes it to Spring Break," said Wethers. "Must be the weather." She was grim, taking me in. She sounded disappointed when she said, "You are unmolested, I see."

"Don't look at me like this is my fault."

"No one blames you. Obviously, Mr. Thierry has issues that will challenge him throughout his life."

I removed the paper ball from my pocket to show them. "He was saying these are everywhere."

Bell said, "We're trying to get a handle on that. There's an assumption that the University is behind it."

"Back up. This is a widespread thing? I thought Thierry was just bullshitting me."

"Crocus, if you're getting your news from Roth Thierry, that's a problem. Our students are collecting the words on their own, holding parties in the residence halls where they try to piece them together."

Nerds. I was jealous, though. "So it's a game, some kind of puzzle."

Wethers said, "We hope so. But we have no idea who's behind it."

"Why does everyone assume it's the University?"

"Who knows? PR stunt. A goodwill gesture. Community outreach." Wethers paused meaningfully. "An *apology*."

Though I knew what she was getting at, the devil in me wanted to make her say what she meant. Wethers and Murgatroyd were old friends, but I'd gone a little sour on the department Chair. After the Doc was arrested, Wethers made me finish my classes as individualized studies. I got my diploma by mail. Proud moment for me, tearing open that envelope with the refrigerator cheering me on.

"An apology for what?"

Wethers' lips pursed in the subtlest smirk I'd ever seen. "How is Liz getting on?"

"I'm not allowed to talk to her. You are, though. Apology for what?"

Her eyes to my hair again. "For Murder Town, of course."

Bell said, "She means the Program. And the kind of people it attracts."

"You mean like Jeaneane."

Wethers was silent. It was as if she was aching for a string of pearls for her to clutch.

"And Roth Thierry," I said.

Apparently, that went without saying, as well.

"And me, right?"

Finally, Wethers said, "I do tire of talking to you about you."

I didn't care. "Well, I was here long before the program launched."

Bell intervened. "It's all about perception, Crocus, and perception is fuzzy." She made a butterfly gesture with her hand, as if the ugly between me and the Chair was a passing vapor. "Doris and I are thinking about how to get in front of this word thing. How to use it to improve the Department's profile, not just to the administration, but to New Royal at large."

I looked at the ball of words in my hand. It wasn't a bad idea, stepping up and owning something people already thought you owned. "Maybe you want to NaNoWriMo it."

"Excuse me?"

"Like the events that the Department hosts for National Novel Writing Month. The write-ins and challenges."

"Oh God, that thing. But yes, something along those lines would be good."

"So, find someone from the department who can coordinate the word collection and analysis in a noisy Student Life kind of way. You want someone to go into the residence halls and provide support for what the kids are already doing, even if it's just pizza nights."

Bell and Wethers traded looks. I'd just about stepped in it.

Wethers said, "Nice thinking, Crocus. How about you, would you do it?"

"No way."

She made herself even taller and more stately, cooing like a Disney villain. "It could be your way of 'giving back.' And we could help you promote *Mean Bone*."

"Bullshit."

It was bullshit, and Wethers knew it. Her face went blank, as if I no longer existed. Still, she gave up too easily. I would have done it, if she'd kept up the pressure.

* * *

And that's how poor John Hock became the puzzle guy.

The next day, Wethers called him into her office, and offered him the rare "opportunity" to become an important part of the culture at NRU.

From what I understood, he tried to reject it but was given no choice. And then, he started to get into it.

The Dean liked the proposal, but failed to imagine the scale of the endeavor. To make things worse, the administration sent out a press release that was imprecise about how the words should be delivered and where. People began emailing the words they'd found to the communications office, and within a week, new guidelines were issued. The words could not be transmitted digitally. Only the original pieces of paper would be accepted for the archive, and citizens were asked to provide provenance as best they could. At first, they mailed or dropped off their finds directly to the President's and Provost's offices, but soon there were drop boxes in the student union and throughout town, mostly at the Subway sandwich shops.

The first count sent a shock through New Royal. A staggering 10,231 words and letters deemed plausible from the same print style and stock. 596 discarded as pranks. 1,188 undetermined.

And the contributions kept coming.

This puzzle was going to be impossible to solve, a fact that only managed to transform casual curiosity into shiny-eyed hunger. The community of New Royal had a new point of focus and there wasn't a single gossipy exchange that didn't bear the residue of the mystery.

Hock presided over "piecing nights," events where everyone gathered to discuss the finds. The events had to be moved out of the residence halls and into common areas like the student center so that the public could contribute. Food trucks appeared, and in general a kind of festival giddiness prevailed, and no one talked about the President, or Russia, or Obamacare. In a way, the piecing nights provided a safe zone where people could be themselves again.

Sorting words made everyone happy.

Except for John Hock, apparently.

I attended a piecing night late in the month, and afterward I hung around outside waiting for Maureen to come pick me up. The participants poured out fast to catch a basketball game of local importance—Buckeyes vs. Lions—so I hung back out of foot traffic.

Eventually Hock came out, huffing like he was in a hurry, too, but there was no thrill in his step. In fact, when he passed under a walkway lamp, he looked sort of washed out. I figured he was just a nervy, overstressed guy, not great with crowds or people in general.

I didn't think much about it, but in a few minutes Maureen pulled up, and I got into the van. She leaned over to give me a peck on the cheek, and then we pulled out, rolling by the faculty surface lot.

"Hey, slow down a little," I said. "Look at that."

The lot was only half full, and it was easy to spot the little Ford—because it was bouncing. As we got closer we saw the driver inside, pounding on the dash as if he wanted to smash it to pieces.

"Someone's a little unhappy," said Maureen.

The van's headlamps swept across the little car and for just a quick sweeping second, illuminated the face of its angry driver.

"Oh shit, that's John Hock," I said.

"Should we offer to help?"

"Uhhhh. No?" I looked at Maureen to see if that was the right answer.

"Thank God," said Maureen, and we giggled about it because we're like that when we're together. Not always nice.

So, that was a mystery, too. A seemingly minor one that should have been easy to figure out, but I was practicing minding my own business these days. It was nice not to be embroiled in other people's drama, even though I knew it wasn't going to last. Maureen was meeting Murgatroyd soon, after which I expected new orders for an old mission.

As it turned out, the angry professor in the tiny, beat up Ford Focus, was raging at a mystery, as well—one that was more than two hundred years in the making.

Chapter 12

At the start, it's a stupid job, almost as bad as maintaining the Department's web page, but Bell and Wethers have assured John that if he makes the right kind of public relations splash organizing word sorting activities for the student body and the public, they'll make a strong case to the Dean to keep him on past May.

He knows they're lying, but the part of him that wants to believe has his critical acuity bound and gagged in a locked closet.

The toughest part of the piecing parties is setting priorities that people will adhere to. If he's going to do this thing, he's going to try to do it right. For a long time, party attendees thought it was important to keep a numerical tally of how many discrete finds there were, and too much energy was wasted cataloguing every *a*, *the*, and *were* fragment. However, as more interesting words emerge, Hock finds himself in the role of imagination coach.

He stands in front of a group of piecers, about thirty in the student center where everything is closed except the Taco Bell. No one is ordering any food, so the paper-hatted servers are hanging over the counter, resting, watching the scene. John gets the sense they would like to join in, but they aren't allowed out of their box.

There's a lower than usual number of participants tonight because every university in the United States is steaming towards March Madness, even if their team is already out of the running. On nights where there are basketball games, the watch parties take priority. Hock's not as attuned to that element of campus culture, having spent most of his academic career at the community college, where the mix is a bit more diverse when it comes to age, class, ethnicity, and affluence. New Royal University is pretty damned white, comparably. Pretty damned rich, too.

The folks assembled before him, four or five to a table, remind him of his former life. There are a few students, but there are just as many folks from town, retirees and other adults who came to campus straight from their nine-to-five jobs. There are two women in pastel smocks, and it strikes Hock as unfortunate that he can't spot the difference between nurses and pet groomers. He thought he was more sensitive than that.

Everyone is there because of the words. An intellectual pursuit that has seized all imaginations, across the board. And Hock is the face of it now. He represents the Department, which represents the University, which has put its imprimatur on the project, such as it is.

It's a big deal.

He reads out from a list that was just handed to him by Mel, from his class:

"Church, Farm, Brought, Occasion, Women, Three, Facility, Thought, Shanties, Growling, Lane, Arrived, Cousin."

Mel has also run a phrase generator, recommended by the poets. There's some very interesting stuff coming from that.

even in the fish she had perished
hard about my father name
mother charred and testament

Everyone scribbles on pads to get the list down. And then each table begins to work out what is possible.

Sentences. It's a joy to see people care so much about sentences.

* * *

March 20, 1805
From the Journal of Abraham Horup

I believe that the combination of notions here—that mysterious sisterhood of nuns and a growing population of orphans under their care—set imaginations on their course. I know I thought often of the isolated facility, populated by spiritual women who watched over abandoned babes and wayward girls, and wondered how they spent their private hours. On occasion, the waywards would come to town on errands, and we would stare at them, wondering what these waifs knew of the world.

I write about this, knowing full well that I expose myself to well-deserved criticism. While the residents of the orphanage were better received than the priests who came before, they were never fully embraced or incorporated into our society. And unlike the priests, whom my parents referred to in animalistic terms, describing them as wild-eyed and unkempt, even in their sacramental attire, the nuns and the waywards could be comely at times and fresh smelling, like laundry. I fear they invited a level of unhealthy fascination.

The nuns' orphanage burned down just as I was preparing to go away to college to learn the law. This was an immense tragedy, and many lives were lost.

The possible causes of the fire were these: accident, arson, or curse. Emotions ran to the outlandish and fantastic tales took hold, especially amongst the very young and the very old. A story emerged that if one were to visit that charred parcel under a high moon night, the screams of the dying might be heard.

I heard them myself and knew it was only a pair of barred owls competing for territory.

Today's work.

I honor Father with another child I have named Peter. The cartman, Micah, has not remarked on the growing catalogue of orphans with my father's name.

* * *

By the end of the session, John is overwhelmed by the theories. This has been his fourth piecing event, and so far, he just doesn't see it. As the players file out, all eager to get to a television to catch what's left of tonight's game, Hock's happiness for them is strained. So many of these people think they are onto something. Even Mel, in her beatnik turtleneck sweaters that she likes to pull up over her chin and down over her knees so it looks like she's nothing more than a pair of eyes under a fringe of straight, black hair. Even she seems stimulated by the quest.

It's great that she's able to set aside her misanthropy, but Hock suspects there's no reward for their effort. His working theory from the beginning is that the words come from an unpublished novel. Or worse, someone's thesis. The best scenario may be one in which the players get bored and wander off before they find out. Hock's going to suggest that the Department award prizes for effort.

Mel's in front of him suddenly, a box in her arms. The shreds. They keep them in their original state, even though they're all recorded in a digital file. The pieces in their fragile condition, are inspirational. "I can take these up," she says. Her whole face out in the world, bright.

Hock gives her his best Big Daddy grin, despite being beat. He says, "That'd be great," and he gives her the main office key, telling her to leave it in his box when she's done.

It's amazing how empowering keys are. Mel reacts as if he's given her flowers.

Now that all his kittens have dispersed, he can stop all the damned smiling. He fishes out his car keys as he quick-walks towards the lot.

Out of the corner of his eye, he sees a familiar silhouette pressed up against the library.

Buonopane has been staying out of Hock's way lately. There was a pattern, wasn't there? Buonopane was so enthusiastic and supportive when Hock was as contingent as contingent faculty can get, but he all but disappeared now that the professional picture was improving.

All but disappeared. The old man thinks he's being stealthy. Hock lets that stand and walks right by.

But now, this traverse is precarious, mentally. It's dark and he's alone, and there's nothing to do but think. As much as he wanted the piecing event to end, it is in class or in front of the participants that he's safe inside himself, allowed to forget what he has done.

He worries the key to the old Ford, takes long strides towards the lot, now half empty.

shanties cousin

steamer settlement

The words crawl up his neck.

He gets into his car, jerking the door and dropping into the seat as if he can shake off the bother. But no. When he puts his shitty Ford into gear, it hits him.

Someone knows.

What rises up in him is tremendous fear, a sort of surging heat. He grips the wheel in one hand, pounds on the dash with the other, and the car begins to shake.

The future is over, isn't it? Almost quicker than it began.

A van passes the parking lot, and inside he sees Crocus Rowe, her bright orange hair recognizable from even this distance.

And she's laughing.

* * *

John Hock sits on the edge of his sagging, unmade bed, head in hands, shaking. He's facing the closet, where he keeps the journal, still wrapped in that old coarse sheet.

Back in the Horup mansion, John had browsed the fragile pages and then, once again when he got the thing to his apartment safe and sound, but there wasn't much to read—just a handful of entries by an inexperienced young man. John hadn't had the chance—or heart—to truly study the pages, not the way he needs to. The book, with a single, idiotic push, had transformed from career-maker to life-destroyer.

And then almost immediately came the job offer. As if one fortune generated the other.

Since then he lays in this bed every night, staring at the closet door, waiting for the book to speak.

He needs to take it out, now. He needs to check to see if what he fears is true.

Except his hands won't stop trembling. There's whiskey, of course, but whiskey doesn't steady him as much as it makes him less careful. If he weren't so panicked, he'd pat himself on the back for being professional above all else. Above being curious and fearful.

He opens his bedside drawer. The non-latex gloves Amanda Carlos provided to him are still in there, wadded up, fouled with old blood from the pins and needles in Viola's goddamned boxes. He should have thrown them away, and he will, but sometimes the Historian impulse is a little stronger than common sense.

He can't use the gloves. He grabs them, takes them to the tiny bathroom and drops them in the toilet. Relieves his bladder on them before he flushes them away.

Hock washes his hands, willing them to still under hot water. He rubs his face in the mirror, like a drunk man trying to sober up. Tries to see what's at the bottom of his gray eyes, but they're just mirrors reflecting mirrors. The more you look, the more unreal you feel.

The whiskey is in the kitchenette.

There are papers to grade on the tiny table where a civilized man would have his breakfast. Hock gently extracts his laptop from the mess, sets it on a chair, and then he stands over the table.

This should feel good. It always looks good when he sees people do it in films. He flings his arm broadly, and sweeps all the papers and pens away, letting them scatter and flutter.

It does not feel good, but now he has a surface to work on.

He slugs two big swallows of the whiskey, which he figures is the medicinal dose. He'll take more later, when it's time.

Back in his bedroom, he kicks away the laundry and boots, clearing a path to the closet. The parcel is inside, sealed in a plastic tub. He carries the tub out, and puts it on the breakfast table. Then he turns on every light in the apartment. He needs it bright in here.

He hasn't touched the journal since the day he brought it home. He doesn't know what, if anything, he can do with it now. His original plan had been to wait a good long time before he "found" the tome, the way historians found everything these days—through a shady, untraceable transaction on the internet. Now he had no plan, though it looked as if someone else did.

The probability makes him sick. If what he suspects is true, he may have to destroy the journal. He pries the lid off the plastic tub and lifts out the bag inside. He shoves the tub away, and opens the bag, slowly removing the sheet bound journal.

There it is again, a lump of ancient laundry, concealing fate.

Before John unwraps the prize, he pauses to think about that day and what it meant. Biggest day of his life, truth be told. The last day of Amanda's.

Has he left evidence behind? Are there traces of his presence in the crawl space of the Horup mansion? Did he leave a stray hair on Amanda?

The answer is of course, most certainly, but it has been more than a month, and Amanda is long buried, and the house is now owned by an investment company that may or may not turn it into a luxury inn. Horup Mansion is not a crime scene, not since Seth Garan Shute was apprehended.

Detective Rasmussen's incompetence is a beautiful thing.

John begins to unfold the linen solemnly.

* * *

April 2, 1809
From the Journal of Abraham Horup

The wagon path through the church's acres was thereafter referred to as Crybaby Lane, and was well traveled, as it was an even path to the center of New Royal where merchants had set up their shops in close proximity to a long, low building we always referred to as "the barracks," which were actually the old stables that we built up with strong walls.

The merchants used the nearly windowless structure as a communal storage facility for those goods. However, as our community grew, shopkeepers built private storage, connected to their operations. My father was fond of saying that there were no thieves in New Royal until we made them necessary.

And after the tragedy at the nuns' orphanage, the barracks were cleared out and restored as living space that would be used as temporary housing for the least fortunate among us. This included babies and children whose parents had perished or otherwise released them from care, as well as older sorts who were expected to provide service to New Royal.

This facility was informally administered by Lutheran volunteers, who were mostly women. The Catholic diocese had pulled up stakes and released its holdings back to my cousin Horup.

Informally, the barracks were called the orphanage.

My father called it the workhouse. I told him we did not have those in America.

Today's work.

No children or wills to process, so I am busy with my history. My Cousin Horup visited in his official capacity, but I did show him this journal and asked him a few questions.

How did he feel about the superstitions concerning the Diocese's many failures? How did he feel about the so-called Crybaby Lane? To this, he had a very sensible and unwavering reply: "It is dirt, young Pete. Just dirt."

* * *

And there, the journal ends.

It is with considerably less solemnity that John pours the rest of the whiskey into a coffee cup and compares his lists. One comes from the shared file that Mel has compiled so far of the words and frequency of words that people report having found. The other is John's handwritten list of "interesting" nouns that he deciphers from the ink soaked words that careen across these brittle pages. The Clerk's hand seems fast and intent, and the loops of his ornate cursive lean left at a tilt that seems almost precarious, as if what is inscribed might suddenly slurp off the edge of the page.

There are too many similarities to ignore, especially these:

orphanage

rectory

But what he should have noticed before now is the stubborn absence of modernity. The words collected from the streets of New Royal never speak to the present, and so they seem timeless, when in fact they are constrained by the past. He, of all people, should have recognized that sooner.

John Hock can only assume that someone knows what he did to Amanda Carlos, and they are using the journal to send him a message.

And that person has to be Crocus Rowe. Somehow she knows about Amanda *and* the journal, but she's keeping it to herself, like the good little Murgatroyd clone that she is. Why pursue justice when you can pursue fame instead?

As he drains the cup, he remembers how she laughed at him tonight, orange hair tilted back while her friend drove her off campus. Did she think he didn't see her?

Or…did she mean for him to see her?

* * *

It seems like alien theater, this sports clothing shop in the center of town where there are no customers, except for John. He wonders if the clerk, a young woman in skin tight leggings, can tell that he's hung over. The prices for the gear, the slippery t-shirts, the shoes, and the energy powders are outrageous. He's not quite sure what he's thinking, coming down here. He'll go to Kohls to get what he needs. As soon as he settles on what that is.

He intends to engage with Crocus privately, and soon. He doesn't know anything about where or how she lives, and he's not going to risk inquiring. But she has her running routine. He can try that.

The clerk, whose youthful, lean body is almost insulting, has asked him twice now if he needs assistance. As he moves to leave, she asks again: "Is there something I can help you with?" Her voice is like a knife in his ear.

Another voice, deep and jolly, answers for him. "Not unless you want to cosign a loan."

Gerald Buonopane is making faces at a pair of shoes on the front display, looking over the top of his glasses at the price. "My, these are dear."

"Dr. Buonopane," says John, almost relieved. He blinks his sticky eyes at the unnatural sight of his rotund ex-mentor looking at cross trainers, dressed head to toe in his mismatched tweeds. The kind of clothing you can't buy anymore.

"Good to see you, Johnno."

John attempts some light banter, but his voice is a little too raw for it. "You looking to buy some new kicks?"

"Now, you know I'm not the sporty type." Buonopane rolls up to John and stands just a hand's breadth too close. "I popped in because I saw you here. You may be this establishment's very first Professor customer."

The young woman behind the counter flashes an indulgent smile.

"Not me," says John. "I was just trying to get out of here. Too rich for my blood."

"Are you taking up fitness, John?"

As inconvenient as the old man is, he can still make John Hock smile. "Only you would talk about working out as if it were a hobby, Jer'."

Buonapane shrugs amiably. "Well, the mere fact that you *are* here, proves that you are a dilettante, no?"

That was borderline hostility, but John chooses to ignore it as just part of the old man's waning, grasping charm. "Let's get out of here, Jerry," John says. "This place can't hold two history professors at one time. There'll be a scandal."

John and Buonopane cross the busy intersection to a chain coffee shop where they will blend in better. John orders a large black coffee, whereas Buonopane orders a green tea and a big M&M cookie. The men sit near the shop's corner fire pit, and in seconds the cookie is devoured. There are crumbs all down Buonopane's jacket. "Well there's that, then," he mutters, brushing away the crumbs.

The coffee is doing its work, and John's brain is almost back on track. He remembers Buonopane in the shadows last night. He thinks he'll make a joke about it.

"Why're you following me, Jerry?"

Only the older professor doesn't take it like a joke. He suspends his self-tidying, and gives John an unexpected, soulful look. "Why the elaborate campaign?"

This is a strange turn. Buonopane seems genuinely upset and…on edge?

"Jer', I'm not at all—"

Buonopane leans forward suddenly and starts hissing his words. "I know what you're doing John, I just don't know what you want."

John looks around, hoping no one has noticed the Buonopane's impassioned but vague, accusation. When he's satisfied that no one cares what two professors have to argue about, he says, "I'm not doing anything."

Buonopane makes a tiny fat fist and pounds it once on the table. "Damn it. Stop with all the lying." That's enough to catch the attention of a pair of teenagers nearby, but only because they find the noise disrupting to their own chattering conversation. "Do you think I'm addled? I get it. You have the book."

For a second, John feels as if a flash has gone off in his face. There is no sound, no air, only blinding light. He doesn't have the wherewithal to say *what book*.

John nods, helpless under the weight of it all. "How long have you known?"

"As long as you've been lying to me." If Buonopane was just a weak little old man when they walked into this coffee shop, now he's a gorilla, trying to decide how best to take his rival's head off. "I knew you were hiding something when you failed to mention Viola's little security system. You spent a week clawing through those boxes. Your hands must have been ripped to shreds."

"You sent me there," John says, slowly understanding. Buonopane set him up.

Paradoxically, Buonopane's disgust makes his mouth water. His lips are shining. "I knew *what* you found as soon as you started this stupid game." He means the words. Buonopane recognized them, too.

"It's not my game, Jerry."

Buonopane bats away the thought. "I am impressed by your initiative. If you had only put any of this energy into your research, you'd be a lot further along in your career."

"It's not my game," John repeats, his anger simmering. "And I bet I'd be a lot further along if you didn't make a habit of bringing up my grad school mistakes every time a hiring committee calls."

"Have you learned to leave the kiddoes alone, then?"

"That's just it, Jerry. The student lied. I never went near her. She *lied*, and that was the finding of the hearing, as well. Jesus, you weren't even there!" John's raises his voice a little, but he's the only one who notices. He takes a second. Then repeats, "It's not my game."

"I've watched you, John. Up there on the microphone like you are calling a Bingo match. You're flaunting it."

John shakes his head. "They're making me do it. The Department."

Buonopane mulls this, tapping his mug with a chubby index finger. "Making you," he says. His skepticism is ugly. "How?"

"Wethers is talking about trying to keep me on, somehow. If I make a go of this."

"Wethers is a cow."

"Well, that's helpful."

"So you are making your mark. Planting your flag, except it's a little toothpick flag that they stick in sandwiches." Buonopane doesn't like it, but he's beginning to buy John's story. "It's undignified, but I suppose this is a good time for a career re-boot. These days there are no unpardonable sins anymore. Not in academia, anyway."

John feels as if he's gone 10 rounds in the ring, but Buonopane looks barely winded, as if this sort of tussle with truth and lies is like wolfing down a hearty breakfast. The old man looks over John's shoulder at nothing, ruminating. "If it's not you, John, then who is it? Who would be trying to get my attention in this bizarre manner?"

Buonopane's vanity manifests precisely the same way as Roth Thierry's mania did at the launch of this thing. They both think the message is for them. There's a phenomenon or syndrome to explain it, no doubt.

"Well, sir. I actually think the message, or warning, or whatever it is, is targeting *me*, to be honest."

Buonopane frowns, takes a sip, frowns at that too. The tea's cold. "You. Why, because you stole the book?"

John knows it's a bit more than that, but for the time being, "Yeah. From what I gather, the journal is part of local legend. I think a few people expected me to find it."

"Like myself."

"Exactly. And when I came up with nothing, well. It just wasn't acceptable that there was nothing interesting in that enormous old house."

"Save the odd dead body or two," quipped Buonopane. "I take it you have a notion as to who our trickster is, and why they want to flush you out into the open."

John nods gravely. "It's got to be Crocus Rowe."

"Murgatroyd's little hag-let?" The old professor's eyes widen, and for second, John thinks he's about to slaughter him with cold, elegant reasons why his suspicions are unlikely. But then Buonopane's low growl surprises him:

"I *love* it."

* * *

For the first time that John can remember, he tells a story to Gerald Buonopane, and the old man is rapt, hanging on every wildly speculative detail. John paints Crocus as an ambitious ingénue, half torn between doing Liz Murgatroyd's bidding and breaking out on her own. Buonopane *tut tuts* once to point out that Crocus did have a book coming out, quite soon, so it isn't as if she is totally inexperienced.

John is finally in his comfort zone, improvising, fantasizing. "Right, props to Crocus, that's if she actually wrote the book herself. I'll bet she got a lot of help. Think about it. If you or I wrote *Mean Bone*, it would be dismissed as exploitative trash. But put Rowe's hair 'do and attitude on the back cover, and you have a publicist's wet dream."

The dirty talk amuses Buonopane. "She's no Aphrodite Jones, but I see your point. And what do you think is Ms. Rowe's goal? Seems a bit extreme just to torment a book thief."

John examines Buonopane's face. It is remotely possible that the old man is being coy, trying to get John to confess to more than he already has. "I have no idea," John says carefully. "But I'm worried. Very worried. What if she tries to connect me to Viola Horup's murder, somehow?"

"But surely that matter is settled."

"The guy confessed, but Rowe is still poking around. She's even been seen talking to that detective."

Buonopane nods solemnly. "I suppose she could string together an interesting, if misleading, story, at that."

"If I've learned one thing teaching in the Crime Writing Program, it's that story is everything, whether it's right or wrong. That's Murgatroyd's brand, right?" John feels as if he's winning the old man over. "So will you help me?"

"Help you. To do what?"

"I don't know. I need to persuade Crocus Rowe I'm not the guy. I need to shake her. I mean it's not about the book anymore, it's about the job. If she starts spinning stories about me…" And here John hopes Jerry catches the overall theme of the day: *Akron was just stories, too.* "If that happens, I'll have nothing. This gig is the last chance I never thought I'd get."

Buonopane hears him loud and clear. "You think I owe you."

"You know you do, Jer'."

The older professor stands abruptly, his knees cracking. He looks down at John as if he's a slug. "My next class isn't until Wednesday. Meet me in my office afterward, say 10:30? And bring me evidence that this Crocus woman is behind all of this. Something other than your gut feeling."

"You have an idea?"

"I do," he says. "Just try to get a grip on yourself, John."

* * *

The problem is, John Hock doesn't have anything other than his gut feeling about Crocus. He doesn't know if he can wait until Wednesday, and he certainly can't be sure that Buonopane has any way of helping him. Nevertheless, John has started compiling a list of fabrications about Rowe, items that may pass as evidence in casual conversation but not in a court of law, and really, how can Buonopane ask for more than that?

Over in the corner of his apartment, the bag from Kohls sags sadly, as all shopping bags do. On the way home from his fateful coffee with Buonopane, John couldn't resist.

For what he would have spent on a single pair of shoes at the sports store in town, he's purchased an entire ensemble: shoes, tracksuit, cap, new shades. The tracksuit is an unfortunate wine color, but it was the least offensive choice on the bargain rack.

He also picked up another bottle of whiskey, just to calm his nerves.

By the end of a long night, scribbling and worrying, the Kohls sack is talking to him in ways the book never did.

We could go get her if we wanted to.

* * *

By morning, he's come to his senses, but he's gone out to the running trail anyway, fully kitted out in his new gear. The morning is crisp but not as cold as it should be, and all around it feels like the world is turning into a sloppy pudding.

His timing's off, it's either too early or too late. There's no one else out there until the trail starts a long slow turn, and he finds himself, of all places, running behind the Honor Farm.

A pair of old men on a bench wave at him as he jogs by, huffing hard, and one of them even give him a thumbs-up. John is at a loss. What is the etiquette here? He chooses not to respond with anything more than a smile of pain as he forces himself to go far enough so that he can no longer see the prisoners behind the trees.

This was stupid. He never intended to run, but anyone can jog, can't they? And this last stretch into the woods—it was all downhill. He leans over, hands on his thighs, trying to breathe. Trying not to vomit.

He hears the old men give a hello shout up top, followed by the regular slap-slap of shoes against the tarmac, and he straightens up. No more time for recovery, he must snap back to his full strength.

A flash of orange through the bare trees. It's Crocus. She's on her way.

John realizes that there is nothing, absolutely nothing, he can or will do, so he just stands there and waits. In the distance is the whistle of a train going through Stackhouse Tunnel. It could be in his head, though. His anxieties aren't very artful.

She comes into the trees in her jeans and NRU sweatshirt with the hood down to expose the bouncing cartoon that is her hair. She does not slow down but veers a bit to create a wide arc around John before she disappears into the trees. She doesn't recognize him.

As worried as he's been of late, he keeps forgetting that he's hit a lucky streak in his life. Perhaps he should test that luck and be a bit bolder, but that's not his style. Fortune, like everything in his life, must come to him.

Like Akron. He was no seducer. The girl, Cecily, was Korean-American, and she was never without a little gold cross around her neck. She just showed up at his apartment. She had been paying him to tutor her in European History, and she came to his carrel in the grad student office once a week, so it was a natural assumption that she was enrolled at the University. He thought that meant she was eighteen at least.

It turned out, she was a mature-looking sixteen, and she'd been paying him to tutor her so she could get a great score on her AP exams. He found that out a little too late. He was telling Buonopane the truth when he said she lied. She did lie, about her age. At least that's how John remembers it. And he did not go near her. She came to him.

Like Crocus is now. She's coming back to him.

Fortune.

She's right in front of him now, lightly running in place. "Heya," she says, smiling. She's breathing these short, accomplished breaths. "I almost didn't recognize you. Sorry about that."

"Hey," says John. Now what?

"You okay?"

"I'm fine. This is just new territory for me."

She nods. "You're doing great, I'm sure. Cool gear."

"Thanks," and then he looks down at her beat old shoes. "You really run in those?"

"I know it's stupid," she says. "But it's what I'm comfortable in. Chucks and boots."

How is it even possible that she can continue moving like that and hold a conversation? "Look, I don't want to keep you, but I'm embarrassed to admit I don't know where this trail goes. I was a little surprised by your friends up top."

"Ha, yeah, but no worries, this all leads back to campus. You can't get lost, but if you do, just follow the train tracks," she says. "Those jerks say anything to you?"

"No, it was just unexpected. Coming that close."

"Yeah well, a prison town's got prisons." She smiles to reassure him. Looks down at his tracksuit. "Awesome color. See you around, Mulberry Man."

She turns again and vanishes into the forest.

Chapter 13

I left home when I was fifteen. My departure was something my mother encouraged to the extent that she gave me all the cash she had in her purse, forty dollars, to give me a good start.

Dad was long gone, presumed dead or in jail, and my mother and I fought all the time, often physically. We both knew that was no good. So, when I told her I was going to travel all summer, she said, "Yeah, great idea." She didn't ask me how, or where, or whether I'd be alone. She just gave me her money and wished me a good time.

Told me to call, if I wanted. Christ, she was tired. Everyone I encountered assumed two things: 1) I was a runaway and 2) because I'm gay. After a while it was just simpler to let those assumptions stand. Otherwise I spent all my time defending my mother's negligence.

I hitchhiked. I had this notion it would be a straight relay race out to the West Coast, that one trucker would take me from Ohio to Wisconsin, and then a Wisconsin trucker would take me to Nebraska, and then a Nebraska guy would take me to Utah, etcetera, etcetera. But that's not how it goes. If you find a ride, you gotta go where they're headed. You can say you want to get to St. Louis, and they can say yeah, but chances are you'll wake up in fucking Altoona, Pennsylvania with a guy's hand up your shirt.

And you gotta say that's cool if you want another ride. Hell, getting felt up is like a Caribbean vacation compared to what happens to some beavers. Beavers are what they call the women—or girls—who hang out at truck stops.

That summer, and I only made it to mid-July, I was raped twice, and the farthest I got was Pahrump, Nevada. Just sixty crummy miles to Vegas, but I never made it.

Because Pahrump was where the guy giving me a ride was like a robot, super clean, looked right through me. When we pulled into a gas plaza in the middle of the night, he showed me a knife and said, "Run."

Like we were playing a game.

I got out right away and started running in the summer night heat, knowing that if he caught up to me, I'd be done. There was no one around, and Pahrump was the kind of town where even if there was, night screams were sort of common.

I ran across dusty properties for a while, but there were too many wire fences, so I headed back up onto the highway, running against traffic that consisted of a truck every few minutes or so.

When I started to feel the heat, knew I wasn't adrenaline-scared anymore, and that meant I sensed the trucker had given up.

That's if he ever went after me in the first place.

I slowed down, tried to figure out which direction was east. And then I saw the headlights way far away, getting big real fast. Followed by the air horn. Not just the short pulls, but long, yowling warnings, held for seconds on end.

I was sure it was him. And he was going to get me.

The truck was on me, lighting me up like a stray dog. I could only see his jaw, his buttoned-up shirt in the cab, but I knew it was him. He roared on, and I fell on rocks and glass in the ditch, knocked over by the wind as he passed me.

It seemed as if he wanted to slow down, but he couldn't. Hell was leaning on him to make his deadline.

When I got back up, I was a mess of scrapes and cuts, but alive.

I had a minute or two to contemplate the risks I'd taken, and the experiences I'd had, before the next truck lit up the highway.

I put my hand out and waved him down.

* * *

Run, he still said in my dreams. It wasn't the sort of story I wanted to tell about myself, but sooner or later, Maureen needed to know. That I'd been independent and dangerously stupid a good long time, and if she understood that, she wouldn't be so eager to encourage me to trust my instincts.

Still, I was lucky with her. And the fact that she was going to see Murgatroyd? I don't think anyone else ever believed in me the way Maureen did.

The day Maureen went down to Chillicothe, I jogged my usual route past the Honor Farm. It was a bright day, and you could hear the drip of melting ice in the trees. Long

Ears was out there with a new buddy, a totally round fellow whose face was covered in freckles, and his tiny eyes just looked like slightly darker freckles in the mix.

Long Ears put up a hand in greeting. "You fin' Crybaby Lane?"

"I did."

"You goin' there now?"

He wasn't supposed to talk to me that much, and I found it hard to ignore him like I used to. He'd become human to me. Shaky Hands had gone to the infirmary and wasn't expected to make it out.

It was good he'd made a new friend so quickly. Howdy, Mr. Freckles.

Jogging in place, I said, "I might, but I might not." Freckles was searching my chest desperately for any sign of bouncing boobs. *Sorry, dude.*

"Well, then you watch out, k?" said Long Ears. "Jus' saw Mulberry Man on his way." He nodded towards the trail.

And I thought we were friends. Now that I'd taken the steam out of his rape humor, he was trying to spook me with a cheesy kid's story.

"Yeah, bye." And I ran on down the trail.

The Mulberry Man was a local thing, said to be a maniac who hung out near the railroad tracks because that's where the wild berry bushes grew. He loved his berries and he loved his killing, wandering the woods with his lips and chin stained purple.

A summer story, not a winter's tale.

But sure enough, those old bastards weren't lying. I rounded the corner and saw John Hock on the trail, about to hurl. He was wearing a ridiculous purple track suit a size too big along with pristine New Balance mall walkers, the soles of which probably added an inch to his height.

Long Ears and Freckles were funny guys. I'd have to rethink my opinion of them. I kept running past Hock so he wouldn't see me laughing. You get a sense about some guys, the ones that get hurt easy.

I looped back, chatted with him a little, but I could see he wanted to be alone in his misery. I totally got that. When you're first starting out running, it's lonely and you like it that way.

I didn't see him again, not even on my way back, so I just assumed he'd given up for the day.

There was a pounded dirt part of the trail that veered off the maintained section, a shortcut to train tracks. I liked that trail in the spring, when there were bluebells everywhere, but it wouldn't have occurred to me to check it out in winter. The conditions would either be icy or muddy, or a combo like today. Except, when I reached the fork, there were shoe prints at the improvised trailhead. Big ones, I thought, but they could have easily been distorted by the sloppy conditions.

John Hock wasn't that dumb, was he? Not in those brand-new shoes…

I paused there, bouncing gently back and forth.

Uh-uh, no way. Wet Chucks were just wet Chucks, but they felt like a death sentence.

I ended up following the prints until they disappeared in the general mess of things, and soon I was picking out the trail by memory more than anything else, head down and avoiding the puddles. I got as far as the first gated access to the tracks, a steep chunky gravel drive guarded with an orange metal bar and plenty of NO TRESPASS signage. I'd been up on the access road plenty of times, and even though it wasn't the easiest climb, it was worth it for the view of the tracks disappearing into the Stackhouse Tunnel, which went through a lump of terrain that almost passed for a mountain in these parts. I ducked under the orange bar and climbed up.

And there he was. The *real* Mulberry Man. He was standing on the access road ahead of me, facing the tunnel, its pure darkness dilating against the rock into which it was carved. I couldn't blame him. There's something irresistible about a straight line that leads to a black dot in the world.

He was a large dude, an easy six feet with a broad back. He wore a long puffy coat, looked like a woman's parka, and above his head, his own personal cloud of breath.

I skidded noisily on the wet gravel. When he turned, I recognized him.

"Hey, Roth." His coat hung open, and he was wearing pale green hospital scrubs.

The implication was unsettling. Had Roth Thierry escaped from the hospital? Or was he just a fellow who liked to dress comfortably?

He seemed to need a moment. He raised a hand, but it looked like he was too exhausted to wave.

So maybe you've been there. You walk into a space, an alley or a park or a section of the public library where a visibly troubled person is hanging around, and you just retreat, go back the way you came as if you'd accidentally walked into the wrong bathroom at the mall. Seems harmless, except there is nothing more heartbreaking than to see the bewildered look on the face of that unfortunate person who drove you away, just by existing.

I didn't want to do that to Roth, so I kept on. I said, "How's it going?"

"I'm tired." He looked down the tracks. He wasn't up for a chat.

"Okay, then, you take it easy." And I walked past him. There was, I knew, another pull off just before the tunnel, so I acted as if that was where I wanted to go.

It was dumb, I guess, but my curiosity had brought me this far, and I was feeling a little defiant. The way you do when you take risks that no one—well, no sensible woman—would take. The simple shit that makes you angry with the world, like not wearing headphones or walking alone at night. Or hitching to Vegas.

I reached the next access drive and at the bottom was another locked orange pipe gate, easy to limbo under. This led to a wet road that ended at the river. It wasn't a real road, but it was a four-wheel path that in summer was popular with fishing types who equated illegal access with success. I picked my way down, then headed in the opposite direction, back to the main trail.

Roth Thierry could get me so easily, and no one would know. By the way, healthy people do not fantasize about their own violent deaths. But there it was, the odd graze of a thought becoming a scar.

The bare trees began to shake, not just behind me but from all around in a consuming vibration. It was the train of course, making one of six daily passes, this time coming out of the tunnel instead of into it. It felt as if this little part of the world was being torn apart by something hungry.

I turned to watch it pass.

A blur on the mud trail just a few steps behind me. Roth had followed me down with surprising grace and speed, and then he was gone again. Impossible. He was too big, and there was nothing to hide behind.

I spun and shouted, "Where are you?" but was drowned out by the train.

Nothing, nowhere. Just the vibrating, howling world. I took a few steps and then I saw his figure, now dark and lithe, emerging from behind a pile of limbs and debris that had been shoved to the side to clear the way.

He...*it* charged at me with unexpected speed, and as I turned to run, the mud shifted underfoot, and my back exploded in pain. I'd never felt anything like it. I couldn't breathe, I couldn't even break my fall.

Yet, falling was nothing. I was flat on my back in the mud, and I couldn't move. There was just white sky, bare tree branches, and intense, overwhelming pain inside me.

Then his body blotted out the light. The last thing I remembered was the sound of the train dying, only to be replaced by the Mulberry Man's roar.

Screaming something about me.

* * *

I guess he got me. I came to, bleary eyed in Emergency intake at New Royal Medical Center, the back of my head feeling like I'd used it to stop the passing train. I was on a transport board not fixed very steadily on a gurney and there was a mob of people I didn't know, arguing across my body. I looked up at a lot of smocks and chins and lights, and every once in a while, the gurney would travel a short distance—I guess down a hall—before whoever was doing the pushing would be stopped and told to go in the other direction or "wait for Jeff" or some other trifling issue.

Good thing I wasn't dying.

A big guy, the only one in green, took over at one point and said, "Hey bro," to me, like he was going to make sure I was well taken care of. *I'm a girl*, I tried to say, but I discovered that I couldn't get any noise out at all. And then I realized that the big guy was someone I knew. He had on a name tag: R. *Thierry*.

"Don't freak out," he said. "I work here. I'm just sorry I couldn't catch the creep doing your beat down. Can you talk?"

I opened my mouth. It was dry and sticky, and I could hear things going on inside the workings of my skull that worried me.

"S'okay," he said. "Pain level, 1 to 10?"

I feel like a box that's fallen off the FedEx truck. What number is that? Lips splitting, and I just pushed out air.

"Got it. I think we're ready for a little more pain management, Carrie." And then he did his little girl giggle.

A young woman was massaging my inner arm with gloved fingers. "Ooh," she said. "You've got some teensy veins."

"Nah," Roth said. "Just Tylenol. She hit her head." He looked down at me and smiled. We were traveling again, making progress. His arms were big and jiggly over a core of hard meat. His skin was raw.

But he didn't smell, so that was good.

They brought me to a room with a half-dozen beds protected by moveable, muslin screens, and it struck me that this was where Jeaneane Lewis had died. Where Professor Murgatroyd had met her own humanity and basically told it to take a hike.

Next thing I knew, I was behind my own muslin screen, Roth was gone, and Carrie was giving me some little pills in a paper cup that were pretty much useless.

* * *

By the time Roth returned, the ER attending was reading my chart. I didn't recognize her, and there was no reason I should. It had been years since I was a regular.

"Ms. Rowe," she said. "I'm Dr. Adnam, how are you?" She held out her hand for a shake. I know Docs are all about the friendly, but that whole handshake thing struck me as weird. Like we were making a deal.

"Is my back broken?" I managed, taking a deep breath and testing every part of it. My spine was singing a little song.

"Feels like it, right? But no, we think it was a spasm."

Roth held up my Chucks, still heavy with mud. "Caused by these."

"Caused by a guy trying to jump me," I argued. "Why were you even out there?"

Roth said, "I like trains. Good thing, too."

Dr. Adnam whipped out her penlight, checking my eyes. "Right," she said. "There is an officer out in the lobby, anxious to see you. Your injuries are minor, which is good news. Nothing broken. You'll be sore for a while, though."

Roth clarified, "Looks like he lost his nerve." He was still waiting for me to thank him.

"You ran him off?"

"Well, he ran off, so I guess so. I'm not much of a runner, myself. Just barely got down there on the trail, and he was gone."

I had a lot of questions for Roth, but the doctor wasn't feeling all that chatty. "We can do an MRI, but I don't think we're going to see any problem with the spine."

"So how long will I be down?" I said.

"As long as it hurts too much to get up."

* * *

Adnam released me a couple of hours later with a scrip for fewer than 10 muscle relaxants. She as much as admitted to me that if I were sixty or older, she'd be writing me a lifetime supply, but they had to be careful with people like me.

I didn't take it badly. In fact, I agreed. I was also supposed to do the ice pack/heat pack dance. Seemed kind of barbaric.

Roth wheeled me in a chair out to the wide, bright lobby, where Maureen was waiting for me with...Rasmussen. They stood when I came out.

Roth observed, "I don't see any flowers or balloons. You sure these are your pals?"

"Cut it out. Is that the guy who took your statement?"

"Yeah, such as it was. I didn't get a decent look at your Mystery Date."

I let Maureen fuss at me and complain about my judgment. She said I'd be staying with her, no ifs, ands, or buts, until I could care of myself.

I said, "What does my hair look like?"

Apparently, the prognosis wasn't good. Maureen said, "We'll figure out something."

Roth handed her a bag with the dressings for my head, the prescription, and instructions for exercise.

"What about my shoes?" I was still in hospital issued no-slip socks.

Roth slapped his own forehead like a cartoon dope. "Oh dear," he said. "I might have lost them."

"Liar."

Big shouldered shrug. "I'll let you know when I find them. Meantime, buy some decent runners."

"I'm not at all sure that I'm interested running anymore."

Maureen made a gagging gesture. No one felt all that sorry for me, and they sure as hell weren't going to let me go down that road.

Rasmussen waited out our tender scene with more patience than I expected.

When Roth said so long, I finally thanked him, in my way. "I'm sorry I thought you beat me up."

"I'm sorry you sort of beat yourself up," he said. "I'll see you out there."

"Hey wait."

He was genuinely surprised at that. "What?"

"Are you back in classes?"

Roth shrugged. "Sorta. I'm finishing with online assignments. Work and all." I'd made him uncomfortable.

Before Roth Thierry had fully disappeared back into the depths of the medical center, Rasmussen said, "So, we doing this here?"

He was not at all comfortable hanging out in the medical center. Not when half the people in the waiting room were wearing paper masks to avoid the spread of this year's flu, which was a doozy. Knocked folks out for a month or more.

Maureen said, "You don't think this was random."

"Stalked and attacked," he nodded.

I looked at Maureen but spoke to Rasmussen. "She told you about the door."

It wasn't a question, so he didn't answer.

I said, "That means someone gives a damn."

"Enough to want to take you out, yeah."

Maureen said, "Holy Christ. Does that mean Crocus knows what she's doing, after all?"

"It's beginning to look like it," Rasmussen admitted. "And believe me, it's as much of a surprise to me as it is to you."

All I could do was sink into the wheelchair, and look up in dismay. "Thanks, guys."

* * *

Once we were in the van, I asked Maureen, "So?"

"Oh god," she said. "Right. Murgatroyd. I'm sorry, Cro, but I was there like all of ten minutes before I got the call you were in the hospital. I just got up and left."

"Damn," I said. "Did she say anything?"

Maureen leaned back and thought. "Not much. Right off the bat she wanted to know how things were going in the program. She asked me about John Hock."

That was interesting. I was beginning to feel the banged up part of my head as a heat island. "What'd you tell her?"

"Just what you told me. That he's a cuddly wuddly type, perfect for the daddy-issue crowd. Then she said"—and here Maureen spoke in a low, patrician drawl that was a pretty decent imitation—"'Sounds like he was born to be sacrificed.'"

I pretended that was funny, but the truth was my brain was zooming.

I said, "How'd she look, though?"

"Serene, Crocus. Serene and bored."

* * *

Back at Maureen's apartment, I discovered that Zero had joined Robert, Bosco, and Mike, and all of them lined up on the counter looked like a pretty rough crew. We would never sleep again, if they had their way.

Maureen put a pill in my mouth and a glass of water in my hand. "You get one day of this," she said. "Then we're back on the trail."

"I need new shoes. You heard the man."

"No, I mean back on the trail of who killed Viola. Who killed Amanda."

We were on the same page, but now things had become a bit more dangerous. "We don't know what we're doing."

"Tell that to the guy who wrecked your back," she said. "Mr. Trouble came looking for you."

"To Mr. Trouble," I said, washing down the pill, thinking about that shadow coming towards me as the train roared past. A kind of purple shadow.

Chapter 14

Steve Rasmussen is spending hours trying to find a nonstop flight to Palm Beach International, but the best he can do is Fort Lauderdale, where he'll grab a car and risk his life on I-95 for almost an hour to see his mother in Briny Breezes. He's in his office clicking away, wondering if another computer will yield a better price. Someone once told him it worked that way.

Briny Breezes is a mobile home beach front town, just fifteen miles away from Mar-A-Lago, which means Steve's mom, Jennifer Thomas Rasmussen Hoy Handlos, had the same damned view of the Atlantic as foreign dignitaries, golf pros, Russian assets, and the president himself. All along that part of the coast are high rises and dramatic mansions, in keeping with the Mar-A-Lago aesthetic, but then you get to Briny Breezes, and that's where your jaw drops.

Acres of little metal boxes, more than 400 of them, most a faded turquoise or pink, all anchored to the ground and never letting go. Back in the early 2000s, each property owner was offered more than a million per lot to sell out and make way for development, and the deal almost went through, except the owners balked at the last minute.

Steve's mom married one of those nutjobs.

Steve plans to go down for a couple of days, maybe fish with Handlos and watch a rocket launch. Of course, nowadays there's the added excitement of high security motorcades coming down the A1A. Handlos says they're carrying the decoy dummies. The president's real inner circle comes in by helicopter.

Steve's just about to pick his flight when he receives a message alert from the general CSU addy, but he knows it's his almost-buddy, a tech named Cheri. She's Canadian, and she always processes his requests ASAP, and the only questions she asks have to do with how he likes the results delivered.

He thinks maybe she has a thing for him. As the lead detective in Homicide, he's supposed to be everyone's crush, but for whatever reason, that's just not happening.

The message is just an attachment. The prints taken at the Carlos scene, specifically the ones inside the basement. And there they are. The ones from the inside knob of the cellar door. The notes: *Carlos.* That is a momentary relief, but then he looks closer. Something off, or rather, not off.

Steve dials up Cheri, and she picks up immediately.

"Heya, Cher'. I'm looking at these images, but I'm not the expert. Can I bounce a thought or two off you?"

"Go right ahead, sir."

That's right, she's the one who calls him *sir.* Definitely crushing. "Yeah, so," he begins. "I know it's not your job to interpret the scenes, but you can interpret the images. How would you characterize these prints, the ones on the inside doorknob?" He pauses to look up the evidence code and reads it out to her.

"Ummm, okay. Got 'em." She clears her throat. "So these are identified as belonging to Carlos, Amanda. There was evidence of layers of prints and smearing—"

"Smearing?"

"Typical of what you find after cleaning. Excuse me, but wasn't this home being prepared for sale?"

"Yeah." Steve hears her. He's obviously keyed up.

"Right," she says, gently. "So the Carlos prints are the 'last' ones, if you will. The top layer. And they're consistent."

"Consistent with what?"

"With closing a door."

"Don't interpret the scene," he says, but even as the words leave his mouth, he's grateful for her insight. Her *incorrect* insight. "Sorry to be so sharp, Cheri. You still there?"

"Yes, sir?"

"So the prints are consistent with what you'd see if someone just closed the door." Which Carlos probably did several times during the clean out of Viola Horup's home.

"Like normal," he added.

"Excuse me?"

At this point, Steve Rasmussen realizes he can't bring young Cheri in any further on this case that is not a case. It wouldn't be fair. He dials back, thinks of another way to get what he wants. "So, no hurry on this at all, because I'm going out of town, but I'm hoping you can do me one more favor?"

"Just name it."

Steve's never seen Cheri, or if he has, he has no clue as to which of the dozen scene techs she is, but he imagines that she's sitting straight up at her terminal, bright-eyed and a little breathless, waiting to be swept up in a Big Investigation. "I'd like you to pull some samples for me—from whatever library you scientists use. I want to see comparisons between prints that are, as you say, consistent with closing a door, and others that are not so consistent. Like when the door is slammed. Or maybe when the knob is grabbed... To slow or break a fall. Cheri, is that possible?"

He's sure he hears a light gasp on the line.

Then, "I'll do my best, sir."

So, weird. An open door, a closed door. How big the little things can be.

* * *

Twenty-four hours later he's in Fort Lauderdale International, where a gauntlet of great, gleaming signs tout Florida's joys, both glamorous and simple, as he drags his rolling bag to ground transport. He's walking too fast for the south, and he's on his cell to his mother, lying. Buying time. He tells her he's come in through Miami after all—on a flight that was $100 cheaper, and she's lecturing him on the concept of false economy. He can play her like a violin, but at the same time, her attack on his judgment drives him up the wall.

Jennifer Thomas Rasmussen Hoy Handlos is 86 years old.

When he finally gets off the phone with her, he punches another number.

"Officer Daigle," Steve says, listening. "Sorry to hear that, but I'm grateful you're still willing to meet with me."

Alas, Belasco won't be there at the cafe where Rasmussen and the cops who apprehended Seth Garan Shute have decided to meet. Belasco's quit the force quite suddenly, although everyone knows that the Shute beating and the subsequent internal investigations took a toll.

Later, in the Green Owl diner, against the backdrop of dozens of crayon drawings of owls done by local school kids, Daigle will lean across the table to confide in Rasmussen: "It wasn't just wild. It was weird."

"Meaning what?" says Steve, slicing carefully into a specialty called the "Owl Stacker," which is basically every breakfast item one would want made into a tower. Vertical food is just tastier, but he doesn't know why that would be.

"Shute going on about his mother, like she was in his head." Daigle is working on a Greek omelet, which is definitely horizontal.

"*Psycho* style?"

"Not exactly, I mean he wasn't delusional, but he kept calling for her, like she could hear him. Shute was crying, and to be honest in pretty bad shape." A half smile on the officer's face. "What's the line? 'Who woulda known he had so much blood in him?'"

Steve is shocked, and part of his breakfast topples over. "What the hell are you talking about?"

Daigle hides behind his hands in a mock defensive gesture. "It's cool, it's cool. That's from Shakespeare, man."

"Yeah? Well then Shakespeare was a sick mother."

"I'm just saying, the guy was a little more delicate than we expected. You know, how the news was like, 'here comes this bad hombre that doesn't have a care in the world,' and then we take him down, and it turns out, he's just a skinny kid, basically." Daigle probes his omelet thoughtfully. "A dumbass."

"Not a killer." Steve wonders if hash browns are the right choice, architecturally, for a tower. He would have started with a biscuit foundation. "Was there something in the way he said he didn't do it that was special?"

Daigle puts his fork down. "So, this is what got under Belasco's skin, I think. What soured him on the job. We're waling on the guy, and the blood is coming, and with each square hit, I know I can feel the tissues start to absorb the impact more and more—you know that flat smack sound you get after a while? Well that happens quicker'n usual, and the perp is starting to cry like a dog, and that sets off our onlookers, a lot of whom are little kids...so there's a whole PR tire fire to put out. We stop, and tell him he's under arrest. And he's bawling, with the blood running down like tears, and kids around us are bawling too, and it's starting to dawn on me that this thing we're doing—catching and subduing a guy who killed an old lady and took off with her cards—this thing that is supposed to make our careers, just might be the biggest mistake we ever make."

"And why's that?"

Daigle's laying two fives next to his plate, ready to bolt as soon as the check comes. "Your man there, Seth Garan Shute. We tell him he's under arrest, and he gets that, sobbing and all, he gets it. Then we tell him why, and the dude is genuinely shocked. The crying stops, hell his breathing sort of stops, and he's looking up at us like he's Carrie with the pig blood all over him. Belasco saw it, too."

"Saw what?"

"Don't make fun of me, but—his innocence?" Daigle's sorry for the term. "I'm not as experienced as you, but I've hauled in some killers before. Shute's the first one I ever saw looked really surprised at the charge."

Steve can't eat and think anymore, and that used to be his thing. Shoveling in the chow and putting together the pieces.

Daigle notices. "These questions, man. They aren't the kind of questions *we* ask, you know?" The officer stands up, looking uncomfortable. "I mean, sounds like you're working for the defense, doesn't it?"

"That is how it sounds, doesn't it?" Steve wants to laugh to ease Daigle's mind, but that never sounds good, deflective laughter. He looks up at him, and decides to just put it out here. "I just feel like I missed something."

"I hear ya," says Daigle. "Maybe, I don't know. Maybe you need to talk to Mommy."

Steve pulls back, suddenly. "*What?*"

"Shute's mother, like I said. You're a little jumpy, man."

And Steve realizes he's holding on to his butter knife very tightly.

* * *

Aside from the low ceilings and the just-hose-it-off decor, Steve's mom's mobile bungalow is very nice. It's clean, bright, and you can see the beach from the driveway. His mom and Handlos, though, they're kind of freakish together. She weighs all of 90 pounds and has a fondness for matching blouses and pants in the kind of strong colors you see in the kids' aisle at Target, whereas Handlos is kind of a lard ass, wears nothing but shorts and salmon pink beaters, and has old fashioned thick-lensed glasses that make his eyes look bigger than they are.

They drink store brand diet soda all day, the weirder the flavor, the better. Steve's mom hates the taste of plain water.

Steve hates the taste of aspartame, but what are you going to do?

Handlos sits on a tiny white vinyl love seat across from the matching sofa Steve is supposed to sleep on. The old man says, "Still got the hair?" And he laughs.

Steve give his step-dad a *you got me champ* smile, and that's as close to a heart-to-heart as they are ever going to have.

"Ma," Steve calls out. Jennifer's in the kitchen, heating up leftovers from Josie's. The leftovers from an entree can make two meals at home because they always order garlic rolls when they dine in. Steve's caught his mom on leftover day one, and he's a little disappointed that he missed the beginning of the cycle. Josie's garlic rolls have chunks of raw garlic on them, and you can't get anything like that in New Royal.

"Ma!"

No answer. Handlos grins, points at his ears. "You can holler all day, she ain't gonna hear ya unless she sees your lips flapping."

Steve gets up from the little love seat and finds his mother in the tiny galley kitchen staring at the microwave carousel going around and around. Today she's a vision in springtime green, with a matching top and capris pants. Her hands are on her hips as if she disapproves of her appliances, and she sort of looks amazing, Steve thinks. Her skin is dark but it glows; it never did that when he was a kid and they were all living in Ohio with Dad.

"Ma."

"What, you want a tomato? We get 'em from the Haitians."

Steve knows she means something by that, but he doesn't want to find out. "No, I don't need a tomato. Thanks, though."

The microwave dings, and Jennifer removes the hot plate as if she can't even feel it. Maybe she can't. As she separates the leftovers—baked rigatoni and calamari, the mashup of last night's meals—into thirds and puts them on plates with a slice of white bread on the side of each, she says, "Then, what the hell do you want?"

Jennifer isn't angry. She's just gotten used to cursing down here.

"You know that guy they caught at the zoo on New Year's?"

She's taking the steaming plates, one by one, out to the dining table, and she makes a fussy noise as she brushes Steve's tummy to get past him.

Handlos speaks for her. "The fella that killed the old woman up where you are?"

"Yeah, that's the one." Steve's not thrilled to see Handlos spring into action, filling three tall glasses with soda. The flavor the hour is peach. Jennifer and Handlos don't drink wine, or any alcohol at all. It's as if they are totally unaware that the stuff exists, and Steve would kill for a Corona right now, followed in quick succession by about five more.

"While I'm down here, I thought I'd follow up on a detail or two." Steve takes his seat, and as gross as calamari is to him usually, this stuff smells amazing. Handlos is buttering his slice of bread from a tub of cholesterol free spread, the only thing on the table that won't kill them all.

Finally, Jennifer sits down, and begins her repast. For all her fussing and scuttling, she's a slow eater, always has been. She grew up in lean times, so now she savors every bite. "I knew you didn't come down just to visit," she says. She could say so much more, but she'd rather eat her sticky pasta.

Steve could say things, too, but he just makes a face at his mother—which she loves.

"Dummy," she chuckles.

The whole meal is mushy, but delicious in a way that makes Steve uneasy, like when he goes to a buffet and there's pizza on it. Good things shouldn't be so easy.

"Ma," Steve says. When she looks at him, he speaks slowly and clearly. "Under what conditions would you send me to an old lady's house to kill her?"

Jennifer smacks her lips thoughtfully, as if the question is perfectly normal. "We talking Viola?"

Steve feels stupid for forgetting. Of course, his mother knew Viola Horup. She'd grown up in New Royal.

"I don't think I'd want you to kill that old biddy. I might want you to ask her some questions, though."

"Like what."

"Like where the fuck we come from."

"Oh, mom."

"She knew, Stevie. Viola knew. She was writing a book about it."

"She said that, sure, but that doesn't make it true," says Steve. "And besides, we know where we come from. We're like Danish or Norwegian, or something."

His mother shrugs dramatically. "That's if Rasmussen is even our name. We have no way of knowing, no records taking it back to the old country."

Steve chuckles. "The old country."

"Don't mock me." She's got calamari banked in her cheek, in no hurry to consume it too quickly, so she talks around it. "Handlos' got all his family's lines written down to, I don't know," she gestures in the air with her fork, "cave man days and whatnot."

Handlos grins at Steve. "She's just jealous."

She shoots her husband a fearsome look. "That better be all I have to be jealous about."

And now Steve sees he's wandered—no, backed into—the secret minefield that is his mother's marriage to Handlos. Handlos laughs at her and she scowls, but they both continue to plow through the leftovers like it's their last meal.

Steve tries to shift the discussion back. "Yeah well, at least we have our families going back a while. The slaves were totally dislocated. The Rasmussens are lucky, considering."

Jennifer stops chewing, and she's still in that way that could mean danger.

Steve gets it. He has certain ways of talking to his mother that he can't resist. Always contradicting her, or diminishing her strong, if momentarily held, opinions.

And then, something weird. She looks up, an almost sweet look on her face. "So Stevie, you ever meet any black folks that claim to come from New Royal back before it was New Royal?"

"No, but—"

Her finger pointing at him, and new light in her eyes. "That's because that story's bullshit, too."

"Oh, really."

"Mmhm." Jennifer's back to her pasta, a smug look on her face. "And Viola knew it."

Chapter 15

No one ever visits Gerald Buonopane, even though his living quarters are about as convenient to campus as they can be. He lives in the little village that the university constructed some twenty-five years ago, a neighborhood of affordable one-bedroom cottages, originally designed as transitional domiciles—places where new professors and visiting researchers would live until they started families or moved on to other opportunities. That was how it was supposed to work, anyway. No one anticipated that it would become a sort of enclave of aging bachelors. Murgatroyd had a cottage one lane over from Buonopane's, but someone set it on fire while she was sleeping one off. They pinned an arson charge on a townie thug, but Gerald has always wondered if Liz didn't do it herself.

Though unaccustomed to visitors, Gerald knows exactly who it is pounding on his door in the middle of an afternoon that can't make up its mind between Winter and Spring. He replaces his suspenders on his shoulders, and eases up from the TV tray where a plate of peanut butter smeared Ritz crackers waits to be washed down with a glass of milk. That John Hock cannot wait until the appointed hour is no surprise.

However, Gerald is surprised by John's condition. He's clearly distressed, wearing some weird purple get up, and tracking gray mud into Gerald's house.

John pushes by his mentor and goes straight to the little kitchen to find a glass and fill it with water from the tap. John drinks it down in one go, chin tilted to the ceiling. The sink is already full of dishes soaking in soapy water, so when he's done, he balances the glass on top.

Gerald watches all of this very calmly, having taken a seat at the kitchen table.

John leans back against the sink and declares, "She's hunting me. What more proof do you need?"

As John describes the details of his morning's encounter with Crocus Rowe, Gerald finds himself drifting. This is John Hock, after all, whose only genuine expertise is in manipulating the truth of any story, so that he is the victim. In this tale, Ms. Rowe tracked him down in the woods of all places, and he had no choice but to defend himself. It's particularly pathetic—John in cheap running jammies, lost in the woods.

He has no more credibility than a student claiming he can't get his assignment done on time because his "roommate" smokes too much pot. Like that student, John just goes on and on with his story, until finally he says, "What do I do now?"

Gerald can't tell the boy he's cooked, that would only panic him. And he should be panicked, especially if Murgatroyd's little minion recognized John in that bizarre outfit. It's as if John is trying get this all over with, whether that means getting caught or not.

Some people can't handle the pressure.

But Gerald can. In fact, he rather enjoys a little intrigue. He says, "There may be a way to neutralize the damage."

"How?"

"Yes, I can help," he says again, ignoring John's question. "But first, bring me the book."

John stares at him. What must be going through his mind, Gerald doesn't care.

"Why do you need the book?"

"I don't need it, John. I want it." Gerald smiles sweetly, lacing his fingers together on top of the table. "You've already established that our relationship is transactional in nature. I owe you, you owe me, etc. I can help you in your current dilemma, but I would like my compensation 'up front' as they say."

He watches the muscles in John's face as they flex and shift.

"Decisions aren't your strength, John. Go, and bring me the book."

* * *

Hock is gone for hours, and Gerald wonders if he hasn't been apprehended by the police. No doubt John's tale of being stalked by Crocus is a reversal of the truth. What do the psychologists call someone whose accusations are always confessions?

But as night falls, John returns, carrying a black garbage bag. Gone is the track suit. John's wearing an underwear t-shirt and blue jeans. A pair of loafers.

Gerald invites him in. "You cleaned up."

"I burned the suit."

"Hmm." Neither approving nor disapproving.

John thrusts the bag into Gerald's hands. "I wanted to burn this, too."

That is what Gerald fears, that Hock will do something incredibly stupid and wasteful just to save himself. Now Gerald feels the weight of the parcel, and he can hardly believe it.

Blessed thing *is* real. Gerald's skin begins to tingle, happiness fizzing in the blood. So this was what it was like to awake from a twenty-five year dream.

Still, the boy can't know what this means. "John, in the sitting room, please. There is much to discuss."

John is sullen as he sits hard on the green sofa that faces the picture window where he can watch the blinking interiors of other cottages in the cluster. He is still in teenager mode, consumed by his own drama. Drama that he created quite unnecessarily. And Gerald's been thinking about that.

He sits in an upholstered rocker and places the bag on the coffee table between John and himself. He reaches in and feels rough fabric. When he pulls it out, he can barely contain his delight. "Did you find it like this?"

"Yes, it was wrapped up in that sheet."

"Where was it?"

"In her study, but not in one of those damned boxes. There was a crawl space in the eaves, hidden by all that garbage she had."

"What else was in the crawl space?"

"A senility cradle. Scared the crap out of me when I saw that lump in the center."

"I don't wonder." Gerald unfolds the sheet until the journal is fully visible. Then he's up, having almost forgotten. He has a pair of white, cotton gloves ready on the bookshelf. As he puts them on, he says to John, "Did you read it? I mean really read it?"

"Of course I did," says John. "And it's pretty disappointing, too. Just a handful of scribbles by a kid."

Gerald freezes, quelling the urge to smack his former protégé. "Then you didn't read it." Why was he surprised? He sits and gently opens the cover to study that first inky page. "You never read closely enough, John. You never ask the right questions."

John is struggling to remain calm. "You promised to help me."

Gerald turns a page. "For example, how did I know, so certainly, where the words from the game originated?"

"You knew the journal existed," John shrugged. "You said a lot of people did."

"So, I just guessed? From *tenant, food, territory*? Am I that good? And is everyone else that stupid? Dozens upon dozens of New Royal citizens poring over their scraps… All of them failing, except me. I'm flattered, Johnno."

Another page. The ink is shadowy, light in places, heavy and clotted in others. Gerald is going to enjoy every moment of this.

John's voice is flat. "So you've seen it before."

A gloved finger rises to signal a correct answer. "Reach over into the drawer of that side table there."

John scoots down the sofa where a lamp sits atop a plain table. The drawer is sticky, but it opens with a tug. "This?" John says, pulling out a manuscript bound with a black spring clamp. He reads the top page and utters, "God damn it."

"Not exactly a running key cypher, but close enough."

"Where'd you get this?"

"From the lady herself. Viola said she wanted expert advice on the material contained therein, but I think she was just showing off."

"Expert advice on what?"

"The social and legal impact of this document, of course." Gerald looks up. "Go ahead, John, ask me what's so juicy about this journal."

John's eyes narrow. He hates this game. "How is this going to help me, Jer'?"

Gerald has always disliked it when John calls him *Jer'*. It's not affectionate, it's a sign of disrespect.

"No need to be so stressed, Johnno. It is safe to assume that Ms. Rowe did not recognize you as her attacker, otherwise you wouldn't have been able to return to your apartment so easily. And, now that this book is in my hands, there's nothing to tie you to it, is there?" Gerald sits back, takes the measure of his guest.

John is squirrelly.

Gerald says, "Or is there more that we're upset about? I feel as if you haven't been fully forthcoming with me."

John drops the typescript on the coffee table with a thud. "How many of these are floating around out there?"

"I have no idea. A few, I imagine, although Viola was obviously careful in her choice of confidants." Gerald is aware that the pitch and tone of his voice has changed to match his mood, which is, of course, barely chained down glee. "John, it is very strange that you're so agitated by this whole episode. All you did was steal a book, is that not correct? And any mischief that Ms. Rowe could stir up, well… Your reaction is extreme, considering."

No answer.

"John?"

It looks like the boy is about to cry.

"You can tell me, John." But he isn't quite at the edge, is he? He needs a push, and Gerald comes up with a big one, preceded by a theatrical gasp: "Did you kill Viola Horup?"

John shouts, "*No*," followed by something unintelligible and pulls his legs up onto the sofa like a child.

Gerald stands, puts his fingers to his lips. "Neighbors," he reminds him.

John clamps his mouth shut, panicking. Gerald comes over and sits next to him, putting an arm around his shoulders experimentally. John trembles, allowing the older man to draw him in for a full embrace. Gerald pets John's back and feels the boy let go, as he starts to weep silently.

Putting his lips to John's ear, Gerald whispers, "Then who, John? Who did you kill?"

Without hesitation John answers, also whispering. "Amanda. I pushed Amanda Carlos down the stairs. I swear I didn't kill Viola."

Gerald strokes John's back, seizing with grief. "I know, boy. Ol' Jer' knows."

John shudders.

Gerald whispers, "I know, I know." The pats become stronger. "I know."

John's breath eases, and he tries to pull away.

But Gerald starts to pound him on the back, clamping onto him. Saying loudly, right in his ear: "I know, I know!"

When John is able to throw Gerald off, he lands backwards on the sofa. "What the hell?"

The man smiles at him with the love of a grandfather.

"Read the damned pages, John. For once in your sick little life, do your damned homework."

Buonopane gives John the gloves.

* * *

Gerald has made John read aloud to him from the original. The old professor corrects his student when he makes a mistake.

When John reaches the end of the April 2 entry, he stops, looks up at Buonopane. "There just isn't much here," he says. "I'm not sure what you expect me to see."

Gerald waits his student out. That's half the battle, resisting the urge to shove John into the obvious. But John is not gifted.

"It's a large tome," Gerald says. He thumbs the typescript that John pulled from the desk, lifting up the first few pages. "This is all you've read, so far. Keep going."

John Hock returns to the original, and keeps turning the unused pages.

And then, the writing begins again, in the same hand, but less adorned and less careful. There are many crossed words and marginal notations.

"Damn," says John. He missed so much. He begins to read again.

Crybaby Lane

* * *

July 12, 1828
From the Journal of Abraham Horup

Highly agitated, I have returned from the deathbed of my cousin Horup. It is past midnight. I am worn out, but I feel I have a sense of duty to the future.

I understand the danger, that what is confessed by night seems foolish by day, but finding this book again seems provident. I lost it more than twenty years ago, almost as soon as it was given to me, but tonight I re-discovered it during a purge of passions. The journal was hiding in the back of a drawer I aimed to heave through a window.

Its reappearance turned my mind and mood. Is it too late to embrace religion?

On this sultry, moth-filled night, I have left a mess for poor Doral. He will come to my side as soon as he hears the news of my cousin.

When I began this journal at the beginning of my career, I expected to keep a daily account of my activities as the Clerk of the Orphans Court of New Royal, not fully understanding that my private fancies would lead to immense tragedy. I thought of myself as a historian with a scientist's eye, but the truth was that I was a romantic, and for that I am truly ashamed.

Tonight, I take the project up again, for private testament until such time as it can be used for recompense, though such a thing is impossible to imagine.

I may need to die first.

Chapter 16

New Royal is, in Spring, two rows of buildings huddling over a road of mud. Horses pull wagons, and one hears the suck but not the hoofbeat, not the *clomp-clomp* that keeps time in higher and drier towns. Logs and planks provide bridges for foot traffic from business to business.

When Cousin Horup, the Mayor, comes to Abraham's office, he tracks in mud and doesn't care. He calls out, "Abe! There has been a Priest."

The Mayor's voice is shocking, but then Abraham is in a delicate state, trembling over his papers. He has been bedridden for days, weak and alone in his apartment above the tailor's shop. An unnamed fever has come to New Royal, the sort of sickness that passes through the very young and old like a common cold, but takes down healthy adults with the swift strength of an ocean wave. The more lively and beloved one is in dance, arts, and conversation, the more dire the affliction.

Today is Abraham's first back in the office since falling ill, and the air is thick with the ghosts of his coughing fits. However, even in his condition, Abraham finds the visit from his cousin thrilling. Unlike Abraham's father, who was narrow and tough like old wood, Horup is broad in the chest and full cheeked, and his hair shines from oil.

Horup says, "I need legal advice, Young Abe. The Diocese wants to return to New Royal and reclaim the holdings that they abandoned."

"They see value in what has been built. New Royal is becoming prosperous."

"And increasing in population. The Catholics love a lot of brats underfoot."

Abraham cannot afford an opinion on that subject, so he demurs. "More people, more tithing."

Horup slaps the desk, and his vigor rattles the office. "So what is the stance of the law on a gift that has been abandoned, Abe? I no longer feel warmth for the Church."

"The more that the property appears to be yours, and used as yours, the more solid your position."

The Mayor agrees. "We start construction in the morning, then."

Abraham enjoys a moment's glory. "Some would counsel that the property is an unlucky plot of land, and that you should leave it to the papists."

"So I have come to you. I believe the philosophy of law rejects the concept of luck."

"Agreed. What most people call bad luck is what we call mistakes."

"And good luck?"

"Opportunity, of course."

Horup is enjoying this conversation. "But you're a churchgoing man, as am I. What is your opinion of God's blessings?"

Abraham taps his brow, still warmer than it should be. "We have His blessings *here*, to do with as we will. Divinity is…administrative in nature."

This is the correct answer.

* * *

The next morning, a boy arrives at Abraham's office bearing a plain courier's casket, wooden with leather binds.

"The Father's papers," the boy says.

Abraham assumes the boy is one of the orphans that has passed through his office. By this time in his tenure, he no longer asks their names. There are, sadly, too many Peters now, and the name has become a sobriquet for any inconvenient urchin, as in *Get away from my pear tree, you little Peter*. It's Abraham's secret shame, one that deepened when his father passed away. The family had dogs all his life, and every one of them was named Andy, but they were one after the other: old Andy would crawl away to the creek to die, after which a new, bouncy Andy was procured.

There was never a pack of Andys all at once.

Not like the Peters.

Abraham accepts the casket. "Why are you giving me this?"

"The Father has gone missing. There's a search party going out. The Mayor says you are to keep his effects in your archives, undisturbed. And I'm to take him back a receipt."

"Of course." As Abraham draws up the document, he asks, "Can you spare any more details about the Priest, son?"

"Only that he rented rooms from the Sorensons, back of the tack shop. He didn't come down for breakfast, so the wife went in. Says she found 'violent evidence,' but no Father Michael."

Violent evidence. "Is there a message from the Mayor?"

"Only what I said."

Then, while Abraham searches for a penny, the boy lights off. He's been compensated well enough, apparently. Abraham places the casket in with his files, and this is where, in spirit-fraught tales, the reluctant hero says something foolish like, *and I put it out of mind.*

But the truth is that little box is very much in Abraham's mind, almost constantly from this time forward, and its mystery is the greatest temptation he has ever encountered.

That in itself is proof that he has led an unchallenged life.

* * *

The search for the Priest ends abruptly, and not because the Father was found. Rather, sometime late in the afternoon, four boys, Peters all, are discovered hiding in the barracks.

Hiding, not living there anymore, for they had been evicted during the height of the sickness, and the barracks commandeered for quarantine. The fever patients housed there had all recovered or perished, and once the barracks were empty again, these boys returned to the only home they knew beyond the orphanage, specter of pestilence be damned.

Abraham arrives in time to watch as the Peters stagger out of the barracks. The state of them, with their shirts untucked and smelling of spirits strikes him as particularly unthreatening. Nevertheless, the oldest, a seventeen-year-old known as Peter Indian, receives a knock on the head as a reward for his cooperation. He is bound before being placed in the wagon.

This action causes the other three to scramble back into the building, where no one wants to pursue them.

Sorenson, with whom the Priest had lodged, is also New Royal's constable. "We can smoke 'em out," he suggests.

Abraham intervenes. "Excuse me, Mr. Sorenson, what makes you so certain that these boys have done wrong to the Father?"

The constable is full of blood, hungry for achievement. "They was in hiding."

"And do you know, sir, the difference between hiding and seeking privacy?" Abraham points to Peter Indian. The boy's face is red from his struggle. "There is no doubt that these boys are bad, but they are still boys."

Sorenson glares. "These ain't just boys, these're Peters."

Abraham holds his ground. "I believe an inspection of the barracks is in order."

"You want to do the honors, Clerk?"

"I am willing. And one day in the future you may come to my offices and manage the records."

Sorenson is confused.

Abraham clarifies, "Because that is *my* duty. And keeping the peace is yours."

"There's only one Horup tells me what to do." Sorenson grins in that way that only a man bent on violence can.

Abraham repeats, "I am willing." He can see that the constable is only barely holding on to reason.

And here Abraham hopes to muster the bravery to enter the house of waifs and disease, but his doubts overcome him. As he approaches the entry, he hesitates.

"Abraham Horup! What in God's name are you doing?"

His cousin at last.

The Mayor is a born leader, decisive and unmotivated by anything other than his own benefit. In one breath, he admonishes Sorenson for putting Abraham in harm's way, and in another, orders that the boys be forced out by any means Sorenson sees fit.

Sorenson is incapable of control. The smoke becomes fire.

* * *

When it is done, put out by a brigade of citizens, the lingering, sickening smell that hangs in the air is the perfume of shock and sadness. Abraham returns to his offices to grieve.

His cousin visits him that night, and finds Abraham dozing with his head on his desk, like a drunkard. Horup taps him with his cane, and Abraham awakens to the sight of Sorenson turning up the lamp flame.

The only mercy is that Sorenson appears spent.

"I worry about you, Abe," says Horup. "You have a tender heart. All societies suffer a foundational tragedy. It is God's punishment for vanity."

Through bleary eyes Abraham watches his cousin inspect the premises, briefly. He is looking for something. "I keep no spirits, cousin."

Sorensen stations himself at the main window.

"You have a bed at home," Horup says.

"I do, but no one should sleep well tonight. They were children."

"Peter Indian has confessed to the murder of the Priest."

"I'm quite sure he has." Abraham keeps a thought to himself—that at no time did anyone behave as if the Priest might still be alive.

Horup leans over. "You are too dark, cousin. You should have married."

"I apologize." Abraham stands and straightens his vest. "Have the Father's remains been recovered?"

"The boy said they drowned him in a river, and he was carried off by it."

Abraham wants to ask, *which river*, but instead says, "Rest his soul."

"Indeed. Now look, Abe, this business is frightful and complicated, but I have a way of making things right, especially with the diocese." Horup's tone is urgent, and that is unsettling. As the most powerful man in any room he enters, he is never furtive or unsure.

Tonight, however, he is strange, just like Sorenson.

And Abraham knows why. He says, "I believe I shall go home. To my bed, as you have suggested."

Relief fills his cousin's eyes as he retrieves his coat and hat.

* * *

When Abraham awakes in the morning, a months-old broadsheet is on the floor in front of his door, and wrapped inside it is the key to the Clerk's office. This means that there is still an office to return to.

As Abraham walks to work, his neighbors have risen, but their eyes are cast down, and no one speaks. The town reeks and will continue to do so for a long time to come.

There are no Peters, not anywhere. They have all fled.

At the office, Abe sees what his cousin and Sorenson have done. They removed three of the cabinets, and replaced them with a fine carved desk that comes from the Mayor's own house.

On it waits a steaming cup of tea.

"Mr. Horup."

The boy comes in from another chamber. He is well-groomed, dressed in new breeches and a clean blouse, and for wishful moment Abraham thinks he's Peter Indian. He is not, though. Peter Indian is in a cell in Montgaul, some ten miles east of New Royal, awaiting his fate.

"I'm Doral, sir."

Not a Peter, then. "You come from the Mayor."

"To assist you sir, yes. With anything you need."

Abraham looks back at the ornate desk and the fragile cup of tea, the scent of which he cannot enjoy. New Royal's poisoned air deadens the senses. "My files."

"A terrible loss, sir. Mayor Horup told me they were stored in the barracks when they went down."

Abraham counts himself lucky. His records have been removed, but at least his cousin has not killed him. Even gave him a boy for his troubles. Family still means something, even to the wicked.

Abraham takes his seat and accepts the tea.

He knows he will remain loyal to the Horup name as long as he lives, but after that, who can tell?

* * *

Of course, Abraham read the documents in the Priest's casket before it and his cabinets were destroyed. He is not an honorable man; he is merely diligent. In the casket were letters, written by Father Emil.

Emil was the young German priest who burned the original rectory down.

Abraham spoke some German as a child but learned to read the language when he was away at University in New England. Father Emil was an unhinged, superstitious man who saw in all things, evidence of witchcraft. He was especially concerned about the nascent community of New Royal, attributing its heartiness to *blutkur*, a blood diet, which is an occult practice. The young Father declared further proof: in his short residency, he claimed to have found artifacts of sacrifice on the lands bestowed to the rectory. He wrote of grave markings, pieces of metal, pieces of bone. He said that a skull had worked its way up through the mud floor of the rectory cellar.

Upon reading these letters, Abraham immediately recalled the slaves that Horup claimed to have freed. Abraham's father had always treated their cousin's tale as a huckster's yarn, and while at University, Abraham was exposed to abolitionist speakers who tended to echo his father's suspicions.

They knew of no slaveholders in the region. In fact, one white-maned, wild-eyed reverend gripped Abraham's arm and said, "Ohio is a place of contradiction, until you see the truth, son."

Abraham was defensive. "Slavery is abolished in our constitution."

"Indeed. So why the many restrictions on colored immigration into your state?"

At the time, Abraham had no good answer to that question, and now that he's read Father Emil's papers, he's even more confused. They seem to confirm the presence of the earlier settlement of slaves, so why would this be something his cousin wants to hide?

Horup's story is, after all, the one glorious origin myth of New Royal—that the blight of slavery was banished when he took over the land. That he made something new and pure in a nearly spoiled place.

* * *

Abraham walks to the old grounds at the end of Crybaby Lane with Doral. It has been years since he's come this far out from town, but he finds the margin still rolling and wild. The sky, as always, overwhelms with great iron clouds ready to crash down on him.

And the stench of the fire still follows. Abraham wonders if he will be able to smell anything else again.

They pick their way through a field of high grasses, vibrating with unseen life.

Abraham does not expect Doral to be a comfortable companion. As a man who has spent his life on his own, Abraham is aware that his habits are peculiar.

"Doral, does something trouble you?"

The boy looks towards the horizon. "Are we going far, sir?"

"Don't be worried. You aren't superstitious, are you?"

"Just. Why are we coming out here?"

"Nostalgia. Archeology."

Though Father Emil's letters contained raving accusations, underpinning all was a clear account of the features of the land his church inhabited. This strikes Abraham as authentic and worthy.

Doral and Abraham pause before a depression in the field where the grasses are dull and bent. A place of burned things.

Abraham gestures with a stick. "Over here is where I lived as a boy, but the foundation is from the nuns' orphanage. See how wide it is?"

There are humps of broken stones in a line, imbedded in the ground.

"It appears ancient," Doral says.

"It does, doesn't it?" Abraham takes his stick and tests one of the stones, sunk firm. "But really, it's been barely a generation. When we came here, there were abandoned shanties and a well that hadn't held water in years."

"The old slave camp."

"You know the story. The shanties were there. And the barns were just over there."

"You kept beasts?"

"I overstate. We acquired a good cow from Horup, and we had our few horses from the journey. They were very tired and never seemed to rally again. We put them under shelters we called barns."

As he speaks, Abraham tries to rebuild the ghost camp from memory.

Father Emil wrote of graves. Abraham's never seen anything like a graveyard out here, and that would have been the sort of thing that his youthful mind would have seized upon.

"Doral, how do slaves bury their kind when there is no churchyard near?"

"The way that families do, I reckon. In a little plot, nearby, where there's peace."

Abraham looks to the trees that guard the entrance to a vast, unvanquished forest. Abraham remembers how his father talked about the value of the timber and how he failed to convince Horup to let him work it.

Horup said he didn't want to live in a logging town, and Abraham's father was very offended by that remark. From then on he had very little to say about their cousin that was not edged with criticism. Evenings he would drink coffee in the middle of the ramshackle compound and stare out into the darkness, towards the trees he wanted to take down.

Doral asks, "How long did you live in the camp?"

"Oh, barely a season. The shanties weren't suitable for cold weather living. By the time the leaves began to turn, there were three proper houses in town and two others framed."

"Was it fun, being a boy here?" Doral enunciates the word "boy" differently than anyone else would. Being a boy is his career.

"There was much work to do."

"Did you ever go into the woods?"

"I don't recall." It's true. Abraham remembers everything about that summer vividly, but the images of the forest are no more precise than dreams. "Have you gone into those woods, Doral?"

"We aren't supposed to, sir. But it's the speedy way to Montgaul if you're on foot."

Montgaul. The next town over. A drab, flat community with few families. Mud everywhere. And a fort on the river that has been recommissioned into a penitentiary, where Peter Indian may live out the rest of his days.

"So, on this speedy path, have you ever seen anything that looked like a cemetery in those woods, Doral?"

"I was never looking for one, sir."

They have only been a short time in each other's company, and already Doral and Abraham are growing close. Naturally, Abraham is suspicious. Doral is a gift in exchange for a signature of receipt and silence. He is also, most certainly, a spy.

Abraham feigns seasonal discomforts out there on those weedy acres, and they return to the offices. When he tries to send Doral home for the day, the boy says, "I live here, now. On the orders of the Mayor."

Doral makes a pallet in an airless closet, no doubt keeping an eye on his new Master.

* * *

A few days later, Abraham sets out pre-dawn, in the blue light. Some of his neighbors are awake, but most are not, and he makes his way to the site of the old rectory, unobserved.

He paces to the rectory foundation stones, under a wavering glow that is taking over the horizon. Abraham has never been brave, but mornings make a man feel safe.

Thus, mornings are dangerous.

There is a downward slope to the tree line, and probing with his walking stick, he makes his way as the trees loom larger with every step.

They are pines, tall, vividly hued, and…full of perfume. This is the limit of the conflagration's ghost, or "Sorenson's stench," as Abraham refers to it.

One remembers the scents of childhood, but the scent of so many pines is wholly new to him. It's a shame in that he doesn't know the genus. His father tried to teach him the trees, but Abraham learned constellations instead.

The gloom lifts as he approaches the forest, and then, as he steps inside, the gloom returns. The passage reminds him of jumping into a pond. The morning, warm in the field, turns icy as the pines fight with the sky.

Abraham treads on a carpet of soft red needles. A man would call the footing unstable, a woman would call it forgiving. And it is in this mood that he realizes he has no idea where to go.

"Sir."

Doral. The boy has followed Abraham. He is only half dressed, in breeches, blouse and vest, but no jacket.

"Please go home, Doral."

"Sir, it's not safe in these woods. All sorts convene in this hide."

"There are no sorts here."

"There are."

"Leave me."

"I will wait."

And so, Doral stands by, bathed in the filter of pine shadows, looking for all the world like an attendant to unnatural men. Abraham wants very much to ask him where he should search, but they must both preserve the membrane-thin conceit that the boy is an innocent.

* * *

A cemetery would be close to the encampment. Abraham follows disturbances in the pine needle floor, where the deer have swept trails through. After only a short way, the forest slopes steeply, boulders jut up through the needles, and there is a cold smell. Abraham recognizes it immediately: water. Down there is some sort of stream. Abraham chooses to walk along the level edge instead.

Even if he finds nothing, he toys with the notion of making a camp here, until the reek of New Royal dissipates.

Shuffling through the needles is thrilling, especially as there is no other sound. Abraham stops from time to time to make sure he is alone. Eventually he comes to a place where the contour is more forgiving, making it possible to descend deeper into the forest without risking injury against the rocks. He spies a clearing, still under the shadow of the tall trees. The space is lenticular, conforming to boundaries provided by boulders and fallen trunks. In the center stands a lone, tall pine.

Is this a natural formation?

He starts down, perhaps too excitedly. He slips twice and loses his walking stick. Then, mid-way down, the stench is back, collected in this bowl of nature. The further he descends, the thicker it becomes.

Abraham has read of bad air produced from decay that can suffocate animals. He holds his kerchief across his nose. Once he reaches the clearing, he searches the ground, kicking away needles.

The slaves would have been illiterate, and their materials sparse, but he sees nothing he recognizes as a grave marker. Yet the ground is free of rocks, as though turned and prepared for use in the past.

Abraham steps beyond the perimeter, the cloth to his face. What has he overlooked?

"Sir."

It is Doral again, this time on the top of the slope, looking down. How has he managed to follow without making a sound?

The boy is distressed.

"Go back," Abraham commands.

"You don't see," says Doral.

And that is true. Abraham does not see. He's too focused on the boy.

But then, he does see. He is now in view of the other side of the lone pine at the center of the clearing. There, leaning against the trunk, as if taking a rest, is Father Michael.

Abraham drops the handkerchief and falls to the forest floor. "My God."

Doral takes off running, fast as he can, back to the Mayor.

* * *

When Abraham returns to his office, Doral, Sorenson, and Horup are there before him. Horup sits at Abraham's desk, as if awaiting a customer, and Sorensen stands at his side. Doral is back in shirtsleeves, holding onto his elbows as if he might fly apart.

Abraham breaks the silence. "I suppose Doral has given you the news. We found Father Michael."

Horup says, "I imagine that was upsetting."

"He does not seem to have drowned. Not unless one can do so tied to a tree."

"Peter Indian was confused."

Sorensen tries to contribute. "Or he meant to throw us off."

Abraham doesn't bother hiding his contempt. "Yes, that seems like just the thing. Confess to a murder and then lie about how it was done."

He looks at his cousin hard. "Perhaps you should kill me." Abraham places a tiny, bent half-moon of metal on the desk. It is the color of an unforgiving Ohio sky. "Because I believe I know what this is."

Horup says, "Sorenson, Doral. Leave."

The boy and the henchman disappear like banished spirits, leaving only the cousins behind.

Horup pulls the metal fragment towards him and pockets it. "You may know what it is, but you don't know what it means, Abe."

"So, tell me."

"Not now," he says. "You're my family, and I would never lay this burden upon you." Horup rises and walks around the desk. He puts his hand on Abraham's neck and pulls him close. "I love you, cousin. I truly do. I even loved your father."

As if that was a hard thing to do.

"Abe, do you love our town, what we've accomplished? We are catalysts of American history. How many names have we had—frontiersmen, colonists, settlers, and now? *Citizens.* That's because of me, Abe. My vision. My fortitude."

He releases Abraham's neck and begins to walk around him, tracing a wide path. He makes a full circle and starts a new one. "And yours, lad. You'll never get the glory Abe, but you create civility with your love of documents and process and regulation. You are the least wild man I know, and you are this town's rock. I see an amazing future for you. You will be a legislative giant, one who cut his teeth on this edge of the West."

"Are you selling me an imaginary gold mine?"

Horup ceases his pacing. "Why do you think I should kill you?"

"Because I know you killed those boys deliberately. Because I know you killed Father Michael."

Horup abandons all traces of false emotion—the glibness, the paternalism, and the concern. "You smell of the dead," he pronounces.

And then he walks out of Abraham's office, into the street.

It takes Abraham some time to understand, but when he does, it's almost unbearable. The truth that he has discovered—about the Peters and the Father— is a truth that everyone else already knew.

* * *

The idea of being in the world, even to cross a street to his apartment above the tailor shop, seems impossible. Like Doral, Abraham makes a pallet of blankets in the unfinished rooms upstairs from the office. As he lays awake that night, he tumbles a handful of metal pieces in his hand.

When Doral returns, Abraham listens for the boy's stealth; the creak of the cupboard door is as familiar as his father's admonitions. Perhaps that is how one lives on, in those unlovely crevices of memory.

Doral makes a thump and swears an oath. Is he drunk?

Perhaps he will initiate Abraham in the pleasures of alcohol one day.

But for now, the boy's master rolls over on his blankets and drops the silvers, one by one onto the floor. He wants Doral to know that he is there.

Clink. Clink. Clink.

They are buttons. Uniform buttons.

* * *

July 12, 1828
From the Journal of Abraham Horup

Since that night I have been my cousin's man, though I have harbored hatred for him all these years. However, justice in the matter of the Peters and the Priest would only come at the cost of Horup, and if Horup were brought down, New Royal would follow.

I no longer loved the light, so I moved into the Court apartments permanently. Doral continued to serve me. When he came of age he married, built a house, and raised a family. My cousin paid him better than he paid me, but I'm no negotiator.

I do not know how Father Michael's remains were disposed, but on my fortieth birthday, I walked back down into those woods. They were much the same, but the great center tree in the clearing had been cut to a stump.

On the return, I visited the site of the former rectory, where shanties and barns once made up a rickety village that we called home for a season. I knew much more about those shanties now, having spent some time studying a variety of colonial surveys. Though the maps were, at times, more improvisational than precise, it was clear that a significant portion of the territory between the Scioto and Little Miami rivers had been divided into land grants for veterans who served in the Revolution.

What is true is this: there were never slave-holdings in New Royal. The shanty village that my father and I helped tear down had been built by soldiers. Soldiers who, for mysterious reasons, gave up their stakes.

On the acres where the rectory once stood, great walls had gone up, and inside those walls the largest free-standing building in Ohio's history thus far.

A prison. It housed three hundred men whose strong backs were put to use improving our roads and working quarries. And when there were backs to spare, leased out to other interests.

It was a vile operation, one that my father seemed to anticipate. There never were slaves on these lands, until now.

* * *

This afternoon I received the summons to my cousin's bedside. At sixty-one years, he was burdened with a cancerous growth that had all but closed his throat. Not two weeks earlier he was robust, walking about, but complaining of a soreness in his neck and an unusually heavy heartbeat.

Now he was dying.

I traveled to his grand home, surrounded with beautiful green shrubs and a rolling lawn kept by men who were professionally trained in English horticulture.

His wife, Lily, met me at the door. She was the third Mrs. Horup and a good deal younger than him. Lily was sharp featured, one of Sorenson's daughters in fact, but she was slim, strong, and the perfect age for widowhood.

She greeted me with an embrace on the brick porch. "He's in his study. We pulled a bed up to the window so he could see, but you know Peter. He's unhappy to be overlooking the gardens instead of town."

I was supposed to laugh at this and share with her a fondness for Horup's cantankerous ways. But she didn't know what I knew about the bitterness that drove him in his golden years. He'd drawn a new will only a month earlier, one that excluded Lily and her children entirely.

The reason given? "The brevity of their affection within the marriage."

After I notarized the revision, I told my cousin I had filed the document in my archives, when in fact I'd put the new will into the stove. I had been doing that sort of thing, dissenting against my cousin via paperwork, for years.

Lily's smile seemed genuinely sad, as if she loved him. She led me up to the study, transformed into a sick room, and now I saw that the "bed" that had been pulled in, was in fact a large white cradle. My father's design, if I recalled correctly. It was intended for the care of an elderly, demented soul. The window under which his bed was placed was a small porthole of heavy glass, set very high. Even if Horup wanted to see out, he wouldn't be able to rise for it. Instead, he was bundled in the cradle, unable to move as the day's light traveled the length of him, by the hour.

Lily was craftier than I knew. This tableau was gentle, easy on the visitor, but certain to terrify the patient.

The growth in my cousin's throat caused him to breathe in a labored whistle, and by this point, speech was impossible. His eyes were glassy as he struggled to take in air, and by his side a pen and book where he could write down his thoughts and commands. Those wet eyes blinked, and I took his hand. The room stank of his sickness and its functions.

I lowered the side of the cradle so that I could kiss his brow. I listened for Lily's retreat. When I was sure she was gone, I said, "I am pleased to watch you die, cousin."

A forced wheeze, and I expected to see panic in his eyes, but when I pulled away, they were full of light. He took his hands away and scraped at the bedclothes.

He wanted his book and pen, which I gave him. I held the ink well, and he stabbed at it like a chicken until I guided his wrist.

A myriad of ink droplets, new and old, decorated the coverlet.

It was agonizing watching him manipulate the pen, but he managed to scrawl *prist* tilting the book towards me.

"Father Michael or Father Emil? They're both interesting."

A frustrated snort, the pen gripped in his trembling fist. He made to write more, but I stayed his hand.

"Cousin," I said. "Do you know my senses were half-dead from the barracks' massacre? I walked right by the rotting corpse of Father Michael, and poor Doral could hardly believe it."

He kept his fierce eyes on me.

"Let me tell you what I saw. Father Michael's cassock, the bark of the tree, and his flesh all blended together, as if he had grown out of the trunk in his vestments. Black, gray, brown. His head was tilted forward, but there was a filthy, braided rope around his neck and another around his waist. His feet hung bare, black, and swollen." I leaned forward. "The flies, cousin. The flies."

The eyes closed, and he stabbed the air with the pen. I helped him dip the nib again.

slver

The silver? He meant the half-moon button I showed him. "It came from his pockets, you old fool."

He'd had the man crucified, but failed to examine his person. Just as he'd failed to interpret Father Emil's letters as anything more than mad man's ravings.

"You are a successful man, Peter, perhaps because you build and burn, build and burn, and you never allow yourself to be distracted by details. You have me for that, after all." I squeezed the hand that held the pen. "But I need just a few details from you, now."

He blinked hard. He understood.

"Give me the names, cousin. Give me the names of those you murdered, and I will preserve the Horup name."

Another hard blink.

"The names, Peter." I pushed his quavering hand to the page. "Or I will tell everything I have learned about how New Royal came to be."

Thomas
Nemuth
Cutler
Shute

I believe these were soldiers my cousin killed in order to seize their land. It is my hope that with these names, I will be able to determine in what regiments they served and track their origins. My studies so far have led me to militias formed in the Virginia territories in the 1770s.

I cannot offer them a confession, but where possible, I will offer support. And land.

These names are my cousin's unspoken confession. When he finally passed, it was an uneasy, fitful death, one that Lily and I watched together.

I now wonder if we were unfair to attribute the original rectory fire to Father Emil's madness. He was hardly circumspect in his accusations. I can easily imagine my cousin taking drastic measures to correct his mistake. The mistake being that of giving the land to the Catholics in the first place.

As for Father Michael, I have yet to decide whether he was sent back to New Royal as a negotiator or investigator. Emil had sent him the buttons, as his letters indicated, and while they would be useful as evidence in criminal proceedings, they could also provide leverage in reclaiming the land. My assumption is that Father Michael was charged with acting in the Church's best interests, and that he was ambushed while looking for further corroboration of Emil's claims.

Either way, my cousin would have taken the same steps. He was monstrous.

Now that he is dead, I will keep my promise to protect the family name and preserve what he has built.

To that end, Lily and I should marry in the autumn. I will take over management of the Horup fortune and enterprises. This will, no doubt, be a difficult transition of power, especially among my cousin's children from his first wife, all of whom are of age now.

There is need to act decisively, with haste.

What I have done in the past was in service of my cousin.

What I do now is in service of New Royal, Ohio.

Chapter 17

John checks the remaining pages to make sure he hasn't missed anything, this time, but all the remaining pages are blank. "This is going to upset a lot of people."

"You think so, John?"

Hock sighs. "Oh, just tell me what you want me to say."

"What have you learned, boy?"

John's tired, but he's come here for help, and whether he's going to get it or not, he has nowhere else to turn. "The main thing is that Peter Horup murdered several soldiers and took the land given to them by the government. Then he established New Royal on land he claimed had been used by slavers."

"And he just kept killing. Old Petey Horup was a born politician, so that's not very surprising. However, now that the myth of our heritage will be dispelled, we will go from pride to shame. Classic American tale. And everything we attributed to his vision, the hospital center, the schools, and any number of charitable societies— most of which have evolved into drinking clubs, by the way—all of that was the work of his mousy little cousin. Of course, what I believe will be of particular interest in this work are the names. Family names still in use today. This is the only document that confirms their connections, their stolen rights. Stolen land."

John shakes his head. "It's terrible, I agree, but too much time has passed, and as compelling as the journal is, it's not a deed. And even so, adverse possession—"

"Is a fascinating doctrine. Think of the politics."

"The politics?"

"Last Fourth of July the Mayor was practically carrying Viola down Main Street like a bride, calling her a 'treasure.' This year he'll probably lead the parade to her grave so we can all spit on it. New Royal has been controlled by the Horups for two hundred years, and now we have proof that they were not founders so much as thieves. And they all knew, you see. *Viola* knew. And she kept her mouth shut to preserve the Horup name. She knew."

John looks at the typescript version of the journal. "So did you."

"Not really. I never saw the original, and I always suspected that it was a test. I thought the manuscript was something she cooked up, like that 'history' she was always promising to write. It's clever, isn't it?"

"What?"

"Viola may not have written a thing, but she kept saying she was busy putting together a history of New Royal, see? Thereby re-asserting that one did not already exist."

"The prison, though."

"That will be a toughie."

"You think they'll excavate?"

"To find the bodies of a couple of Revolutionary war soldiers? Oh, that is too much to hope for," says Buonopane, wistfully. "The 'vile operation,' as our man says."

John is looking at the journal, his face slack and pale. "You can't help me, can you? You just wanted the journal."

"If you're crying, lean back a bit. I don't think I need any more of your DNA at this point."

John's response is a very satisfying jolt to life, his dark eyes darting, scared.

"It's a joke, my dear. Just a joke."

"Then stop screwing me around, 'Jer."

"Calm down, calm down." Gerald eases up, smiling at Hock's outburst. "I told you, we may be able to neutralize Ms. Rowe. Show her up as the wannabe muckraker she is."

"How do we do that?"

"Well, let's be clear-headed about this. She's trying to flush you out because she knows you have the book."

"So, we burn it, right?"

"You're not listening, John. As long as the book is missing, she'll keep up the pressure. She's already ramped it up with these 'rare drop' words."

"Rare drop?"

"Christ, John, you're supposed to be on top of things. You're the game master. 'Rare drops' are what they are calling the pink words. They just started showing up. Nouns, proper names, and the like. It'll only be a matter of time before someone finds a 'Horup' in the gutter. And then where will we be?"

John looks lost.

Buonopane takes pity on him. "This is bad news and good news, John. Bad news because time is running out. Good news because this"—he points at the journal—"is all she has. She's rattling you, hoping you'll make a mistake."

Which John has. "Do you plan to go public? With the typescript, I mean. You can end this whole thing by solving the game."

"No," says Gerald. The last thing he wants is to draw attention to himself in this matter. "I have a much better idea."

"Which is?"

"We return the journal."

"Are you crazy?"

"Well, not inside the mansion of course, but as close as we dare."

John clearly regrets placing his trust in his old mentor. He runs his hands through his hair and grimaces.

"John, go home and get some rest. You need it badly." Gerald rises to escort John to the door. "Then return in the morning, as early as you can. This will all be over soon."

* * *

After he watches his protégé drive off, Gerald returns to the journal, rewrapping it lovingly, carefully, in the muslin. Reading the discolored folds for the order. As he closes the last, he sees something he hasn't before, and the realization makes him want to sing.

There, on the old, coarse linen, a few tiny drops of color form a crescent on a faded corner of the fabric. He has seen this pattern before.

Is that, could that be, *John's* blood? And Viola's revenge, such as it was. A marvelous little constellation of guilt. Too subtle for Rasmussen, but still, the detective deserves a shot.

"My girl, my girl, my girl," he croons. "Talking 'bout—"

* * *

He was in that wicked cellar when they returned, and he could hear the clack and creak as they walked across the floor, overhead. They'd only just left for dinner, and were supposed to attend a church concert after. Did Viola decide to give it a pass? He could tell her footfall from Helen's. Helen had a sturdy, deliberate step, one that vibrated the boards, whereas Viola liked to flit and float, her shoes tapping lightly but frenetically in patterns that suggested that she was bouncing from corner to corner. She never seemed able to settle.

And that's when he heard Helen's muffled, "Hold on, I'll get that," followed by Viola's voice rendered in senseless bubble sounds that were impossible to interpret.

167

Crybaby Lane

At first the bubbles came in clusters, but Helen popped them one by one, dominating the conversation.

Gerald was unafraid. He snuck in from the outside cellar door and had been doing so for a week, and it would be easy enough to leave that way, undetected.

Still no sign of the journal.

He'd just pulled another box down from a pyramid of them jammed under the stairs, and he had it half unpacked. Now he would gently replace the junk in the order he found it—a telephone book, a tin vase, an empty syrup bottle—and as he reclosed the box, he saw something that stopped him cold.

A half dozen dots of blood on the corner of the cardboard flap. He looked at his glove and saw the pin prick wounds that managed to ooze through. He hadn't even felt it.

It was a concern. An infuriating concern.

He tore away that corner of cardboard and put it in his pocket.

He should have left then and there, but sadly, his temper got the best of him.

Chapter 18

Marla collects the words when she spots them, scooping them up from the curbs, checking the shelves and floors at the Kroger, usually finding a half a dozen of the little strips before anyone else can. She used to read them before jamming them in the trash, but no more. It hurts too much to know what she's set in motion.

At home she sticks to her routine, tries to ignore the world outside, but she does watch television. Fires, storms, chemical attacks. It's all so far away and unreal. The only thing that really penetrates is the ringing of her phone because it's always either Seth or Huebinger.

And Helen comes around, like tonight. They sit together quietly or sometimes they watch television. Marla always gives Helen the old, burgundy LazyBoy, the best seat in the house.

They are both dying inside, thinking about Seth and what he must endure. What he will endure for many, many years. There are times, especially when they've made a decent dent in the Franzia, when Marla wants to relieve Helen of her burden, but how? There's no changing the fact that Helen is a gossip. Just as there is no way to change the fact that Seth ended up killing that old crow.

What's missing, of course, is Marla's part in all this.

Wine's pretty good for that, like makeup to hide a bruise, but it should be reapplied every day.

Marla does have news, though. "There's a plea deal in the works."

Helen, ever the optimist. "Oh, that's good."

"Voluntary manslaughter, on account of—" and Marla taps her head.

It's awfully hard to put a happy spin on brain damage, so Helen rises from the LazyBoy and hefts the Franzia. It's done. She takes it into the kitchen, despite Marla's soft protests, and when she drops it in the trash, she sees the mangled strips of words floating amongst the microwave containers and empty chip bags.

There's a pink one in there, and Helen nudges it with the corner of the box so she can read it: *Lily*. Leaves it in there, with the rest of the trash.

Helen knows what those words are, and she's got a good idea where they came from.

When she comes back in, Marla has switched to some show about witches and werewolves going to school. Helen settles into the big old chair, and places a fresh box of wine between them. "Your trash can looks a lot like mine, Marla," she says, before refilling her friend's glass. It's supposed to be a joke about how they drink too much, but it isn't.

They watch the show up to the point where there's a young woman making potions, but she looks more like she should be selling insurance, so Marla switches over to a medical show. She and Helen never watch more than twenty minutes of any program, and they almost never catch the beginnings or the ends.

Helen usually stays until Marla starts to nod off.

Tonight is a little different, though.

Marla's reaching for the remote again, and Helen stops her: "But *why* d'ya think he did it, Marla? Do you know?"

"I don't know why," says Marla. "I can't even imagine it."

Helen stares at her old friend. This is the biggest mystery of their lives.

Marla leans forward, like she's been pushed, and her hair swings down in a blunt gray curtain all around her face. The muscles in her back and arms tense, and anyone else would assume that she's having a stroke.

But Helen knows Marla is just crying hard. As hard as she can without making a sound.

* * *

First thing in the morning, Marla gets off the bus at the stop outside of the NRPD station. When she enters the complex, she's recognized by a few of the officers, and the uniformed woman behind the desk seems a little confused when Marla asks to meet with Detective Rasmussen.

Marla supposes it is unusual, for the mother of a soon-to-be convicted killer to want to speak with the man who made the case against him, so she leans forward and says to the young woman, "You can frisk me if you like. I don't mind."

An odd light goes on in the young woman's eyes. "He's down the hall. Right side, his name is on the door. Do you need someone to take you?"

Ah. So, they're not all crazy about Detective Rasmussen around here. Marla passes on the escort and makes her own way down the prefab corridor that smells of carpet chemicals. Most of the offices are open, and as she walks by the occupants look up at her, in dread that she's come for them, like the angel of death or boredom or work. Rasmussen's door is closed, but when she knocks there's a grunt in response.

He's in there, behind his desk, wearing a sweater and a sunburn.

"No wonder you're hiding," says Marla. "Ohioans hate it when you go south, and they hate it even more when it shows."

"Mrs. Shute? I'm not sure it's a good idea for you to be here before the trial."

"Seth's going to prison," Marla says. "Won't be no trial, as I hear it. May I?" Pointing to the chair.

"Of course." Rasmussen rises in haste, knocks some forms to the floor and pretends not to notice. When she sits, so does he. "Is there something I can help you with?"

"I love Seth," she says.

Rasmussen stays quiet.

"I don't know why he did it, you know. I mean, a mother knows everything about her children. It's funny because they spend so much of their time trying to hide the truth about themselves—cigarettes, masturbation, thievery, drugs, or being queer—but mothers know." Though only in her fifties, Marla knows she talks and acts like she's in her seventies. Work and Seth have aged her.

"I can't help your son."

"I know that." She has something to say.

The detective has something, too. "You sent him."

"I did."

Rasmussen rises again, closes the door for privacy and returns to his side of the desk. "Why?"

Marla is ashamed to say it. "To get a book. One Helen told me was in that house."

"Helen?"

"Helen Nemuth. She was Viola's home nurse," Marla begins. "And she and I go back a bit. We worked in a nursing home together, but the home shut down and then Helen lucked into working for Viola." Marla focuses on the linoleum floor. It needs a wax. "I work at the Kroger now."

Rasmussen nods. He has no right to that rosy tinge on his nose, cheeks, and neck.

She continues, "Anyway, Helen's been at Horup's a few years. Long enough to see a thing or two."

"I'm sure."

"And she and I are still buddies and all. So she tells me things."

"Mrs. Shute, are you sure you don't want to talk to Seth's lawyer?" But Rasmussen is already getting a pen and pad ready.

"No, thank you. Like I said, the boy is going to jail. There's nothing I can do about that. But there's still the matter of the book."

"Right."

"It never turned up, did it? When they were cleaning out all of Viola's trash." She hits that last word hard and flat.

"I'm sorry, Mrs. Shute. I don't think there is any book." Rasmussen smiles sadly. "My mother was asking about that, too. I was down to see her this weekend."

"Your mother?"

"Yes, she was the one who told me Ms. Horup was supposed to be writing a history. I think that was just wishful thinking."

Marla swings her head. "The only writing Viola ever did was signing checks, Detective. She didn't need to write a history of New Royal, because she already had one."

"Excuse me?"

"Abraham Horup's diary from the 1800s. You know why that's important, right?"

The detective isn't used to being quizzed, so he falters. "There aren't any records from back then. All the official documents were destroyed by flood."

"By fire," Marla corrects him. "Except for this one book, handed down through the Horup generations and kept hidden."

"Come on, Mrs. Shute. Why would they keep the only history of our town a secret?"

"Must be something in there that the Horups never wanted to get out. Something that a couple hundred years can't change. The Horup that wrote it, he was the town's first clerk of records."

Rasmussen leans back. "So you sent your son in to find it."

"Yes." Her throat tightens at the memory. "Right when the first snowstorm of the season started, I told Seth to clean himself up and get on out there to Horup Mansion, offer his services. Helen was angry when he turned up, but Viola liked him right off the bat. He's a good-looking boy when he's not been beat half to death."

Rasmussen shakes his head. "Seth doesn't find anything, gets his hands wrecked in the process, and then kills Viola, anyway?"

"It doesn't make sense to me either, but there you go. The only thing I can think is he had a fit of some kind. It's not like he didn't do it."

"It was your friend Helen who told you about this Horup book?"

"Yes."

"A book no one else has seen except her, is that right?"

172

Marla takes a moment. She wants only to say what she knows is true. "I don't know that she ever saw it, but Viola sure did like to talk about it. You think Helen has the imagination to make something like this up? The book is real, Detective Rasmussen. Believe me."

"Believe Helen, you mean."

"You want me to bring her in here?"

"Uh, no." He tilts, looks Marla in the eye, and she wonders why he hasn't kicked her out already. "Ms. Shute, let me be honest with you here. I wish there was a book. Something with all the answers in it, but there isn't. There *wasn't*. That's just one of those stories that is just too good not to believe. From what I've learned about Ms. Horup over the past couple of months, she was charismatic, *theatrical,* if you will. If she told Helen there was a book like you're saying, why would she do that?"

Marla stares at Rasmussen. How can he not believe? This is his heritage, too. Otherwise, Viola's life and death would amount to a total waste. Seth's too. Marla's heart aches for the both of them.

Rasmussen will answer his own question, something he's generally inclined to do. "Because that's what Helen wanted to hear. About this book that's bursting with secrets. Viola Horup made it all up, probably with the best intentions at first."

"This visit was a bad idea," Marla says. She gathers her purse and gets up from her chair, declining to look the detective in the eye. No doubt he's looking all sympathetic, and Marla is tired of sympathy. But then she asks him, "Why'd you say 'best intentions at first'?"

"In my line of work you see a lot of liars. They usually change things up, depending on the weather in the room. My guess is Ms. Horup probably started believing in the book once she started her decline."

"What decline, Detective?"

"Well, her dementia, of course. Or whatever it was that turned her into a hoarder."

Marla has to laugh at that. "Viola got weak, but not in the head. Not like you're talking, anyway. She wasn't a hoarder, Detective."

"They took out some fifty boxes of things she packed away, Ms. Shute. Most of it was junk, you know that."

"I do, but I also know Viola wasn't 'in decline,' as you put it. She lived in that house all her life, never had to lift a finger to make her way." Marla sits back down. "Then last October she tells Helen she's moving to Florida after the New

Year. Said she was 97 and didn't see why she had to tolerate another Ohio winter. That's when she started packing things up. She was planning to move."

"Planning to move," Rasmussen said. He seems to pity Marla.

"Yes."

"But the garbage—"

"She thought she was going to haul everything in that house down with her to a condo near Mr. Trump's, and she wasn't going to be bothered by something as tedious as making decisions. So, she packed it all. Got to be her hobby. Her problem wasn't that she was in decline, her problem was that she was rich for nearly a century. That's a mental condition all its own."

Rasmussen mulls the new information. "Wait. Is that why you sent Seth when you did?"

"Yes sir, she was getting close to finishing up. Damned shame too. What with the mild winter we ended up having this year?" Marla thinks about this, starts to tear up. "She didn't need to be in such a hurry, after all."

* * *

After Marla Shute leaves, Steve Rasmussen feels like he deserves a break, so he takes a walk to McDonald's. As soon as pushes open the glass door, the counter girl calls out to him, shouting down a line of customers.

"Hey, Detective, somebody left you a package."

Steve comes up to her and says, "What do you mean?"

"I came in to open, and this was propped up against the back door." The girl reaches below her counter and hands him a heavy, large envelope that's wrinkled and stuffed full. It has RASMUSSEN in black marker across it.

He stares at it for a while, gauges the heft of it.

Someone from the line says, "Well, open it."

Has no one in this establishment ever heard of the "See something, say something" campaign? This package could contain a bomb or poison powder or anything.

Except it can't. It's painfully obvious what it is.

And Steve flashes back to Christmases with his mom, back when she was just Jennifer Thomas Rasmussen, but his dad wasn't around anymore. There were a few strained holidays when Steve didn't know where to point his anger, and he was at that age where he was too old for most toys and too young for anything he really wanted, like a car. The presents people gave him were usually sweaters or personal grooming items or things that no amount of wrapping could disguise, but his mother would try her darnedest to get some excitement going. *Come on, Stevie. Let's see what you got!* And what he said then is the same thing he says now, only this time he is not trying to hurt anyone's feelings. This time he's buying a minute or two to think:

"It's just a book. No big deal."

He grabs a coffee to go, and the counter girl can't believe he doesn't want more. He's late for a meeting, he lies.

As he walks back to the department, he texts Cheri. He might need a lab person on standby.

Before he reaches the foyer, he's worked himself into a pretty hot state. Steve is always being accused of not being curious enough, but that's bullshit. He's plenty curious about a lot of things. He just doesn't like it when people try to do his job for him.

Like now. With this damned book.

Chapter 19

John follows Buonopane's instructions, but the little Ford Focus was never meant for these conditions, and John fears that they'll get stuck. They've driven past Horup Mansion just as the sun is rising behind it, and turned down a half muck, half ice farm road. He's not sure, but it looks like there's a light on, third floor.

"Are you sure, 'Jer'?"

"Just a little further."

Gerald Buonopane is dressed for a monsoon or a mountain climbing expedition, and John resents that. The old man should have warned him.

Aaaaand, it happens. They are stuck.

"God damn it, Jerry!" John hits the steering wheel with the palm of his hand.

"No worries, no worries, we'll be in and out in a jiffy. Just don't spin the wheels or you'll bury us."

The men get out of John's car and assess the situation.

"A good push or two, is all we'll need," says Buonopane, slinging the strap of the gym tote over his shoulder. "We're lucky it's getting colder. This place would have been like quicksand only a week ago."

John is skeptical, looking around at all the torn-up ground. "Why does anyone come out here, anyway?"

"It's prettier in Spring."

Buonopane begins his trudge to the trees, his boots laying waste to the uneven churn.

John picks his way forward. He's wearing his work shoes, and if he's not careful, this will be the end of them.

* * *

They hike along the tree line, and John observes how the terrain becomes steeper as the trees become thicker. This was where Peter Horup walked, this was what he saw nearly 200 years ago, more or less. And when Buonopane stops ahead, John knows why. They've arrived.

Down there is the ring of trees and the clearing where Father Michael died. There is a worn place, a beginning of a path down, but John isn't enthusiastic.

"Here," he says, "you better let me carry the bag."

Buonopane wants to protest, but there's too much sense in John's suggestion. The older man will need to hold onto trees to keep his balance on the way down, and the weight of the bag is likely to throw him off balance.

"Thank you, John." That twinkle in the old professor's eyes is irritating as hell. John swings the bag strap over his shoulder and starts down, finding it necessary to grab the odd tree trunk himself along the way.

Behind him, he can hear Buonopane's labored breathing.

They find themselves dead-ending on an outcropping of rock that, from above, wasn't discernible against all the gray. John frowns. "Sorry, I thought that was the path."

Buonopane looks at the narrow line in the debris. "A path for something," he says, ever positive. "Just not for us. Here, let me get my water."

John hands the bag over, and Buonopane sets it down on the rock, squatting over it, fussing with the contents.

"I suppose you brought a picnic along, too."

"Not quite." And the professor suddenly rises.

John feels the barrel of the gun at his temple before he sees it. "Jesus," he shouts, knocking Buonopane's hand away. The last thing he sees, before he falls backwards off the rock, is Buonopane's bewildered disappointment.

* * *

He comes to, only to find Buonopane hovering over, muttering to himself.

John can't move his head, it's stuck. He's still in the woods, though.

"You're awake? Well that's no good. I'm not a monster." Buonopane crouches and manipulates John's hand, folding his fingers around something that John only understands on a cellular level.

"Oh wait," says the old man. "Not yet." He stands again and John can see the gun, just laying there next to him, balanced on a small, fossil pitted boulder. He can't reach it.

Buonopane points at the boulder's unusual markings and says, "That's the work of Ordivician rain. Keep focusing on that."

But John cannot. He looks up to the sky, the bare branches trying to reach across it. And then suddenly, it starts to snow.

Pink snow.

Chapter 20

At 19, I was doing better. Going to guidance counselors and not threatening to punch them out. And I was looking into health services careers. Not like being a doctor or even a nurse—that was out of reach for a kid like me—but something like a tech or emergency services, which was where I landed, for a short time, anyway.

I supposed that was why Roth Thierry was an orderly, given his vulnerabilities. You go with your strengths, and you don't reach too high.

I was doing all right until I read a story about a guy they caught in Nevada who had killed and buried a fourteen-year-old in the desert. He was a truck driver, known for his neat, preppie appearance. The article suggested he was being looked at for another dozen similar murders. Young girls who had lost their way.

And then I saw the mug shot.

It was him, Mr. Tidy. The man who told me to run.

I decided to keep my mouth shut. No one would have believed me except mom, and that would have killed her. I wondered how many girls there were out there like me. Who lied about the men they'd encountered, just so they wouldn't upset their moms. The world seems to prefer situations that are clearly terrible or good.

The in-between stuff, not so much.

* * *

I had to wait until I knew that Maureen would be closing the store. Luckily there was a piecing party that night, offering me the opportunity to observe Hock from a distance, perhaps even camouflaged by the crowd. What I didn't want to say to Maureen or Rasmussen was that I was sure Hock was my guy, and to be honest, I wanted a little time alone with the creep.

I arrived at the Student Center at six p.m., my back offering frequent reminders that I should stand up straight, not slouch. My whole punk thing was being chipped away, bit by bit. I now had decent running shoes that I spray painted black so you couldn't see the logos, the reflective strips, or how thick the soles were, and I hadn't bothered to recreate the match-tip majesty of my coxcomb. My hair was combed flat, straight back.

I noticed Mel looked a little uneasy behind her box of scraps. John Hock was late, and she was going to have to start without him. The crowd that had assembled was even larger than the one I'd seen before—at least a dozen or more tables filled, forcing students who were trying to grab dinner to sit at the perimeter or on the steps leading up to the Financial Aid offices.

She laid out her materials. Ten minutes after the piecing was supposed to have started, Mel tried to crack a joke about how long you were supposed to wait for a professor before assuming class was cancelled. Was it 10 minutes? 15?

She started the session without him.

I looked around and saw that among the white scraps piled on each table, there were a few little pink ones.

"Who all's brought a rare drop?" she asked.

A half dozen hands went up.

"Well, let's take a look!" And as the lucky few approached her table, applause broke out.

I had no idea what was going on, and while normally I need to put my nose into everything, tonight I was distracted.

I wanted to find John Hock. And he sure wasn't there.

* * *

When I got back to the apartment, I grabbed the mail but something fluttered out from between the glossy coupon mailers and pleas for support from the NRU alumni office. I might not have noticed, except Zero pounced out of nowhere, ready to kill.

He had a little pink piece of paper between his fat black paws. I took it from him.

It read: *Crybaby Lane.*

I sat with it a bit. Ate a frozen pizza and played with Zero. Listen to screaming children careening up and down the hall. By nine, all of that had stopped. It was a school night.

By ten, Maureen would be closing, going back to her place. When we were apart, we usually talked before she went to bed at eleven or twelve. That gave me a little time, right? But no running. Heck, I needed to be careful *walking.*

I scrolled through the recent calls on my cell. There weren't many. I found the number I needed.

Roth Thierry was understandably surprised to hear from me.

"Hey, Roth, you having a good day or a bad day?"

180

"I am on good streak, I'd say. It's been a week since I felt like screaming at a bus or a dog." He giggled. "Is there something I can do for you?"

"You got a car?"

"Sure, I have a car," he said, sounding a little offended. "They just don't let me drive it."

"Oh, okay."

"So I'm no use to you then?"

"I didn't say that," I said, checking the apps on my phone. "I'm sending you an invite, Roth. To follow me on *Find My Friends*."

"Wow," he said. "We're friends, now?"

"We are," I said. "I have two kinds of friends, Roth. Ones who tell me not do stupid things"—I opened the app and saw that Maureen had gone offline, which was usually the case when she was working—"and you."

* * *

I don't mind the night, but other people do, and they are especially suspicious of hooded, tattooed punks in low light, so for the first time in my life, I summoned an Uber to take me across town to the wooded side of campus. I had to convince the driver I was headed towards the Field House, as he didn't like leaving me out there. Even I can rent the patriarchy pretty cheaply for a quick fix.

The walking was okay, but I was a little nervous, as it was quite a way out there. It wasn't that cold, but it was getting colder and going into freeze mode the next week—just in time for Spring Break, was everyone's complaint.

Babies.

Halfway to the Horup mansion is when it started to feel like I was making a real jackass move. These side roads were dead dark, with zero traffic, and it was taking a whole lot longer for me to get out there than I thought it should. And running, with my tender back, would be bone stupid. I picked up the pace, told myself I was merely fast walking. I had this urge to call Roth, let him talk at me about his bullshit theories just to take my mind off how spooky this was getting.

Okay, I do mind the night, especially when it's all trees and shadows and owls. I should have waited for Maureen. I should have brought her along. But then, she wouldn't have liked anything about this trip.

I checked my phone. I was running out of time.

When I made it to the mud road with the brambles encroaching on either side, things were even darker. So dark that I didn't see the little Ford Focus until I was right up on it.

Crybaby Lane

I remembered that this was Hock's car, and that the last time I saw it, he was having a bit of a tantrum. The car was dark, and the hood was cold. I looked inside to see if Hock wasn't passed out in there. He wasn't and that struck me as a very bad sign.

The car was stuck. I looked for foot prints in the slop, hoping to find evidence that he'd gone back to the main road, but no. There were a lot of prints going on up ahead, though.

Who goes to Crybaby Lane and never comes back?

I was about to find out.

* * *

Maureen never took me all the way down, so I had no idea what I was doing now. I just had this feeling, as I stood at the edge of that improvised trailhead, that whoever put that slip of paper in my mail slot meant for me to go all the way. I didn't wonder whether it was a trap or not—I knew it was. I mean, anyone would.

But I also knew that I was alone. I could feel it.

"Hello!" I called out. "I'm coming down. Don't kill me, okay?" I picked my way down and found it was easier without all the snow. I reached the fallen tree where Maureen and I shared our first kiss and then moved on ahead where she said there was an overlook. A flat rock jutting out over the clearing.

If I didn't have my phone, I might have walked right over the edge of it.

And fallen right on top of John Hock's dead body.

At least I assumed it was Hock. I lowered onto my stomach to get the light closer. When I saw that the top half of his head was, um, *integrated* with the forest floor, it scared me so bad that I hollered.

And dropped my phone.

I gripped the edge of the rock. My phone landed mostly upright in about the most awful location imaginable—the back of what used to be the man's mouth. The screen lit up his ragged, lower jaw like a slumber party prank gone wrong.

That was bad enough, but the poor bastard was covered in little slips of pink paper. Covered in words.

Literally. You either love or hate that word. It means "in the strictest, non-exaggerated sense," but if you look at the word it means words themselves—their exact meaning.

I'm not a subtle person, I underline this stuff when I see it.

It was as if a crossword puzzle exploded all over him.

And then, oh god. My phone started to ring. I rolled over and stared up at the darkness, counting. Ten buzzes and then it stopped. That was the signal.

Might as well let Roth do what he was supposed to do.

It was better than trying to get my phone back.

Chapter 21

Maureen told Crocus she'd be working late, and she will, but that afternoon she has off, so she takes the van down to Chillicothe to see Murgatroyd. Again. Crocus only knows about the one time, when Maureen turned back after the attack, but in fact she's been down to see her lover's mentor three times so far.

Which in prison terms makes her a regular.

Visitation at the Women's Reformatory is supposed to be as comfortable as possible, because everyone here is a low-risk offender. Most of the inmates are in for drug-related crimes, and most of them have families. The visiting area is soft and open, with sofas and toys. Several of the inmates are on the floor, playing with their children when Maureen is led in.

Murgatroyd's in a square upholstered chair in the corner, watching the women on the floor. Her hair is more gray than black now, and even though she's already a trim woman, she seems very thin and a lot older than her fifty-five years.

Fifty-five. Murgatroyd just had her birthday in prison.

A year is a long time for a woman like her.

Maureen has gone through all the security checks, and now she enters the room, crosses over, and hugs Murgatroyd. It's all for show, like Maureen's a family member. Murgatroyd's bones have become scary sharp over the past couple of months.

"You not eating?"

"I eat." The professor's once burning eyes are dull.

Maureen knows the score. "You getting any drink in here?"

"I'm on medication," Murgatroyd says. "I don't miss it."

"Yeah, well. Walmart had bottles of wine for $2.96. I bought one in every flavor, for when you get out."

Murgatroyd blinks slowly. It's what passes for laughter these days. "How's our girl?"

Two toddlers from different families start running around the room, giggle-screaming. Everyone, save Maureen and Murgatroyd, finds the ruckus life-affirming.

"A little gun-shy," says Maureen. "Whoever took a run at her, didn't do any damage, but he sure did a number on her head. Could have been some rando creep, but not even Rasmussen thinks that's the case."

"Impressive, seeing as he tends towards paths of least resistance." Murgatroyd pauses. This is where Maureen is supposed to laugh. She doesn't. "What is it?"

Maureen wants to reach into her pockets to show Murgatroyd, but everything from her pockets is in a bin with a guard out at the check in. "Little pink slips started showing up this week. Just a few, but get this. They have names on them. 'Peter,' 'Doral,' and 'Sorenson' were the ones I heard about."

As Liz absorbs the information, it is as if life is returning to her veins. "No 'Horup'?"

"Not yet."

"This is excellent news, Maureen. Someone is reaching out, and I think I know who."

Chapter 22

The heat is sobering, but it's also making Liz a little sick, especially as she's waiting for a piece of heavy construction machinery to make its way across the road just blocks from her cottage. The university is building another "neighborhood" of cottages at the top of the hill, meaning the professors are creeping ever closer to campus proper.

It's a pretty little subdivision, but the dust from the new site hangs in the air, and Liz is sure some of it is getting into her car through the vents.

Finally, the tractor clears, and Liz zooms across the intersection a little aggressively, then glides down into a cul-de-sac.

Her front door is unlocked, and when it swings open, she finds Gerald rather inconveniently cooking her dinner.

It's some sort of fish, and the smell, which would otherwise be delicious, doesn't sit well on top of the Bourbon residue. No wonder Viola has managed to stay so trim. Gerald's wearing a barbecue apron and his shirtsleeves are rolled up. He's smiling through a cloud of sizzle.

"Hey, babe." He waves tongs in the air, something brown in its grip.

"What a surprise," Liz says, stomach rebelling.

On the little yellow table, an open bottle of wine. Dark and red, and probably expensive. And there is a modest bouquet of white mums in a drinking glass. He couldn't find a vase.

Gerald lives one cul-de-sac over, and he and Liz have been seeing each other for a month now. He's almost a decade older than she is, and sort of delicately attractive, with curly brown hair and the lively eyes of someone who never needs to worry. Gerald already has tenure.

Apparently, they are at the break-in-and-cook stage of their relationship.

"What are we having?"

"Swordfish steaks," he answers, proudly.

Liz bolts for the bedroom.

When Gerald can break away from his efforts, he comes to find her. She's laying sideways on the bed, looking up at the ceiling, with the little window AC unit on full blast.

"You all right? Where did you go?" He sits on the bed, removes her hand from her stomach, so he can put his there instead. He reeks of the food he's cooking.

"I went out to Horup's Farm."

"Really?"

Liz nods, her eyes closed. "Command performance. When Viola Horup requests your presence, you obey." Viola was the University's biggest donor, which was appropriate, since the Horups founded the institution a hundred and fifty years ago. Back then it was a teacher's college or "normal school" as they used to call them.

"What did she want?"

Something in Gerald's tone makes Liz open her eyes. He left his apron in the kitchen, and now he's lounging beside her, his collar undone. If she seduces him can she forego the fish? Probably not.

"She wanted me to listen to a story," Liz says, guiding his hand closer to where it will do her some good. She's not a domestic sort of woman, and playing house doesn't turn her on. Gerald should realize that by now.

"I'm still cooking," he says, as a meek sort of protest. "What story?"

Liz props herself up on her elbows. "What else? How the Horups built New Royal, blah blah blah." Liz summons her strength and wraps her arms around Gerald's narrow but strong chest, hanging onto him like damsel to a fireman. "Mmmm, you smell like cloves under the swordfish."

"Ha. You smell a bit like bourbon."

"She was pouring the stuff down my throat, so I'd sit still."

"Ah," says Gerald, beginning to understand Liz's condition. "So let me get this straight—you went to a rich woman's home, drank all afternoon, and listened to stories? Sounds horrific."

"Yes, and now my lover has cooked a gourmet meal for me. I should write about all the abuse I've suffered."

Gerald kisses her deeply, which he sometimes does when he can't think of a witty comeback. Liz knows she's a handful, and she feels bad for coming home in this state. It's as if she's been cheating on him.

She pulls away. "Wait," she says. "Take a look at what she gave me." She rolls off the bed and retrieves her bag from the floor. She withdraws the typescript, and hands it to Gerald. "This is more your area, anyway," she says.

"What is this?" He starts flipping through the pages.

"My guess is it's a load of horseshit," says Liz.

* * *

Liz and Gerald last the summer, but it's only because they aren't teaching, and their social lives are limited to each other's company. Once the Fall term begins it's apparent that theirs is a mobile-home style love, with no foundation. Where they stand within the culture of their departments is a big factor, as well. Gerald Buonopane is beloved by students and his peers, ranking very highly in the unprofessional polls published in the student newspaper, while Liz is developing a reputation as a no-nonsense disciplinarian. In a few years, when her looks start to fade, an upset student will call her "bitch" to her face after discussing a paper, and from then on, that sort of thing will happen nearly once every semester.

But at the end of things with Gerald, Liz notices something else that's pushing them apart. Just the slightest dark smudge in his moods, which are generally so sunny, and an increasing independence of thought that is also remarkable, given how clingy he can be.

He's been studying the pages from Viola, repeatedly asking questions of Liz that she can't answer with any certainty. One of them is, "But why did Viola confide in you?"

"She likes me."

"No one likes you." It's their joke, becoming more and more brittle as the leaves change colors.

Gerald is convinced on even days, skeptical on odd ones. He wants Liz to take him to Horup's farm so he can try to wheedle a glimpse of the original from Viola.

"Please, Jer'," Liz says, "You know I can't just pop over. She sets her appointments weeks in advance. And you also know she's not going to show *you* the journal." Liz is aware of how that sounds even as she says it, that Gerald is unworthy. It's the little cuts in the day time that lead to night time fights, and accusations from Gerald that Liz is jealous of his popularity.

It's the worst thing he can come up with, and she thinks that's charming and pathetic at the same time.

But the journal, the journal, the journal. "Why won't you help me, Liz?" He's tried on his own to meet with Viola, explained his expertise, but she is a tiny brick wall of *no, thanks*.

The last denial comes the weekend of homecoming at NRU. Gerald has approached Viola at a fundraising banquet, and across the room, Liz watches Viola's white hair move once, from left to right, all the while maintaining a terse grin for the public.

Gerald's been shot down again. When he returns to their table, Liz reminds him, "She has no incentive to show you the book, Jerry." This does not make him feel any better, and he sullenly saws into a piece of roast chicken breast.

"She's 81," Liz says, trying another tack. "Look at her. It won't be long." They've talked about this before, how they'll have to wait until the last Horup kicks the bucket for the existence of the journal to be confirmed.

Liz also reminds Gerald that if the book *doesn't* exist, they'll never know. She finds the notion amusing, but he does not.

Later that night, they break up, very successfully.

Chapter 23

I waited a while, but no police cruiser came. I was getting ready to climb up out of the woods and walk my frozen ass back to town when I saw a flashlight up top.

"Cro! You down there?" A rescue party of one: Maureen, looking just like she did that night at Viola's, in her North Face zip up, scarf, and ratty cap that mashed her hair down.

"Damn it. Roth was supposed to call the cops if I wasn't back by eleven."

"Yeah, well, Roth Thierry knows that if there's one person with less credibility with the NRPD than you, it's himself. He called me."

Ugh. I forgot to tell Roth not to call Maureen. "Okay, but don't come down here. I'm coming up."

"Why?"

"Uh," I look down at the shadowed mass that was John Hock. My phone's screen had gone dark, which was a mercy. "Dead guy?"

"What?" She was starting down anyway. Quick as a deer, too, which made sense, seeing as these were her old stomping grounds.

"No really. I'll come up."

"Why didn't *you* call the cops, then?" And she was already on the rock with me. I tried to hold her back, so she wouldn't see what was down below. It was all a little too déjà vu.

"'Cause my phone's in the dead guy, Maureen."

She stepped to the edge, anyway. Her flashlight lit the body up head to toe. "Holy shit."

"I think it's John Hock."

Maureen surveyed his broken body, covered with little pieces of pink paper. She paused the light on Hock's chest. His arm was folded over it, over the pink slips, and in his hand gripped something dark: the gun he used to blow his brains all over the forest floor.

"Why did you come down here, Cro?"

I reached into my back pocket and pulled out the little pink slip that said *Crybaby Lane* on it. "I got this in my mail slot. I thought it was an invite. Didn't know it was a suicide note."

"God damn," Maureen said, shining the flashlight on it.

I did not think our relationship was going to survive this, not if we had to spend another winter night being interrogated. "Let's get out of here."

"Um, your phone."

"Are you serious?"

"It's your phone."

"He's kind of *using* it, Maureen."

"Fine, I'll get it." And she started backtracking to access a better way down.

I called after her, "Do not do that, Maureen. They'll give me my phone back after he's processed."

She was already another level down, crossing parallel on a path she knew from childhood. "I bet they won't."

"Why not?" She'd left me in the dark again, so I started after her.

"Because Hock's no suicide," she panted, climbing up on a boulder then hopping down on the other side so she could approach the body feet first. "Which makes this a murder scene."

She scanned all around him with her light until it landed on the explosion of bone and blood that was his skull. She took a few steps closer and bent over to disturb as little as possible, gripping the corner of the phone that rose from the gore like a tiny iceberg.

"How do you know that?" I tried to pretend I didn't hear that sucking noise of release.

She made her way back to me, holding the phone by the corner the way you hold a mouse your cat just killed. "It's kind of a long story," she said, "And you're not going to like it."

Maureen took off her ratty knit cap, and put the bloody phone in it for me to take. "You can keep the hat, though."

"The story," I said.

"The story, yeah," she said, starting the long slow slog back up the hill. We were heading back to the van. "Starts with me getting a call back in January. From Murgatroyd. She wants to make sure I know you didn't write *Mean Bone*."

* * *

190

That first call was the Doc ordering Maureen to visit her at Chillicothe as soon as she could schedule, and she wasn't supposed to let me know. Maureen thought it was blackmail, but when she got there, the Doc explained that what she really wanted was for me to keep on the Viola story. She thought I'd just fade out on it without help. She needed someone on the outside to keep on my back.

Murgatroyd told Maureen that she knew *for a fact* that Seth Shute didn't kill Viola, but she didn't offer up what that fact was. She said I'd figure it out if I just stuck with it, followed my nose. And that it was going to be my opportunity to legitimize myself. All I needed was a nudge or two in the right direction. So, at first, all Maureen had to do was make me *want* to succeed.

This was before we found Amanda Carlos, so it was also before we were even a couple. The Doc knew we would be, though.

But then I started spinning my wheels, not getting to where the Doc needed me to go quick enough for her tastes. That's when she came up with the idea of the words. She knew the journal was out there in someone's itchy hands. Viola had warned her, and she'd dismissed it as an old woman's fantasy, but no more. Not now that Viola had been murdered.

The game was a way of applying a little pressure.

"So she gave me a list of words from the journal, and I went out to Montgaul to get them produced and duplicated. Then she gave me an account number and an email for a guy who ran day laborers to do the distribution work. The idea was to wait and see who would recognize the words."

This was crazy, but somehow the idea that Murgatroyd was behind this mess made sense. Still, Maureen was right. I was pissed off. I yanked my seatbelt on and tossed the cap with the bloody phone in it onto the dash. "And what? You were just going to point me at him?"

Maureen turned the key, and the van rumbled to life. "Well, yeah, I guess so."

As the van moved in reverse, I watched Hock's car grow ever smaller in the distance. I was trying to decide how hurt and angry I was supposed to be. "All this bullshit, just to make something of me."

"I'm sorry we did that to you, it was stupid." Maureen threw her arm over the back of the seat and looked out the rear window as she picked up speed. "But I think you're missing the point."

"What, that there's a guy dead back there, covered with pieces of your cute little game?"

"Right, except those aren't ours," she said. The van hit the ruts like a boat bouncing on rough water. "And you were right the first time."

"About what?"

"*Crybaby Lane.* It was an invitation."

Chapter 24

I wasn't sure what weirded me out more, the idea that someone was trying to get murder mojo all over me, or the fact that Murgatroyd had a boyfriend back in the day. The first idea felt more natural than the second.

We rolled into Murgatroyd's old neighborhood with the lights off, and waited at the top of a hill where we could look down at all the cottages lining the curving asphalt drive. It looked like a river at night. Most of the cottages were dark because of the hour, but some were twinkling with light. Buonopane's was one of those. He was working late.

Maureen said, "He had the typescript of Viola's book to work from. Our words just came from Liz's recall, and she was very selective, but to be honest I thought her choices were too neutral to get attention. But his words were names and places. Real bell ringers. And then he made them pink, like he wasn't messing around."

She took my hand. "When you pulled out *Crybaby Lane*, I almost got sick."

That seemed at odds with the nerve required to pluck my phone out of Hock's cratered skull. I pulled out of her grip, not yet ready for normal. "So, I'm just supposed to go on up and knock at his front door. Then what?"

"Then be yourself, Cro."

"He's a murderer."

"He's a fat, *old* murderer. And we're two lean, young not-murderers."

"The murder part is pretty important, Maureen. What a person can do and what they're capable of are two entirely different things."

She gripped the steering wheel, frustrated that I wasn't more enthusiastic about rattling Buonopane's cage. "Yeah, well you've been telling me for weeks that you're the incredible hulk."

She was right about that. I just wasn't sure that my temper could be weaponized. "Where are you going to be?"

"Right here in the shadows. We got this, Cro."

"It's all shadows, Maureen." I started to get out of the van, but Maureen pulled me over for a kiss.

"Wait," she said, and started fussing with my hair, pulling it up straight where she could. "That'll have to do."

The little neighborhood of professors was supposed to be charming, and in the bright light of a Spring day it was. Every little house was a different color from the ones next door, and flower gardens and neatly trimmed hedges abounded. But if you took away the light—and I mean even when the day was partly cloudy—the whole place became strange, just a little *off*, like a stage set. When Murgatroyd's home burned down last year, I half expected the whole subdivision to go up in flames, just for effect.

As I walked up to Buonopane's cottage, my steps were silent, and that bothered me, so I knocked on the front door. *Loud.*

When he opened up, he announced, "It's two o'clock in the morning," but he was grinning. And he was wearing a close-fitting metal cap with golden rivets and a nose guard. Other than the hat, he was in wool slacks and a linen shirt, and a pair of suspenders hung slack off his belt.

"Is that a Viking hat?"

"It's a Spangenhelm. A student gave it to me. A replica, of course, but the design is authentic. Do you like it?"

"I guess."

He removed it, revealing a sweaty scalp and a few hanks of hair plastered over it like pennants. "I've been waiting for you."

"Is the get-up supposed to freak me out?" I walked past him, into the cottage.

"Liz's little thug," he said, appreciatively. He was not the least bit fazed by my brazen routine. "It's a sign of mental illness when you confuse a bit of whimsy as a threat."

"It's a sign of mental illness if you think your threats are whimsical."

The sitting room was dim, but lights were on elsewhere in the hallway and the kitchen. Same floor plan as Murgatroyd's old place, but Buonopane seemed to favor old colors. Not old fashioned, but old, like greens that had become mossy over time and reds gone to rust. And of course, there were little cairns of precariously balanced books everywhere. He placed the helmet atop one of those.

"I'm right, aren't I? Liz sent you."

"After a fashion."

"Good. So, she got my messages. Because I certainly received hers." Buonopane dropped himself onto a love seat, put his feet up on the coffee table. He was entirely in shadow, just a voice emanating from the rotund shape of him. "Do you know we lived for twenty-five years just one street apart, Liz and I? Barely speaking, barely making eye contact when we crossed paths, which was quite often."

I said, "But once upon a time…"

"*Mmmph*," he growled. It was the dirtiest sound I'd ever heard, in prison or out. "I'd invite you to make yourself comfortable dear, but I don't want you to be comfortable."

"That much I've gathered." I stood with the light behind me. "What messages?"

"Via the journal, of course. Via the *game*."

He used the long *I* pronunciation for "via." Any second now, he was going to break out the old *mwahh hah ha*. But first, a long, thoughtful silence before he said, "Tell Liz I miss her."

"I'm not allowed to. Conditions of my parole."

He wasn't listening. "Tell her, it's been fun."

"I can try to get a message—"

"Tell her, there was never anyone else. Not like her."

I stopped arguing with him. "Sure."

"Sure," he whispered. Like the word was new to him. "I'm not a bad man, you know."

"Well, now you see, Professor, that's about the scariest thing you can say to someone you just met."

A sigh from the sofa.

I said, "I found John Hock's body, you know. Down on Crybaby Lane."

"His body? That does not sound promising."

"It shouldn't. Someone covered him in pink words—those are yours, right? And then they made it look like he blew his brains out."

Buonopane grunted as he leaned over to turn on a lamp on the side table. "Blew his brains out," he repeated, with a gentle smile. "Do people really speak like that?"

"I do."

"Well, then. If you don't know already, you will soon. John Hock was a student of mine. We'd tried to reconnect, but as you know from your own experience, he was unstable. Yes, he confessed to his little encounter with you. How are you doing, by the way?"

That thing, where you can see the architectural plans of a lie, but you can't read them because you aren't an architect, yourself—I was going through that. Buonopane's face was softening, transforming into the least threatening visage imaginable, and I knew it was an act, but there was no stopping the performance now.

"I'm fine." My mouth was dry.

Buonopane looked away, as if he had regrets. "He was steeped in that scheme of Wethers', so I had to tell him. That this whole word game was merely an elaborate, drawn out duel between old lovers. Well, you can imagine that didn't sit well with the boy." Buonopane tried on a little frown, just for me. "He has had a troubled past."

"You're trying to tell me it was a suicide," I said.

The old professor sat up, leaned forward, his fingertips together. "I'm afraid I pushed him a bit far. I showed him my pink words, the 'rare drops,' as they call them. In fact, when I came home this evening my supply was missing. I assumed John had taken them to punish me. I just never imagined how far he gone he was."

This was ridiculous. "Except someone dropped this in my box." I took the pink strip out of my pocket and showed him.

Buonopane peered at it, then up at me. "I can only assume John wanted you to find him. He was a little obsessed with you, you know. He was convinced that you were taunting him. That you knew his secret."

"Which was what?"

Then the old man batted his eyes like an embarrassed child. "Well, he never said for sure, but he hinted around the subject quite a bit. It's my belief that he killed Amanda Carlos."

"Bullshit."

And suddenly, Buonopane was distracted, looking out through the picture window at something new. Had he spotted Maureen? He said, "Who the hell is that?"

Out there on the little asphalt cul-de-sac, was Roth Thierry, standing under a street lamp, looking lost. He was checking his cell, trying to figure out what direction to go.

"My back-up, obviously." I was joking, of course, but Buonopane didn't seem to take it that way. I went ahead and wiggled that loose tooth. "Did you think I would come down here alone?"

But then Roth got the bead he was looking for, and walked away, up the hill where we'd parked the van. Oh, well.

Buonopane said, "As your second, he's not very good, is he?"

"No," I said, watching Roth's huge bulk melt into the night. "He's just terrible."

"I suppose you feel vulnerable, now," Buonopane said.

I half expected him to have a gun trained on me, Peter Lorre style, but no. I said, "I don't actually. But I am a little irritated with you."

"I believe I've been a perfect gentleman, considering the hour and the circumstances."

"Uh huh. Except you are a complete lying sack of shit."

He sat there on the sofa, unperturbed. If anything, he was even more sweet looking. "You're confused, my dear. You're the liar, and while I grant you, it takes one to know one, your reputation is already…oh, heck let's use that word again—*vulnerable.* I do wonder how many bodies Rasmussen will let you stumble across before he starts to notice a pattern. He's slow on the uptake, but he's bound to notice the significant increase in his workload now that you are without proper supervision."

I stood my ground. "That sounds like a confession."

"Everything sounds like a confession when you shine the right light, but that's not the point." He stood, reminding me of his bulk. "Ms. Rowe, I know you didn't write *Mean Bone.*"

I did not respond.

He liked that very much. "Not *that* sounds like a confession."

I tried to recover. "Why do you think I didn't?"

"Because the book is a piece of prevaricating garbage that reeks of Liz's rationalizing. There's also the matter of her ice-in-the-veins prose."

He'd turned from sweet to spoiled, just like that. Years of living with a broken heart will do that to a person.

"So," I swallowed, pretending to be rocked, "Can I count on you for a cover blurb?"

The explosive, avuncular laugh. "That's the spirit."

"When did you read it?"

"All the program heads received advanced copies so they could prepare to refute any negative characterizations of the University. My department chair thought I deserved a peek. My question though, is why did Liz set you onto me?"

I was on the verge of telling him it wasn't about him, it was about me, and my potential career, but then it struck me.

Buonopane was right.

* * *

As I walked the hill towards the van, Maureen was standing in the middle of the street, on her way down, her thumb poised over the keypad of her phone.

"Don't hit that last 1," I said.

"Jesus, Cro, are you okay?"

"Let's just get out of here."

When we reached the van, I was only half surprised to see Roth Thierry sitting in the middle of the second bench.

"Look what you caught," I said to Maureen, climbing in.

"I found *her,*" Roth said.

Maureen gripped the wheel. "You going to tell me what happened?"

I pulled the safety belt over, clicked it in. "I'm not totally sure, but I think he sort of confessed to killing John Hock."

A mighty thump from the back seat, and Roth's giant head was thrust forward between the seats. Maureen hadn't told him.

"Sorry, Roth," I said. "Hock's dead. We found his body down in the woods."

Roth's mouth hung slack. "He was directing my independent study."

Maureen said, "Crocus, you're shitting me, right?"

"I wish I was."

"But why would he just—?"

"Buonopane is pretty sure no one will believe me," I said. "And I think he's right. We don't have any proof. We're just going on Murgatroyd, and I'm beginning to think she set us up."

Maureen's jaw flexed defiantly. "What are you talking about?"

Roth's breath filled the cockpit. It wasn't great. "I think we've been fooled, Maureen. Maybe Liz wants me to stand on my own two feet, but her main goal is to get Buonopane. He was the first person she thought of when Viola was killed. For some reason."

All three of us stared down at his cottage. The light inside blinked out.

Roth said, "But you didn't get him."

"No, I did not."

Maureen said, "Should I go back to her? Find out what to do next?"

"Nah. I don't know about you, but I'm tired of having her play me. I need to talk to someone who was there."

"Where?"

"With them, in the past."

Chapter 25

As I walked across campus the next afternoon, two powerful elements charged the air. One was Spring Break, about to start the following week. The other was the news that John Hock had died. Maureen and I had made Roth call in an anonymous tip.

Half the classrooms in Jarvis were unoccupied. The Thursday and Friday before break were like Easter Monday—not a thing but definitely a thing. Those classes that were in session were sparsely attended and very low key. Wethers had sent out an alert to the faculty, charging them with the duty of breaking the news.

Myself, I was ragging on three hours of sleep. After we dropped Roth off at his house, Maureen spent the night at mine, but we didn't talk much, and when I woke up I felt more exhausted than when we hit the sack in the first place.

There were lots of hushed conversations happening in the hallways, and already flowers being delivered to the front office.

I trod quietly down the hall to Alma Bell's office and tapped on the door. When she opened it, she looked like I felt. Defeated.

"Can I come in?"

"Yeah. Take a seat."

She'd put a potted plant on the sill of the much-desired window. Seemed like the obvious thing to do, but Murgatroyd had never kept a plant in the office.

"Any news?"

"Not yet," she said. "Just plenty of rumors. Apparently, it's quite a messy scene."

I nodded, innocently.

"So, I need to ask you about the Doc," I said.

"Oh, Crocus—"

"It's relevant." I tried to be as precise with my thoughts as possible, and if that meant setting off alarms, so be it. "Did you know about the Doc and Gerald Buonopane?"

"Gerry?" A little life to her sad face. "His name is popping up a lot these days. Yeah, they had a summer thing that turned ugly."

"Ugly enough that the Doc still holds a grudge?"

Bell's eyes narrowed. "Grudges are unreasonable. Liz has every right to resent Gerry to his grave. He all but destroyed her career, a fact she's reminded of with every paycheck. Well, she used to be reminded."

"Did it have something to do with Viola Horup and a journal?"

Bell looked at me very seriously. Instead of asking me how I knew about the book, she said, "What's this about?"

"I'm not totally sure yet, but let me ask you this. If the Doc had a chance to mess with Buonopane's head, like big time, would she be willing to go to prison for a few months to cover her tracks?"

Alma Bell sat back and looked at me as if I told her one of the secrets of Fatima. "Damned straight she would."

* * *

March 2002

Liz is trembling.

She looks through her files and it's gone. The journal typescript that Viola gave her is gone. She throws a sweater on over her shirtwaist dress, and walks over to Gerry's cottage, and she barely has it together to knock like a civilized person. She's probably being watched by her neighbors, all of them her colleagues, as well.

It's brisk, and there are dandelions and crocuses already. Liz's hair blows into her face.

When Gerry comes to the door, he's in jeans and a cardigan, layers to hide the fact that he's a little plumper since the break-up.

Liz points her chin at him, and he lets her come inside.

"I'm sorry the place is a little untidy," he smiles.

"You bastard," she says quietly.

"Took you long enough."

"Where is it?"

He crosses his arms and tries to look casual. "Does that really matter now?"

Liz runs her hand across her forehead. "It's bad enough that you accosted her at the banquet—"

"Accosted? Please."

"But you went to Viola's *house*?"

"She didn't let me in."

"Gerry! This isn't some *faux pas*, this is my career. I just heard form Doris that there's a flag on my tenure dossier. Apparently, an unnamed donor wants me to undergo an ethics review."

Gerald's smiling. "Perhaps that's appropriate."

"She gave me those pages in confidence. I only shared them with you because…"

"Because you loved me."

"Because I felt sorry for you, you ass. Now, where is it?"

"Seriously Liz, what good will it do?"

Liz's hands are in the air as if she's forgotten what they're for, normally. "I'm going to return the pages to Viola. I'm going to tell her you stole them. I'm going to apologize to her."

Gerald is trying to look somber, now. "And exactly none of that is going to work."

Liz knows that. From what Doris told her, Gerald terrified Viola, standing on her porch, screaming until he was red in the face, slapping the screen door with the pages. Viola hid in a closet, while Matz shoed Gerry away.

Liz asked if Gerry was going to be fired, and Doris said, *No, but you are. Viola blames you.*

That was so like Viola, too. She was of an era where Gerry's behavior was "passionate." His intensity only validated the journal's importance.

Liz needs to talk to Viola, set her straight.

But first she wants the typescript back. "Where is it, Gerry?" but she doesn't wait for him to tell her. She knows this house as well as her own, and heads straight back to the little office that overlooks a drainage pond crowded with snow geese.

She's not quite prepared for what she finds back there.

He's behind her. "It's just my research, dear."

"There's a difference between research and obsession, Jerry." Liz leans over his desk, piled with mountains of documents, most of which were copies of military manifests and private letters dating from the 1700s, all with that unmistakable blown out blur you can only get from microfilm. Beneath those, were surveyor's reports and building plans stacked across each other as if vying for rank. But behind the clutter was Gerry's corkboard, where, between the calendar that was still turned to January and a list of final exam dates and times for the current semester, a series of three photographs are pinned in a vertical line.

Each one is of Viola Horup, either leaving or entering the mansion.

Liz can feel her ex-lover's body heat flow forward against her back. He's too close. "When did you get a long lens, Gerry?"

"A treat for my birthday."

In the first two pictures, Viola is mounting the long brick porch at the front of the estate. There's no way of telling when they were taken. Viola is wearing sweater sets in each, one blue, the other white, and the grass is bright green, almost Spring-like, but then that's how Matz keeps things over at Horup's Farm. Always timeless, always Spring. The third picture is a curiosity, showing an angle of the mansion that is unfamiliar to Liz. Here, Viola seems to be crossing a patio furnished with Adirondack loungers, but the shot has been taken from below, as if at the bottom of a hill, and the mansion is made to look almost monstrous behind her frail body. It's already swallowed the sky, and now it wants Viola, too.

Liz knows she will regret asking, but, "Where was this taken?"

Gerald isn't ashamed. "From the woods."

"Crybaby Lane?"

"Very near there, yes." And it's in that moment that he slips his arm around Liz's waist, and then the other across her throat. She has just enough time to gasp, as he pulls her straight up.

It's a practiced move, one that she and Gerry have practiced together in fact, though in a more recreational context. She refuses to panic, even as he tightens his grip. The only real danger is if he gets too excited and goes too far.

As a kid, Gerald Buonopane must have been a real terror on the playground.

When he releases her, he laughs a fake laugh, and that's when Liz realizes how touch and go things might be. She straightens her skirt, smooths her blouse. Gerry is slow wheeling away from her, and the look on his face: he surprised himself.

"To hell with it, Gerry," says Liz. "Keep the pages. But if anything happens to Viola? You better know I'll make sure you're suspect Number One."

Gerald's eyes are shining. "You just put a target on your back, sweetheart."

"They're in fashion these days," says Liz, walking away from him. "Mine matches the one you just put right between your own eyes, in fact."

* * *

"Whoa, wait," I said. "So Buonopane chokes the Doc and has secret pics of an eighty-year-old woman in his man cave? Why didn't she call the cops?"

Alma sighed. "Welcome to Women's Career Day. She couldn't afford the attention."

"But what about Viola?"

"She never spoke to Liz again, which was sad, but rich people are like that. They don't like it when simple folk become complicated. Liz's ethics review turned out just fine, but the whole thing was so awkward. Back then the Department administration blamed her falling out with Viola for the slumping charitable donations."

"That's not fair."

"No, it isn't," Alma said. "After Liz finally got her tenure, she just put her head down, and kept doing her own thing."

"For twenty-five years?"

"She was pissed off. Stayed that way, too. And they only lived one street apart from each other, all this time."

"You put it that way, a year off civilian life is just a drop in the bucket."

"Some relationships are a long game," Alma said. "Your turn. What's Liz got on Gerry? Does she think he killed Viola?"

"Uh huh. And I think he killed Hock, too."

Alma leaned back in her padded chair, considering all of it, and I expected her to tell me how ridiculous I sounded, but then she said, "Got anything to take to Rasmussen?"

I shook my head no. "Nothing but my good name."

Alma's grimace was far from encouraging.

Chapter 26

Roth Thierry's mother always called him her wild card. Not her wild child or her wild thing. Those were different, somehow. A wild card is something you deploy or chance upon, and he's never really understood what that meant.

The last twenty-four hours have been rocky, and now Roth has given in. On his third beer, being eyed by a bartender he only sees every six months or so, but who remembers Roth very clearly, anyway.

He's not supposed to drink, but nothing else is working. His pills, the CBT, nothing. He's so tired, but his thoughts are racing. His head is an old paper bag with a squirrel inside.

And he has to use the toilet every hour.

Of course, he hasn't slept. Not even when he gave up on his narrow bed and put his ratty, old duvet on the floor. He sleeps on the floor when his back acts up.

John Hock is dead. Covered in words. What could that even mean?

There aren't a lot of bars like Huck's left in New Royal. It's a shotgun of an establishment where the windows are blacked out so that the gray machines aren't visible to the street, and it's easy to lose track of day or night. At twenty-seven, Roth is easily the youngest customer, and even though he's usually escorted out at the end of his infrequent visits, he's always welcomed back, albeit begrudgingly.

John Hock is dead. Covered in words. Roth signals for another beer, and the bartender, Gunner, has to show him that he's only a third of the way through the beer he already has.

"I'm not drunk," Roth says. And that's mostly true. He's just trying to figure out the impossible.

"Man," Gunner says. And he waves his hand across his face. "Maybe you need to get home and freshen up."

Roth has no idea what the guy is talking about.

A beer and a half later, Roth is wobblier than a man of his size should be. Gunner tells him to call a friend to come get him. Roth tries to explain that he didn't drive, but the thoughts and words tangle together, especially when he tries to describe his friend situation. He wouldn't be at Huck's if he had any.

And then he remembers the pulsing blip that was Crocus down on Crybaby Lane. Was that just last night? Impossible.

He reaches for his cigarettes, taps one out and starts to light up right at the bar.

"Hey," says Gunner. "Outside."

"Why?" Roth laughs. "No one else is here, man."

"Outside."

"Jesus, okay." And Roth slides off his stool, grabbing the edge of the bar until he's got his land legs again. He puts on his parka and once outside, he lights up and looks down the street at a traffic light changing yellow to red, even though there isn't a car in sight. "Shit's pointless, man," Roth says, to a generic imaginary companion. He feels like he's the last man on earth.

Behind him, he hears the locks being thrown, and above, the light that says Hucks in neon, with no apostrophe, sizzles out.

"God damn it," Roth yells, realizing he's been shut out by the second to last man on earth.

* * *

Roth does not remember walking all the way to campus and across it, but here he is in the dark that never eases up, scuffling along between buildings. He has the wherewithal to step back when a campus security vehicle cruises by, but by the time he's into the village of professors' cottages, he's not nearly as stealthy. That is, he feels like he's getting drunker, somehow.

He stumbles against a fence he can't see, and the racket sets off a dog two houses down, but these days no one pays attention to their dogs anymore. Roth shouts, "Shut up!"

This does nothing to quiet the dog.

No big surprise he's made it to Buonopane's street. His body seems to know the way by now, and there's definitely unfinished business to attend to. He makes his way to the History professor's front stoop. Pounds on the door with the heel of his hand.

It takes a while for the porch light to come on. When the old man opens up, he's in a striped robe and shower sandals. He doesn't appear to be wearing any pajamas, even though it seems clear that Roth has woken him up.

Roth says the first thing that pops into his head. "You sleep naked."

"And you sleep in your clothes, apparently," Buonopane says.

"I was here with Crocus before. Don't be scared."

"I'm not scared. Why have you returned? Did you lose something?"

Roth stands there for a moment, his mind a complete, momentary blank. He knows he needs to remember why he's there. He also knows that this blankness is a mercy, one that he should cling to, but—

"No, I found something." And he fumbles inside his parka. He hands a dark thing over to the professor. "What is this?" Roth says. "What does it mean?"

Buonopane holds the cell phone up in the light. It's covered in dark, dried blood. "Interesting," he says, and he presses the power button, but the unit is dead. "Where did you find this?"

"In the van. That's why I'm confused."

"Understandably," says Buonopane. "I supposed it's bricked."

"I don't know."

"But that might not be important," says the professor. He smiles strangely. "How do you suppose it got in this state, eh? Or is this some new sort of Goth accessory?"

Roth senses that the man is joking, but he can't get why anything about a bloody phone would be amusing.

Buonopane says, "There's no more sleeping tonight, I suppose, so you may as well come on in. And who knows, maybe I have a cord that works."

* * *

While the professor rather noisily searches through junk drawers in his kitchen, Roth sits on the sofa in the front room, his knees out and parka hanging open. The professor had muttered something about Roth looking like he was walking around in an unbuttoned bear costume. The bloody phone is on the coffee table. There had been a winter hat, too, but he doesn't remember what he did with that.

When the professor returns, he has two kinked up power cords dangling from his grip, and his robe has opened over his chest and round, bare belly. There's just a tiny patch of gray curls hovering like a cloud over the man's gut. Otherwise he's smooth as a baby.

"Here we are," he says. "One of these should do the trick." Buonopane retrieves the phone and starts matching plug to jack, undeterred by the gore. "Success," he declares, and he waddles back to the kitchen to plug it in.

Roth rises to watch. The professor's kitchen is gold and brown, and for some reason it reminds Roth of a men's shoe shop. Buonopane leans over the counter, peering at the phone, as if it needs his encouragement.

"Fingers crossed," he says to Roth.

Roth crosses his fingers. "Professor?"

"Yes? Oh! I think we're getting a glimmer of life here." He turns his attention to Roth. "What is it?"

Roth's condition so far has been a loose affiliation of unstable ailments, but now there's a migraine coming on to pull it all together. There's a hum and whir that will soon become a swarm of bees. "Crocus says you killed John Hock."

"Does she?" Buonopane's smile is open mouthed, unsettling. "She's a strange person though, don't you think?"

Roth isn't in any position to gauge what or who is strange. "Did you?"

"John Hock committed suicide," says Buonopane. "Or as your friend, Ms. Rowe, put it, He 'blew his brains out.'" And the professor makes a flourish at his own temple. "She certainly doesn't shy away from crude imagery, does she?"

The phone buzzes, and the ghostly outline of a battery flickers across the screen.

"There we go," says the professor. "We're in luck. Oh, fascinating."

"What is it?" And Roth is in the kitchen next to the professor, staring down at the blood encrusted phone.

The phone's wallpaper is a picture of a redhead holding a black cat up to her face.

"Well, mystery solved, then. That is Ms. Rowe's lover, is it not?"

"That's Maureen," Roth confirms. Is she and Crocus together? Of course they are. Maureen came to the hospital. It was one of those obvious things that Roth tends to miss. It's frustrating, only being able to see the world one piece at a time and not all at once, the way everyone else did.

Roth feels the first crashing wave of sadness hit while the migraine strengthens and pushes confusion up the shore. Professor Buonopane's shifting moods don't help, either. He's moved on from his state of tolerant curiosity, and now, as he looks down at the phone and Maureen's crooked smile beaming up at him through smudges and streaks of horror, his good humor is gone, replaced by what appears to be a grim understanding.

The professor says, "Well. I suppose all we can do now is wait."

Ain't that the truth, Roth wants to say, but he's just about drowning under the second wave.

* * *

It's not even light out when the noise wakes him. Roth's on Buonopane's sofa, at first unfamiliar, with his knees up and his head bent at a painful angle. Everything looks greasy and unfocused until he starts breathing again. He hears her familiar voice, feels the cool morning air from an opened door.

"I believe you have something that belongs to me." It's Crocus.

"I do," says the professor. "I was this far from calling the police."

But Crocus isn't having any of it. "To tell them what, exactly?"

"To tell them to collect that giant sack of shit."

"Roth?" That's Maureen, stepping in. "Are you okay?"

Roth forces himself up, rubs his face. It's sore, like it gets when he's been crying.

Crocus remains on the threshold, ready for a fight, but Buonopane is himself, still in his robe with nothing underneath. Still in control and unflappable. Maureen has moved past them both and now stands over Roth.

"As much as I enjoy your state of confusion," Buonopane says, "you should know, he brought your phone to me."

Crocus and Maureen exchange intense expressions that make the old professor laugh. He raises his voice to a cartoonish, feminine pitch: "*I thought you destroyed the phone!*' '*No, I thought you did!*' And on, and on."

"I took it from the van," Roth croaks. "Sorry."

"Such are the perils of improvisation," says Buonopane. "Get him out of here."

Roth rises, unsteady, cramping. He believes he's crapped himself, just a little. Maybe Maureen doesn't notice, her being around animals as much as she is. She takes his arm in two places, guides him towards the door, and both Crocus and Buonopane step back to give them plenty of room.

As they pass, Roth can see the first glow of dawn, and where everyone else would see the beauty in it, he feels dread. "You should just take me straight out to Mannen," he says, and Maureen agrees. Mannen is the state hospital, where Roth Thierry is a frequent guest.

Crocus bends sideways, looking around the slow moving mass that is Roth Thierry, and says to Professor Buonopane, "I'm not getting my phone back, am I?"

"No," he says. "And I don't suppose you will ever explain to me how it got to be in its current state?"

"No."

"Ah, well. Perhaps that's not important. Perhaps all that is important is that you want your phone's secrets kept secret, as it were. I can manage that, provided our relationship remains stable."

"Yeah, about that," says Crocus. "Hey, Mo?"

"What?" Maureen's van is just out front of Buonopane's cottage, waiting.

"You and Roth go on ahead. I'll catch up to you later."

"Crocus—"

Crocus is smiling. "S'okay, Mo. I just need to get a few things settled with the Professor."

Chapter 27

Buonopane didn't put up a fight, but he was not happy to see the van pull away without me, either. "I hope this won't take long," he said. "Your friend is tiring. Extracting information from him is like playing cat and mouse with a demented Labrador retriever."

"He was one of John's students. He's grieving."

"Really?" Buonopane was only mildly interested. He walked back into the sitting room and wrinkled his nose over the sofa. "Good lord. To the kitchen, then."

The kitchen and the dining area were connected, and Buonopane invited me to take a seat at a tiny, gold-flecked Formica table over which loomed an old-fashioned cupboard of spices. He plopped down across from me, exaggerating his fatigue, though his eyes were puffy and red-rimmed.

A night with Roth Thierry, eh? Good. Buonopane deserved it.

"Well?" he said. "Go ahead, drop your bomb."

"No bomb. I just wanted you to know that I had a nice long chat with Alma Bell."

"Alma? Oh my, that must have been fun. Memoirists and their abstractions."

"Yeah but, memoirists are good at remembering, too. It's sort of their job. Anyway, she filled in the details for me, about your relationship with Liz."

Buonopane's smirk was constitutionally unavoidable. He put his elbow on the table and rested his chubby, whiskered face in his hand.

So punchable.

I added, "And your relationship with Viola."

His eyes were at half-mast, as if I was singing him back to sleep. "And your Eureka moment?"

"That you killed her."

"Mmm," he said, sounding bored, but he straightened up. "Good luck trying to convince anyone of that. Your credibility is quite strained, even without the distracting addition of a bloody phone. You know, when you said you'd found John's body, I never imagined you rolling around with him on the forest floor."

"Right," I said, struggling to sound cheerful. "So this is, more or less, an academic conversation."

"The best kind." He looked around his kitchen, gaze resting on the empty coffee carafe in the dish rack. "Shall I put on a pot?"

"Please."

I watched him fuss over the sink, pouring the water and measuring out the grounds. He was stalling, but I don't know why. Once he'd pressed the button on the machine, he sighed, leaning over the sink, his robed back to me.

He said, "Do I need to be armed for this conversation, I wonder?"

"I'm not."

"No?" He turned, flashing a quick grin. "I always imagined you had a little stiletto tucked in your boots."

"Not me, I'm not allowed."

"Oh, right. I keep forgetting. Still, I think I should retrieve my gun. For civility's sake."

"If it makes you more comfortable," I said. "But a gun? That's a little disappointing."

"Historians love guns."

"Just assumed you were a Katana man, is all."

"That hurts," he frowned. "I'm not sixteen, you know."

He didn't wait for the pot to finish, but poured our cups prematurely and intentionally. The portion he served me was undrinkable. From his cupboard, he pulled down a container of powdered creamer and a squeeze jar of honey. He dropped those on the table.

I was a little uneasy about his quick, sweeping movements. The only thing holding the robe closed was a fuzzy sash tied in a lazy, overhand knot that his belly pushed against.

I picked up the creamer. "'Best by May 2012.' You don't have many guests, do you?"

When he sat down again, he had turned sullen.

"So the pink words were yours," I said.

"I told you as much. John took them from me."

"Right, you keep saying that like even you find it hard to believe. But the problem with games—puzzles, treasure hunts, all that shit—is that there are solutions. Guaranteed solutions. And people get confused and start thinking that's how life is going to be." I picked up my cup, tilting it to test the viscosity of the sludge it contained. "But when all the pieces start to come together, that's when

212

you need to be suspicious. Because pieces don't come together on their own. You gotta pull 'em together and then tie 'em together."

Buonopane sniffed. "I'm a professor, Ms. Rowe. Have been for thirty odd years. Your existential musings aren't very interesting or original."

"Okay, sorry, I'll try to get to the point then. Can you tell me what really happened to Viola Horup? Is that sufficiently existential?" I refrained from calling him a piece of fuck, but he managed to pick up on my mood, anyway.

"You're only making yourself angry, Ms. Rowe. Working yourself up. Anger is dangerous, and leads to poor decisions." He grabbed the honey like a brute, strangling it until nearly half of its contents was in his cup.

A demonstration.

He continued. "Poor Viola would be alive today and unpacking her boxes of moldy potatoes and mismatched shoes in sunny South Florida if her assailant—oh, let's call him Seth, shall we?—if *Seth* had been able to keep his temper in check."

"You're going to play it off like it was an impulse control thing?"

His head bobbed. "It was no secret Viola was finally pulling up stakes and moving on. Possibly taking the untold history of New Royal with her. That would be frustrating for a lot of people."

"Seriously. You're saying the journal was worth killing for."

"Oh, not at all. The book's revelations might upset the status quo in New Royal, but—as my deceased protégé John Hock, once said—the information is de-fanged by sheer age. As so many of us are."

"De-fanged my ass," I said. "If you're talking about you. Or Murgatroyd."

He was cheering up again. "Or Viola, for that matter. Even at her extreme age, I never thought of her as old or weak, and to be frank, I'd begun to think of her as an adversary."

"Because of the journal."

"It would have been crucial to my research, yes. If proven real."

"And the only way to confirm that was to see the original."

"Exactly." He took a long swallow from his cup, keeping his eyes on me. "Not enjoying your coffee?"

"Not really," I said, pushing the cup forward. "After you and Liz had your showdown all those years ago, were you ever tempted to go back to Viola's? Maybe sneak in while she was away?"

Buonopane thought about that. "No, but I could have. There's an outside hatch to the cellar, just like in the *Wizard of Oz*. And from there you can use the servant stairs to go anywhere in that ridiculously puritan mansion."

He laughed at me. "You're surprised at my candor, Ms. Rowe. Just remember, there's a difference between teaching and confessing."

"As long as we've found our groove. Academic discussion, and all." I continued, carefully. "So what do you *think* happened on December 26, Professor Buonopane?"

"Oh, that sounds very official. Nice," he said. "What I believe happened is this. Ms. Horup came home early. Our villain, Seth, was trapped in the cellar, perhaps with bleeding hands. John told me that the boxes she'd packed up were littered glass, razors, and pins. To discourage plunderers no doubt."

"That must have been frustrating."

Buonopane grinned at me. "I'm sure it would have been. Very."

"Enough for Seth to lose his temper."

"Those are my thoughts, yes."

I nodded and stood, more than ready to leave. And grateful that I didn't have that stiletto he feared. "Thanks, Professor. Thanks for helping me think this through."

"My pleasure."

"Poor guy just snapped, then. I guess I need to tell the Doc that we don't have much of a story here," I said. "Because if it was you—if you had killed Viola, it wouldn't have gone down that way at all."

"Pardon?" His grip tightened around his coffee. He didn't think I noticed.

But I did. "Well, kind of person you are—someone who cases the comings and goings of an old woman, someone who creates his own little word game to communicate with his ex behind bars, someone who stages a suicide and then sends me out to stumble through it—*that* kind of person doesn't just have a melt down and conk an old lady on the head because he has a temper. Nope, that kind of person is more methodical."

Buonopane didn't even take the time to argue. He was up, robe flying open at last, and I thought he meant to take a swing at me, except he tried to shove past me instead. Going for that gun, no doubt.

I put one arm out to stop him from getting by. The other? "Hold on, Professor. I got nothing on you, and you know it."

His eyes fluttered wide.

"Except your nuts." Which felt like a handful of rotting fruit. Not my favorite way to subdue a guy, but effective. "Sit back down. We're still talking."

Buonopane swallowed, considering his options.

I gave his unit a quick squeeze and said, "Just a quick refresher. I have a history of creative violence."

He nodded, and I let go. He returned to his chair.

I crossed to the sink and washed my hands, talking over my shoulder and generally keeping an eye on the old bastard. "Here's what I believe, based on your weak little story. Because I'm thinking it's all lies, except for the time, place, and cast of characters."

There was a dish towel hanging below the sink, but I chose to wipe my wet hands on the back of his robe, across the shoulders. "I think you *planned* to kill Viola, so you could have as much time as you needed to find the journal. You hid in the cellar until she was alone, and you pulled her plug. Except you didn't expect Seth Shute, who probably came in through the front door with his own damn key."

Nothing from the old man. I couldn't even hear him breathing. I stared down at his scalp with the hairs plastered over it, wondering what was going on underneath.

"Come on Gerry, did you hide again? Did you watch Seth go through the same damned boxes you'd already inventoried? Did you watch his hands bleed just like yours did? More importantly, did you watch him find Viola's body?"

I put my face right next to his, and he leaned away, making a sour face, as he pulled his robe over his lap. He said, "There was no reason to remain. That would have been an enormous waste of time and energy."

Which was apparently more important than the waste of a long, rich life. I stepped away from him and took a slow stroll around the table.

I said, "You must have been disappointed."

There was a butcher-block knife holder on the counter, and next to it, a matching rack for slotted spoons, spatulas, and the like. I bypassed the knives for something with a little more creative. The metal tenderizing mallet was small but nasty, with a pleasing heft to it.

Buonopane was both confused and upset by my selection. I came back to him, tossing the thing from hand to hand.

"This is ridiculous," he said, attempting to rise.

"Down," I said, smacking the mallet head into the palm of my hand. "Ouch, that does smart."

He resettled himself.

I said, "So you thought the journal was out of reach, until another opportunity rolled up in the form of John Hock. Except when he found the journal, he didn't come running to you like he was supposed to."

Buonopane kept his eyes on the mallet. "He was always such a corrupt little bastard. He killed that Carlos woman, you know. She caught him as he was trying to sneak off, and he panicked. Sent her down those stairs."

"So Hock is the one with the so-called *uncontrollable* temper."

"I believe you experienced that first hand."

"You know what," I said. "Who the hell cares? When the bodies start piling up, people like Doris Wethers think *I'm* the problem, but that's complete bullshit. You people—you and Murgatroyd and Viola? You people invented messed up."

I suppose I had raised my voice, because Buonopane cowered, his shoulder raised as if that would stop me from tenderizing him to a pulp. There he was, this roly poly nothing of a man, quivering in a robe at his kitchen table.

But he was also a murderer. A multiple murderer who was likely to go free.

I was enjoying scaring him, and that was not a good thing. For me, this stuff tended to escalate. I was on the verge, but then a low familiar buzz stopped me. It came from a kitchen drawer.

"Stay put," I said.

Buonopane put his hand up in a *whatever you want* gesture.

I found the buzzing drawer and yanked it open.

It was my phone, with a text from Maureen trying to peek out from behind John Hock's blood.

The message read: **Lawyer emailed. Murg out 05/05.** Just like the Doc predicted.

Buonopane eyed me from the table. "Bad news?"

"Good news, really. Liz is getting out on early release." I pointed the phone at him. "Which is probably bad news for you."

"Only if you give her another twenty-five years to work out her next move. I'm not worried about Elizabeth Murgatroyd, believe me." The professor put his chin out. "Or you, for that matter. Go ahead and have at me. You'll only end up back in jail."

He braced for a malleting. It was almost cute, really.

"You're right about that." I placed the mallet back on its rack. "But I'm taking my phone back."

He said, "I don't need it. A little advice though: don't google 'How to clean blood off a phone.'"

"So noted. I'm out of here," I said, jamming it in my back pocket. Buonopane cringed as brown flakes sloughed off and floated down onto the linoleum.

The last of John Hock.

"Should we expect something big from you soon, Professor? A 'Secrets of New Royal' expose', perhaps?"

He tilted his head. "Not out of the realm."

"Where is the journal, anyway?"

"It's in safe hands," he said.

How precious. "Like I give a damn." Cryptic was another flavor of coy, showing how needy he was. I walked out of the kitchen, and towards his front door. It was getting light out, already, and it would be time to change the clocks soon. That was another thing I didn't need to worry about anymore, now that I was no longer a student.

Too bad not everyone was willing to accept that.

Professor Buonopane followed me out. He even reached forward to open the door for me.

He said, "When is Liz getting out?"

"Early May, it looks like."

"Just in time for your book launch." Buonopane thought that was interesting. "Well, then, I have one more question for you."

"Yeah, what's that?"

He chuckled, and his whiskers glinted in the morning light. "Where's the party going to be?"

It was quick. So quick that I don't remember actually hitting him. All I know is that he was smiling in one second, huddled and groaning on the threshold in the next.

Instinctively I took off running, and when I reached the top of the hill, I turned and looked down.

He was still there, on the ground, half in, half out of his cottage.

Motionless as a bag of garbage.

Even if he was still alive—and he should have been, it was just a sock in the nose, for cripe's sake—I'd be going back into jail just as Murgatroyd was getting out.

Please move, please move, please move.

His arm dragged slowly across the stoop, and my heart just about exploded. He put his hand flat, and lifted his face.

That was a lot of blood, but there was no mistaking the fact that he was looking up at me with fire in his eyes.

I waved bye-bye. "Sorry, man," I called down. "Party's canceled."

Chapter 28

Steve Rasmussen has opened a second beer, but he's sipping it slowly. He's relaxing in his den, listening to a re-broadcast of the game, and trying to read Abraham Horup's journal, but the handwriting is terrible, and the spelling is even worse. There's a grilled cheese sandwich and a bowl of chips on a tray table next to his chair, and every so often he has to blow crumbs off the brittle pages, which isn't as bad as when a page just folds and breaks just because he turned it. That's happened a couple of times, so he has the scotch tape nearby, just in case.

He justifies having taken the book home with him because if it was genuine, whoever dropped it would have done so at the office. His real office.

Nah, this is a load of horse shit, even though some of it's good reading. Whoever left this for him is yanking his chain. Probably Crocus.

Still, Viola was a decent writer. She knew how to capture that old-timey feel. And who knows, maybe she did have the goods on her great-great grandfather? No doubt there were family stories, just like there always is. The stuff you don't let outsiders know.

It's past midnight when he gets to the end, and he hiccups when he sees the list of names:

Thomas
Nemuth
Cutler
Shute

Steve grabs a ballpoint, and circles 'Thomas' in blue ink. That's his mother's maiden name, though common as hell. Still, you can never go wrong telling people what they want to hear. When he finishes reading the journal, he examines it for signs. A thing like this could have come from anywhere, he decides, and he drinks the rest of his beer.

When he takes his bottles out to the recycling bin, he puts the journal in the trash, as well. No good can come from it. Whoever gave it to him thought there were still investigations going on, but there aren't. Cheri's been reassigned to another lab, so the doorknob thing is dead. Seth Garan Shute confessed, and even his mother thinks he did it. And poor, stupid John Hock. Doris Wethers should have listened to Professor Buonopane. He tried to tell them Hock was troubled.

Steve goes to bed, only to wake up an hour later. He's being selfish.

* * *

Marla Shute comes to the door a lot quicker than he expected at this hour.

"Detective," she says, and behind her a light flickers. The television's still on. "What's wrong?"

He can smell her breath from where he stands. It's warm and fruity. "Everything's fine, ma'am, sorry to give you a start. I just thought I'd leave this with you." He hands her the journal. He wishes he still had the sheet it was wrapped in, but he used it in the garage to cover his motorcycle.

He says, "I don't think it will change anything, but you might find it interesting."

A woman calls from inside, "Marla?"

"Just a minute, Helen." Marla holds her sweater closed over her breast with one hand and uses the other to bring the book up to her face. "What is this?"

"Creative writing," says Steve, nodding his so long. "I hope it brings you comfort."

Seth Garan Shute's mother is confused and tipsy on her doorstep. "But wait," she says, "Where are you going?"

"Headed home." He gets into his car and looks at Marla, the state of her. Everything askew. And in her hand, the only thing she wants, other than Seth, and she can't have that.

What was it, two or three in the morning? He started the engine. Seemed like as good time as any to give his mother a call.

The End

Acknowledgements

Names are important, so thanks to Debra Lattanzi Shutika for being a particularly generous vector for so many of my character names, and for giving me access to the creative minds of her students in English 301. A special thanks to Sydney Megan Rowe and Michael Hock for lending me their family names—I hope you two meet one day. Also, thanks to Tamara Harvey, Samaine Lockwood, and Joy Fraser for helping me name this darn book.

In the support category, thanks to the Chessie Chapter of Sisters in Crime for giving me so many opportunities this year, and to Erin Fitzgerald for knowing when a flash wants to be a novel.

Finally, I want to thank everyone at Pandamoon Publishing for their faith and enthusiasm. You make this fun.

About the Author

Laura Ellen Scott is the author of four novels, *Death Wishing*, *The Juliet*, and *The Mean Bone in Her Body* plus *Crybaby Lane*—books one and two of The New Royal Mysteries series. An Ohio native, Laura is based in Fairfax, Virginia where she teaches fiction writing at George Mason University.

A proud member of Sisters in Crime and the Association of Crime Writers, Laura is happy to connect with readers at her Facebook page at https://www.facebook.com/LauraEllenScottAuthor/ or through her website at https://www.lauraellenscott.com/.

From the Publisher

Thank you for purchasing this copy of *Crybaby Lane* by Laura Ellen Scott. If you enjoyed this book by Laura, please let her know by posting a review.

Growing good ideas into great reads...one book at a time.

Visit www.pandamoonpublishing.com to learn more about other works by our talented authors.

Mystery/Thriller/Suspense

- *122 Series Book 1: 122 Rules* by Deek Rhew
- *A Flash of Red* by Sarah K. Stephens
- *Fate's Past* by Jason Huebinger
- *Juggling Kittens* by Matt Coleman
- *Killer Secrets* by Sherrie Orvik
- *Knights of the Shield* by Jeff Messick
- *Kricket* by Penni Jones
- *Looking into the Sun* by Todd Tavolazzi
- *On the Bricks Series Book 1: On the Bricks* by Penni Jones
- *Southbound* by Jason Beem
- *The Juliet* by Laura Ellen Scott
- *Rogue Alliance* by Michelle Bellon
- *The Last Detective* by Brian Cohn
- *The Moses Winter Mysteries Book 1: Made Safe* by Francis Sparks
- *The New Royal Mysteries Book 1: The Mean Bone in Her Body* by Laura Ellen Scott
- *The New Royal Mysteries Book 2: Crybaby Lane* by Laura Ellen Scott
- *The Unraveling of Brendan Meeks* by Brian Cohn
- *The Zeke Adams Series Book 1: Pariah* by Ward Parker
- *This Darkness Got to Give* by Dave Housley

Science Fiction/Fantasy

- *Becoming Thuperman* by Elgon Williams
- *Chimera Catalyst* by Susan Kuchinskas
- *Dybbuk Scrolls Trilogy Book 1: The Song of Hadariah* by Alisse Lee Goldenberg
- *Dybbuk Scrolls Trilogy Book 2: The Song of Vengeance* by Alisse Lee Goldenberg
- *Dybbuk Scrolls Trilogy Book 3: The Song of War* by Alisse Lee Goldenberg
- *Everly Series Book 1: Everly* by Meg Bonney
- *.EXE Chronicles Book 1: Hello World* by Alexandra Tauber and Tiffany Rose
- *Fried Windows (In a Light White Sauce)* by Elgon Williams
- *Revengers Series Book 1: Revengers* by David Valdes Greenwood
- *The Bath Salts Journals: Volume One* by Alisse Lee Goldenberg and An Tran
- *The Crimson Chronicles Book 1: Crimson Forest* by Christine Gabriel
- *The Crimson Chronicles Book 2: Crimson Moon* by Christine Gabriel
- *The Phaethon Series Book 1: Phaethon* by Rachel Sharp
- *The Sitnalta Series Book 1: Sitnalta* by Alisse Lee Goldenberg
- *The Sitnalta Series Book 2: The Kingdom Thief* by Alisse Lee Goldenberg
- *The Sitnalta Series Book 3: The City of Arches* by Alisse Lee Goldenberg
- *The Sitnalta Series Book 4: The Hedgewitch's Charm* by Alisse Lee Goldenberg
- *The Sitnalta Series Book 5: The False Princess* by Alisse Lee Goldenberg

Women's Fiction

- *Beautiful Secret* by Dana Faletti
- *The Long Way Home* by Regina West
- *The Mason Siblings Series Book 1: Love's Misadventure* by Cheri Champagne
- *The Mason Siblings Series Book 2: The Trouble with Love* by Cheri Champagne
- *The Mason Siblings Series Book 3: Love and Deceit* by Cheri Champagne
- *The Mason Siblings Series Book 4: Final Battle for Love* by Cheri Champagne
- *The Shape of the Atmosphere* by Jessica Dainty
- *The To-Hell-And-Back Club Book 1: The To-Hell-And-Back Club* by Jill Hannah Anderson

48662234R00131

Made in the USA
Middletown, DE
24 September 2017